# Echoes

## A Modern Fairytale

# Books by Connie A. Walker

## Young Reader

*Timmy and the K'nick K'nocker Ring*

## Teen Fantasy

*Echoes: A Modern Fairytale*
*Dark in the Forest: Another Modern Fairytale*
*Sunshine and Shadows: Another Modern Fairytale*

## Fantasy

THE WOLKAREAN INSCRIPTION

*The Spire of Kylet*
*The Eyes of Landor*
*Triumph at Serpent's Head*

THE WOLKAREAN ENIGMA – Coming Soon

*Revelations of Riddles*
*Sorcerers in Shokareen*
*Temple of Rulianthabah*

# Echoes
## A Modern Fairytale

Connie A. Walker

**Press Forward Press**
Fiction Division
5060 S 710 West
Salt Lake City, UT 84123

ISBN: 978-1-940802-09-1


LIBRARY OF CONGRESS CONTROL NUMBER:
2016946033

First Edition: August 2016
Second Edition: October 2021


Cover Design by Bud Spencer, SUMO Graphics

Printed in the United States of America

This book is dedicated to my granddaughter, Natasha Ann, who asked me to write a contemporary fantasy.

# Chapter One

Today is my first day back at school since the accident.

I hope I survive.

Literally, I hope I'm still alive when the last bell rings.

Mom pulls up to the curb. When she pushes the button on her key fob, the hatchback to her silver minivan opens. She gets out of the vehicle, walks around to the back, and works the hoist.

I glance around.

Last fall, when we moved from Chicago to the small college town of Shawon, Colorado, I was stunned to discover how beautiful the Rocky Mountains are. It's not just professional photography on The Science Channel that makes them look good. Rugged peaks reaching up and piercing the sky are just as breathtaking as steel skyscrapers.

I was even pleasantly surprised with the high school. It is only two stories high and is spread over an entire block. The main building has three sections that face the street, with the cafeteria, auditorium, and music rooms hooked onto the back. The gymnasium is separate, and so are the "shops"— woodshop, auto shop, ceramics, and metalworking—in order to keep all of the unpleasant odors associated with them out of the classrooms.

I was prepared to like it here. I was going to learn to ski this winter. In the spring I hoped to find a social club that hiked up the canyons.

It didn't turn out that way.

Instead, I ended up in Denver, first in a hospital and then in a physical rehabilitation center, where my Uncle Frank and his family could look after me. My parents traveled back and forth to visit as often as they could.

At least that's over now. I can live at home again as long as I continue with my physical therapy.

Luckily, as small as Shawon is, Mountain View Hospital has a good physical therapy unit and a wonderful staff.

This morning, big cotton-ball snowflakes drift lazily from the clouds.

Even so, kids are hanging out in the parking lot and clustering in front of the building beside the doors. When the hoist in the back of our van squeaks, they all stop where they are and turn to stare.

My mother warrants a few stares. She was nineteen years old when she had me, so she's only thirty-five now. She hasn't changed much from the perky blond cheerleader in her high school yearbook. I get my honey colored hair from her, though mine is natural and hers has to come from a salon now.

Under different circumstances she would dominate the scene, making the boys gawk and the girls jealous.

This time, I steal the show.

I can hardly believe my parents are making me do this.

The principal said the school district would provide me with a home tutor until the end of the school year, but my father turned him down. He said it was important for me, psychologically, to have contact with other teenagers. He said I was already too isolated just by being new.

Dad might have reconsidered if I'd shown him the hate mail that started arriving at the hospital as soon as the doctors decided I wasn't going to die.

But I figured my parents had enough to worry about without me piling more on top. They had my two younger brothers to contend with, plus their new jobs, a new town, and a new house with an unfinished basement and stacks of unpacked boxes—not to mention the inconvenience of an injured daughter who needed care in a city a hundred miles away.

I didn't even get to come home for Christmas.

When I hear wheels thud against the wet pavement, I open my door and wait while Mom brings the wheelchair around. I use my arms to pull myself onto the seat, hating life, hating my useless legs, hating my mom, hating the kids at this school, hating everyone in the world who can walk.

Reaching past me, Mom grabs my backpack and hands it to me. "Your father will be here to pick you up at 3:15."

I nod silently. *Yeah*, I think, *and then he has to rush back to work for another two or three or four hours. I'm not a daughter anymore. I'm a burden, a problem, an affliction.*

"If you need anything, Karissa," Mom says, "call me. Principal Haskell said you can keep your cellphone as long as you don't use it during classes, not even for texting."

"I know, Mom. You reminded me yesterday."

"Don't forget your medication is in the nurse's office."

"You told me that yesterday too."

Mom lowers her voice. "I know this was a terrible thing to happen to you, especially so soon after starting at a new school, but I'm sure you'll make friends now that you can attend classes. Just keep a positive attitude."

"Positive attitude, right," I mutter. "I'll be sure to put that at the top of today's To-Do list."

Glancing at her watch, Mom gives my arm a pat. "My first client isn't until 9:30. I have time to go in with you if you want."

"No," I tell her quickly. "I'll be okay."

The only thing I can think of that's worse than coming back to school is having my mother come with me.

"All right. See you tonight." Mom's boots squish through the wet snow as she walks to the driver's side of the van. A moment later she's gone, leaving me in my own personal nightmare.

I push a lever on my right armrest and guide the chair up a little slope from the blacktop to the sidewalk.

The maintenance crew must have been warned that I was coming back today. Someone has sprinkled Melt-It-Quick on the handicapped access ramp that runs from the sidewalk to the landing in front of the main doors. Newly fallen snow is collecting along the edges, but the center is only damp.

At least my parents got me a motorized wheelchair—an unnecessary, but appreciated, luxury.

The physical therapists consider it a triumph when you can manipulate one of those manual chairs, the kind where you turn the wheels with your hands. They say it gives you more maneuverability and independence. But those chairs are lightweight, and even though my sitting balance and my upper body strength are both adequate for me to handle one, coming back to this school I need the protection of something heavier, sturdier, and stronger than my own muscles.

Behind my sunglasses, which I wear because my new anti-depressant makes me light sensitive, my eyes dart from one group of kids to another. They display a wide variety of coats, jackets, and parkas in a rainbow of dark colors. Some of them have hoods pulled up, hiding all of their faces except an occasional nose or chin. Others wear caps or hats. However, most are bareheaded, and the snow dusting their hair makes them look like participants in a senior citizens convention.

No one smiles.

No one nods.

No one rushes over to tell me how glad he or she is to see me up and around again.

That's because no one is glad.

They don't want me back.

They want Josie Peters back: captain of the cheerleading squad, senior class secretary, last's year's Junior Class Sweetheart, brilliant young singer and dancer, and most popular girl in school.

Everyone wishes I had died instead of her.

I am *not* being paranoid.

After I was moved out of intensive care, each day, a nurse or nurse's aide would come into my room, beaming at me, to deliver the mail. I guess I got more than most people because they always said something like "You

3

certainly are popular" or "Your friends must really miss you."

They didn't know that only the letters postmarked Chicago wished me well.

The others made it clear that I was a bug on the sidewalk, which the authors would be happy to step on and crush. Today the students reinforce the message by watching me fumble with the front door until I manage to pull it open on my own.

I don't ask for help.

I'm already too conspicuous.

I pretend I'm not frightened.

I remind myself that no one is likely to harm me while I'm on the school grounds. I just need to stay in view of lots of kids and teachers, so no one can get me alone, especially not the football team. Kenneth Nelson, their captain, was Josie Peters' boyfriend.

The hate mail arrived off and on all of the time I was in Denver. It followed me from the hospital to the rehabilitation center and was comprised of nearly three-dozen threatening letters. Half of them were really vile and had a picture of a football pasted at the bottom, no names of course. The last one didn't have any words. It was a hand-drawn picture of me angling through the air toward the goalpost. Rushing to catch me was a pack of wild animals—bears, tigers, lions and wolves—with claws extended and mouths full of razor-sharp teeth. They were all wearing football jerseys.

I didn't throw any of the notes away. I put them in a shoebox, which I then placed on the bottom shelf of a bookcase in my room. I stacked some old stories I had written in grade school on top.

If something happens to me, if I disappear or die under suspicious circumstances, I hope my parents or the police will find the letters when they search my belongings. Something in one of them might help the police catch whoever is responsible.

Since the car crash, my perception of death has changed. I'm not afraid of being dead, ceasing to exist, or facing God for judgment.

What I dread is how much pain I might have to go through first. The human body can endure a great deal and still live. I know. I've been there. While I waited for the paramedics, I prayed to die.

If an evil person wanted to make someone suffer, he could make the agony last a very long time. That's the only thing that frightens me about the hate mail, not that someone might kill me, but that they might do terrible things to me first.

My hands are shaking when I pull off my gloves, remove my sunglasses, and unzip my jacket. If people notice, I hope they'll assume I'm shivering from the cold. I can't afford to appear weak, or at least no weaker than I actually am.

I glance down at my schedule.

I can't remember if C Wing is on the right or the left of B, which is the central section and includes the administrative offices, the nurse's room, and the faculty lounge. I guess it depends on whether the person who labeled the wings stood at the front door looking in or in the office looking out.

The first bell rings. Suddenly the halls are filled with a jostling mass of adolescent bodies.

I inch the chair forward slowly.

I have a fifty-fifty chance.

I take a right. Right is right.

"Hey, look where you aim that thing," a brunette girl shouts as she cuts in front of me and darts into the nearest classroom.

I tip my head back so I can see the number above the door: C-2, my homeroom.

Two more kids dash around me just as the second bell rings. I roll in behind them.

"Karissa Day?" the teacher asks as if she's never seen me before. I suppose she doesn't remember what I look like. I had only gone to this school a few weeks before the car accident. Nevertheless, you'd think the wheelchair would be a dead giveaway.

I glance down at my schedule and locate her name.

"Yes, Ms. Hews."

"The faculty decided it would be easier for you to go straight to your first class and have homeroom there." She hands me a transfer slip.

I must look vacant, because she comes over to the door and points.

"You go back that way, past the front office, into A Wing. It's the third classroom on the left, A-5."

"Thank you, Ms. Hews."

As I navigate through the building, I keep my eyes roving. No one else is around. There goes my brilliant idea about staying close to other people. I drive my wheelchair at maximum speed, slowing down only when I pass the office. Can you get detention for driving a wheelchair too fast? Maybe it is equivalent to running in the halls.

The loudspeaker sputters.

Mrs. Fulton, the Vice-Principal, says, "Good morning, students. We have just a few announcements. One of your classmates has returned to school today after a prolonged absence. I want all of you to be kind and helpful. Karissa Day is in a wheelchair. Be aware of her presence and give her the right-of-way in the halls. Your feet are more flexible and less cumbersome than her chair."

She pauses.

I want the ground to open up and swallow me.

"The decorating committee for the Sweetheart Ball will meet—"

It is absolutely the worst day of my life.

# Echoes: A Modern Fairytale

Considering it wasn't too long ago that a rescue crew had to cut through a smashed-up car to get to me, that's saying a lot.

I am a reasonably attractive sixteen-year-old girl. My chin-length, naturally curly hair is the color of golden honey, which goes well with my dark blue eyes. I am not too tall or too short. My weight is in proportion to my height, and I have nicely rounded breasts and hips.

I am a junior in high school, have always been a good student, especially in English and math, and I have a pleasant personality.

I shower regularly, brush my teeth, and dress well.

I am not a leper, a lunatic, or a serial killer.

Now, try convincing the student body at Millard Fillmore High School of that.

Hardly anyone talks to me, except for teachers telling me where to park and asking me if I know who Millard Fillmore was. Since we went through this in the fall, I could have told them he was the thirteenth president of the United States, but why ruin their fun? Being high school teachers, they need to get their happiness wherever they can.

A few kids make rude comments about how much space the wheelchair takes up and how inconvenient it is to dodge around me in the halls. Other than that, mostly they ignore me.

During lunch, there is only one table in the back of the cafeteria that doesn't have chairs crammed around it. I get a bowl of soup, crackers, and a banana, and then head for it.

As I pass the table where the jocks are sitting with the cheerleaders, they stare at me like I'm Public Enemy Number One. Kenneth Nelson glares at me while he punches his left palm with his right fist.

I sit alone, but I can't eat.

When a group from a nearby table gets up, I follow them out. I dump my lunch in the garbage barrel, all except for the crackers.

I go to the nurse's office and take my antidepressant, an anti-anxiety pill, and a couple of ibuprofen. I've been off the heavy-duty painkillers for a while, but my muscles still ache and feel twitchy. The ibuprofen helps.

I force the crackers down first because the doctor told me not to take the medication on an empty stomach.

# Chapter Two

For most of my life on Monday nights, my mother and father have stayed at work late in order to deal with problems that developed over the weekend or to get a jumpstart on the rest of the week.

But in the mysterious way of parents, because I am miserable after my first day back at school and because I want to isolate in my room and suffer, this is one Monday when both of them come home by 5:30 so we can have an old-fashioned sit-down dinner.

Jeremy and Bennett, my two younger brothers, are as unexcited about it as I am. We kids look forward to these weekly reprieves from parental dominance. We fix whatever we want to eat from what's in the refrigerator or the freezer. The boys watch television or play video games. I eat in my room and read.

Regrettably, our family is not a democracy. At 6:30, we gather around the dining room table for a dinner of pork chops, mashed potatoes and gravy, green beans, and salad.

After things are passed around, Mom tells Dad she has a new client.

Dad says he's picked up a new one too.

They are not talking about the same thing.

My mother is a self-employed accountant, working out of a little office she rents downtown. My father is a clinical psychologist, recently hired to run the Student Counseling Center at the University and to teach a few classes in the Psych Department.

Mom sorts out people's money.

Dad sorts out people's minds.

That's a family joke. Ha. Ha.

My parents are an odd couple.

Dad has a long, serious face and thinning brown hair that's starting to go gray. He wears tortoise-shell rimmed glasses that hide his dark brown eyes and long lashes. He's average height and on the slim side. If you took two-dozen men off the street at random, put my dad in the middle of them, then asked any fifty strangers to choose which one is the shrink, they'd all pick my dad.

On the other hand, Mom looks like a blond, bouncy, beauty queen. If you put her in a room with two-dozen women and asked fifty people to select the one who has a bachelor's degree in accounting and an MBA, and who graduated *summa cum laude* (with highest honors) in both programs, there would not be a single person who chose her. She doesn't look like she can add two plus two without counting on her fingers, but she can add, subtract, multiply, and divide numbers in her head faster than the average person can with a calculator.

"How did you do on that science exam?" Dad asks Jeremy, who's in ninth grade.

"Haven't got it back yet," Jeremy mumbles around a huge bite of potatoes. He's got Dad's long face and Mom's blond hair, and he's smarter than both of them put together. He's had a straight A average since kindergarten. He's talented musically, too. Right now, his voice is changing and he has zits, plus he's painfully skinny, which only seems right since he got all the brains in the family. It wouldn't be fair if he got all the good looks too.

"Don't talk with your mouth full," Mom says automatically.

Jeremy swallows. "Dad asked me a question," he says defensively. "Aren't I supposed to answer?"

Talking to Mom is the one area where Jeremy's brain switches off. They argue about the stupidest things, and he never wins. If it looks like he's getting the upper hand, Mom plays the *Dad-card*, knowing Dad will support her even if he thinks she's wrong.

Bennett, always the peacekeeper, interrupts before Jeremy and Mom can get going.

"I need to write a report about someone with an interesting job," Bennett says. He's in seventh grade, small for his age, quiet and gentle. He has brown hair and eyes like Dad. He's started to squint lately, so he's probably going to end up with the glasses too. "Can one of you drive me down to the Fire Station so I can interview the Chief?"

"When is your report due?" Mom asks a little coldly. I think she's irritated because Bennett cheated her out of a good fight with Jeremy.

"Tomorrow."

"This is pretty short notice," Dad says. He's always calm. "Did you think to make an appointment?"

Bennett shakes his head.

"How long have you known about this?" Mom asks, still sounding snippy. (That's one of the words Dad uses that I really like.)

Bennett just shrugs.

"Natural consequences," Dad says to Mom. She nods.

Dad tells Bennett, "You'll have to choose someone in the neighborhood, someone who lives close enough that you can walk to the interview. If you had asked for a ride immediately after you got your assignment, we could have negotiated a time that was convenient for all of us. Plus, you could have made an appointment with the Fire Chief, thereby assuring that he would be available."

Dad talks like that, like he's always in lecture mode.

Then, in order to reinforce his displeasure with Bennett, Dad turns away from him and looks at me.

My brother goes back to eating, not the least bit disturbed. I wonder if he really has a report due, or if he was simply distracting Mom and Jeremy. It's probably the latter. He's too conscientious to let homework go until the last minute, and he hates quarreling enough to bend the truth now and then to prevent it.

"How was school for you today, Kari?"

Dad always telegraphs what kind of answer he expects. He wants me to say something positive and uplifting. I'm the eldest, and I'm supposed to set a good example. Right now, he's counting on me to reestablish a pleasant dining atmosphere.

Sorry.

"It was horrible," I tell him. "Everyone looked at me like I killed Josie Peters with my own two hands. They hate me. They think I should've died instead of her."

"Karissa," Mom says, "you know that's not true."

"It is true," I snap back at her. "Even some of the teachers gave me dirty looks. I'm the new girl. She was the homegrown, school favorite. They think she should be alive and I shouldn't."

"Survivor's guilt," Dad says.

"What's that supposed to mean?" I throw my napkin down beside my plate. "Now you think I've got some kind of psychiatric disorder? I'm already the poor pitiful wheelchair girl. I don't need to make up stories to get attention."

Dad looks at me with his psychologist face.

I hate it when he does that.

"Kari, honey," Dad says, "it's easy to misinterpret situations when we feel conspicuous or out of place. Going back to school in a wheelchair must have been uncomfortable for you. If you give it some time, I'm sure you'll find out that people aren't as hostile as—"

That does it!

I explode.

"I'm not one of your patients," I yell at him. "Stop trying to shrink my head."

I spin my chair away from the table and race for my room—or for what passes as my room now.

9

# Echoes: A Modern Fairytale

My original bedroom was upstairs, but since the house doesn't have an elevator, my parents took the couch and chairs out of the den and moved my bed and dresser down here. They cleared everything out of the bookcases and filled them with my books, stuffed animals, CD player, and CDs. They even bought me a small flat screen television and a DVD player.

They left the desk in the corner. It's nothing fancy, but it's okay for my laptop.

The floor space in the den is actually a little bigger than my upstairs room because the den doesn't have a closet.

No big deal.

My t-shirts, jeans, sweaters, undies, and nightgowns are more convenient in a chest of drawers anyway.

The nicest thing about the den as my bedroom is that it has its own three-quarters bathroom (that means a shower but no tub) and is handicapped accessible. The door is wide enough for even a fancy motorized wheelchair like mine.

It was like this when we bought the house. If I think about that too long, I always get goose bumps and end up wondering about fate or destiny.

The entire bathroom is covered in pale blue ceramic tile except for the ceiling and one darker stripe. At about my eye-level there is a row of dark blue tiles that goes all the way around the room. Solid-colored tiles alternate with pictures of tropical fish and seashells. It's really pretty.

The shower stall has a built-in bench that extends on a metal bar. I maneuver onto the seat from the wheelchair then pull a lever to slide the bench back into place. The plastic shower curtain is weighted at the bottom and is covered with sailboats and lighthouses to go with the rest of the decor.

The showerhead is on one of those long flexible cables. The taps are right by the seat, and so are three recessed shelves for soap and shampoo and whatever else I might need.

I appreciate the setup. It makes it so I can handle my personal business without help. I hated it in the hospital when nurses had to lift me onto the toilet or into the bathtub.

Tonight, though, I'm not in a grateful mood.

Tonight, I'm in a "life sucks" mood.

I lock the door to the den and call up the games program on my PC.

I don't play those shoot 'em up, jump and dodge, race and kill games. I like the ones that require a little brainpower and not just good eye-hand coordination.

I prefer things like cribbage, chess, backgammon, Scrabble, or one of a dozen different types of solitaire. When I get bored with those, or when I'm too agitated to concentrate, I go back to the old stand-by, FreeCell, at which I have a 96% win rate. (My longest run of wins without any losses was 995).

I choose backgammon.

The computer wins six games in a row.

I win zip.

It's consistent with the rest of my day.

I finish my Calculus homework. I enjoy math and I'm good at it, like my mother, but it doesn't fill enough time to be an effective diversion.

I try to read in my World History book, but it's hopeless. We don't have a test coming up for another week, and if there's no pressure, I just can't get into history, especially the wars. They seem totally idiotic to me. Why can't people just play nice!

I wheel over to the dresser, open the bottom drawer, lift out sweaters and sweatshirts, and stack them on a shelf in the nearest bookcase. Then I pull on a loop of string and lift up the false bottom that I made out of cardboard and contact paper. Underneath are some letters and notes from friends that I want to keep private, plus some papers I wrote before we left Chicago. I take out a short story I've been working on, "Lark and the Secret Doorway," and then replace the false bottom and the clothing.

When I first printed out this particular piece, I left space on some of the pages for pictures. The story is a fantasy, and I've already done some of the illustrations. I love drawing mystical creatures: dragons, trolls, unicorns, and elves, but especially fairies. They can be beautiful, or they can be horrific, and their wings can be as fancy or as plain as my imagination devises.

I put my laptop in the middle drawer of the desk and get out my pencil box. I start reading my story to put myself in the mood for sketching:

*Lark heard music playing inside her closet.*

*When she went to investigate, she realized the sound was coming from a shadowed corner beneath her good coat. She got down on her hands and knees and put her ear to the floor.*

A knock on the door makes me jump.

"Kari?"

It's my dad.

Of course it is. He doesn't believe families should ever go to bed angry. He thinks it's psychologically unhealthy.

I shove my story into the drawer with my laptop and go unlock the door.

# Chapter Three

Despite my protests, Mom takes me back to school the next day, another day of hell.

I go to P.E. for second period. Yesterday Mrs. Scott just had me sit and watch the other kids play basketball. Today, after she marks the attendance sheet, she tells me I can go to the library if I want.

I ask why I can't just transfer out and have study hall, but Mrs. Scott says since P.E. is required for juniors, if I want to graduate next year, the records have to show that I attended her class, even if I don't stay and participate.

Ordinarily I wouldn't mind—I like to read—but it means going from the gymnasium and across the parking lot when no one else is around.

Suddenly, when I'm halfway there, a group of boys jog straight at me.

My heart flutters and my hands tremble.

Mr. Ellis, the assistant coach, points to his right, and the guys detour around me. I don't look at the faces, so I don't know if Kenneth Nelson is among them.

When I get to the safety of the main building, I'm so relieved I could cry.

The library is on the second floor and is a long room full of big windows. It extends the entire length of B wing.

I use the faculty elevator.

There is a double row of tables and chairs in front of the checkout desk, and a small, single row about halfway down the stacks. I'm just on the other side of a rack of reference books when three girls come in and plop down on some chairs in the short row. I spy on them between volumes R and S of the *Encyclopedia Britannica*.

It is the first time I hear the name Neeve Maynard.

"He's the Taylors' new foster kid," a snobby rich girl named Kimberly says to her equally snobby friend Brenda. They're both wearing designer jeans that probably cost more than my entire wardrobe. Kimberly is willowy thin and has sleek black hair in a medium cut. She sports long, professionally sculptured fingernails, and their deep cranberry color matches her lipstick.

"I know," Brenda says in a whisper. She might be Kimberly's clone except her hair is auburn. Both girls are extremely pretty. "My brother, Jason, has P.E. with him. He says Neeve's back is covered with scars, like he was tortured!"

Kimberly shrugs, looking bored. "He was probably in a car accident like Josie Peters, except he survived."

"No." Brenda tosses her head, and her auburn hair swishes around her shoulders like in a shampoo commercial. "Jason says the scars are in patterns. There are ovals around his shoulder blades and crisscrossed lines on his lower back. He has scars around his wrists and ankles, too, like he was tied up. He even has scars on the bottoms of his feet."

Emily, the third member of the trio, is stocky and plain. Her clothing is expensive, but not flattering. Her hair is a mousey mess. I think Kimberly keeps her around for contrast.

When Emily speaks, she sounds as if she's missed most of the preceding conversation, latching only onto Neeve Maynard's name. "He's awfully good looking," she says with an audible sigh. "He reminds me of Orlando Bloom in the *Lord of the Rings* movies."

"Well, duh," says Kimberly sarcastically. "He's tall, has long blond hair, a gorgeous face, and intense eyes." Her tone mellows, and her lower lip juts forward in a little pout, as if she's just had an uncomfortable revelation. "Too bad he's in foster care. My father would never let me go out with him. Dad says nothing good ever comes out of foster care."

"Maybe he's on drugs," Brenda, the clone, suggests. She grabs Kimberly's arm in her excitement. "On television, drug dealers are always torturing people who owe them money."

"How sad," drab little Emily says. "Imagine someone that handsome getting involved with criminals." She looks over at Kimberly with big puppy-dog eyes. I almost expect Kimberly to pat her on the head or scratch behind her ears.

I don't listen to the rest of their conversation.

I think Neeve Maynard must be the blond guy in my World History class. He's the only person at school who looks as if he might be as miserable as I am.

There are still thirty minutes of class left, so I wheel to a table in front of the checkout desk, reach into my backpack, and pull out "Lark and the Secret Doorway."

I start reading where I left off last night:

*Lark crawled forward.*
*She reached out with her hand.*
*Where was the wall?*
*Suddenly she emerged from the shadows into a meadow full of spring*

*flowers. She sat back on her heels and looked around.*

The bell rings.

I head for Calculus. It's the same old, same old: formulas, equations, add, subtract, multiply, and divide.

From Calculus I go to lunch and then to World History.

I watch Neeve Maynard enter the classroom just as the tardy bell rings.

I know it's him because the guys sitting in front of me whisper his name. His eyes flash in our direction.

The guys shut up.

I don't blame them.

There is a lot of anger in that glance. But Neeve couldn't possibly have heard what the boys said about him. I didn't catch anything except his name, and I'm a lot closer to them than he was.

Neeve sits diagonally from me: two rows over and one chair up. He is tall enough that I can see him easily over the heads of the intervening students. His long blond hair is pulled back in a neat tail at the nape of his neck. It hangs maybe eight inches down his back.

During class I watch him out of the corner of my eye. Emily was right. He certainly is good looking. But there is something scary about him. Every now and then he tenses, and I can see the muscles and veins stand out on his arms and neck.

I look for the scars that Brenda said are around his wrists, but he wears a watch on his right wrist and some kind of braided leather band on his left. His hands are big with long fingers. I'm sure, if someone wanted to harm Neeve Maynard, they would have to tie him up first. He looks strong enough and angry enough to snap bones without difficulty.

Despite all that, when Mr. Mitchell wanders in my direction and Neeve follows him with his eyes, I sense something vulnerable and sensitive beneath the bitter expression on Neeve's face.

He's angry, but he's hurting too.

Misery loves company, they say.

Maybe we could be miserable together.

I try to catch his eye when class is over.

He looks past me like I'm invisible.

Then he's out the door.

Miserable, yes.

Together, no.

I wake up with my stomach tied in knots.

After school this afternoon, I have a physical therapy session scheduled with a guy named Randall Gregory. I suppose he's good enough at his job, but he doesn't have any personality. He is the silent type and is not at all friendly or sympathetic.

It's bad enough knowing I have to go through this process, if I ever want to walk again, but having to do it without a little supportive and distracting conversation while we work makes it hard to endure.

Almost everything we do hurts, and even when I'm working with the physical therapist I like best (her name is Abby Madison), often a sound or a comment or a physical sensation will trigger flashbacks of the accident, and I end up a quivering, sobbing mass of remembered fear and pain before the session is over.

On top of that, there are no guarantees that all of this stressful effort will make me ambulatory again. Sometimes I just don't think it's worth it. I wish everyone would leave me alone and let me decide when I'm ready to take the next steps. (Pun intended.)

On my way to homeroom, I'm in such a bad mood that I don't watch where I'm going.

A dark-haired girl steps absent-mindedly out of the office. She is staring at a piece of paper.

I almost run her down.

She looks at me in bewilderment.

"Which way is Wing A?" she asks, glancing from right to left.

She is so preoccupied that she doesn't realize how close I came to turning her into roadkill.

"I'll show you," I tell her, anxious to make up for the near mishap.

She smiles and a deep dimple appears in each cheek.

I ask her, "What room are you looking for?"

"A-5, Mr. Ullom for homeroom and English."

"We're in the same class," I say.

I ease forward and she walks beside me.

"My name is Juanita Flores," she says. "This is my first day here."

"I'm Karissa Day. When we get to homeroom, I'll fix the map the secretary gave you. I remember how confusing it is. I haven't been here too long myself."

"Do you like it?" she asks.

The answer is *no*, but I hesitate to say it. Juanita is the only person who's spoken a kind word to me since I came back. I don't want her to label me a negative moron and write me off. I need a friend.

"It's not bad," I answer. "The mountains are spectacular, and some of the teachers are exceptionally nice, but I miss my friends in Chicago."

"I can understand that," she says. "We just moved here from Roseville, California. I lived there my whole life and knew just about everyone in my school. My parents say teenagers are the same everywhere. They expect me to find new friends as if they were shoes. You know, wear out one pair and buy another. It doesn't matter, shoes are shoes."

We laugh at the innocence—or stupidity—of parents.

"This is it," I say when we reach the classroom. I roll to the back row where there is a desk waiting for me without a chair. Juanita gives a slip of paper to the teacher and then takes the empty seat next to me.

"What's he like?" she asks in a feeble whisper, looking at Mr. Ullom nervously.

I remember feeling the same way at first.

As a middle-aged, balding, and paunch-bellied man, Mr. Ullom is almost a stereotypical high school English teacher. He even wears half-moon reading glasses low on his nose.

What makes him unusual is a port wine birthmark on the left side of his face. It starts between his temple and his eye and droops toward his mouth, looking a bit like an over-sized teardrop. The left eye is pale blue and slightly off center, unlike the right one, which is hazel. All together they make him appear a little sinister.

"He's great," I tell her. "English will be your favorite class."

While the vice-principal makes the morning announcements, I fix the misleading information on the map of campus for Juanita.

When the bell rings, ending homeroom, about half the kids leave for other classes and a new group enters.

Juanita leans over and whispers, "Why doesn't everyone have homeroom in first period class?"

"I don't know," I say, shrugging. "Maybe the administration just wants to keep us confused."

As usual, as soon as he's taken the roll, Mr. Ullom begins English class with a joke:

"A women's club decided to give a Christmas party for the children in an orphanage. They collected donations of clothing, toys, and treats from the local businesses. On the day of the party, the women met with the children, a few at a time, to distribute the new clothes.

"Small bags of candy were left on a table, but none of the women explained what they were for or if they would be passed out later.

"After each child was given a new outfit to wear, he or she was invited to choose something from a large toy box on which was printed the message: 'Take only one gift or you'll end up on Santa's naughty list. His elves are watching.'

"One of the older orphans looked around and then snatched up a piece of paper and a crayon. He wrote a note and propped it up on the table beside the candy: 'Hurray! Grab a bag while the elves are watching the toys'."

Juanita looks over at me as she laughs.

"Today," Mr. Ullom says, "we're going to talk about—"

A boy raises his hand.

"You have a question, Thomas?" asks Mr. Ullom.

"Not really. I just wanted to say that I heard a similar joke told about a basket of fruit and a woman on a picnic with her Sunday school class. She tells the kids the fruit is for lunch and they have to wait to take a piece until all of the food has been prepared. Then she tells them God is watching the basket, so the kids steal a platter of cookies instead."

Waving her hand in the air, a girl says, "I heard a joke like that, too, except it was about a minister on a college campus who gave a sermon on the evils of drinking. He told the students that angels were always watching to see who went into the bars, so the kids planned a kegger in the park."

Mr. Ullom nods. "Like any story that is passed along orally, jokes are often altered, either accidentally or purposefully, by people who've heard them. The essence, however, is usually retained.

"Consider the three jokes mentioned this morning. In each version we have different people concerned with different aspects of similar situations. Whether it's charity women and orphans, Sunday school teachers and picnickers, or ministers and college students, the characters are focused on the specific circumstances that are important to them.

"This is called point of view, and that's what we're going to discuss today. I hope all of you have read William Faulkner's 'A Rose for Emily.' Open your textbooks to page 178, and let's see if we can spot all of the places where the point of view switches."

Before Juanita and I separate to go to second period, we agree to meet for lunch. As I head for the gym so I can check in at P.E. before going to the library, I'm actually cheerful.

Unfortunately, as noon approaches, my dark mood returns.

I just know that Juanita won't show up for lunch. Someone is bound to tell her about Josie Peters and what a jinx I am. I look for her in the halls, but I don't see her.

I go through the lunch line, taking only chocolate milk and a bagel. I watch the doors, but Juanita doesn't come. I sit alone at the table in the back and feel sorry for myself.

Lunch period is half over when Juanita rushes through the cafeteria door, spots me, and waves. There isn't a line at the register, so she breezes through with a salad and a soft drink.

"This place is a madhouse," Juanita says as she plops down beside me. "Thanks for fixing the map. I would never have found the band room without it. Ms. Christopherson kept me after class to quiz me about my experience with marching band. I was beginning to think she would never let me go."

"What instrument do you play?" I ask her, trying to sound casual. I'm so glad to see her that I have to rein myself in to keep from giving her a hug. I've been lonelier than I've admitted to myself.

"Drums," she says, "and chimes and xylophone and cymbals, you know, percussion. Anything you hit to make a sound." She giggles. "I'm the only

17

girl with four older brothers. I'm really good at hitting."

I laugh. "I'm the only girl with two younger brothers."

"Hey, we need to stick together. Us against them."

It sounds great to me, and I beam happily.

Juanita and I spend the rest of the lunch period trashing guys in general and brothers in particular.

We keep each other laughing the whole time.

When I roll into World History, I am still feeling good.

Neeve comes in and glances in my direction.

I smile at him automatically. He does a double take and then looks away.

Later, I catch him sneaking peeks at me over his shoulder, but he doesn't meet my eyes.

On any other day, I might have felt rejected.

Today I don't care.

Maybe I don't need a companion in misery.

Maybe I've found a real friend.

# Chapter Four

When I go back to school the next day, my entire body aches.

I hate physical therapy, but I especially hate it with Randall Gregory.

To distract myself during the session, I let my thoughts drift to Neeve Maynard. I can understand the fury that flashed through his eyes when those boys in World History were whispering about him.

Maybe foster care is better than nothing, but how much support and affection can you get from people who are paid to take care of you? Besides, how can you trust anyone after someone has tied you down and cut you up bad enough to leave scars? Anger and hostility seem logical responses to his situation.

Even though he's not interested in me, I would like to get to know him.

He needs a friend who is nonthreatening.

I doubt there's anyone less threatening than a cripple in a wheelchair.

There has to be a way to catch his eye.

When I get to homeroom, Juanita is already there. She tells me about her classes yesterday.

"Is this entire faculty obsessed with Millard Fillmore?" she asks. "Every single one of my teachers asked me if I knew who he was."

I laugh. "At least you'll only have to go through it once," I say. "When school started last fall, I got the whole Millard Fillmore, thirteenth president of the United States, from all my teachers too. Then when I came back after my accident, I had to go through it all over again."

Juanita doesn't say anything right away. I think she's waiting to see if I'll reveal more about what happened to me. I don't, and she doesn't push. I guess we both realize we're not that kind of friends yet.

"When I went home yesterday," Juanita says, "I read a couple of articles about Fillmore on the Internet. I could only find two significant things he did. The first was assuming the presidency when Zachary Taylor died, and the other was appointing Daniel Webster as Secretary of State. Why on earth is this school named after him?"

"I don't have a clue," I tell her.

As usual, I go to the library during P.E. and sit at a table in front of the checkout desk.

I decide to work on my story.

I plan on being a professional writer someday.

Before I can find a pencil, the library door opens and Kimberly, Brenda, and Emily parade in.

They walk past me like I'm a cockroach.

I leave my backpack on the table and circle around several racks of books until I'm hidden behind the encyclopedias again.

Ready to eavesdrop, I wedge my fingers between two books and open a crack so I can watch too.

I learned yesterday that Kimberly and her friends help out in the front office when extra hands are needed. They stuff envelopes, put notices in the teachers' mailboxes, enter data in the computer (as long as it's not confidential), and prepare handouts or fliers for distribution—things like that. If there is no work for them to do, they come to the library, supposedly to study.

I guess things have been slow lately.

Maybe the office staff is taking a long breather after the hectic holiday season. Anyway, the trio has been here nearly every day. Usually they don't say anything interesting, but I keep hoping they'll mention Neeve again.

Today I'm not disappointed.

"You'll never believe this," Brenda says, "but Danny Bower got a peek at Neeve Maynard's file in the Social Services office."

"You're right," Kimberly says, "I don't believe it." She gets a nail file from her purse and smooths out a chip in the nail of her right index finger.

"It's true," Brenda insists. "Lynda Miller told me she got it straight from Danny's sister, Heather."

"Either they're mistaken," Kimberly says, "or one of them is lying."

"But—"

Kimberly holds up her hand to interrupt Brenda. "My dad is a lawyer, you know, and he says those records are kept locked up. He's been involved in some of the lawsuits against the foster care system and that was always a big issue."

"But Danny's mother is a supervisor at Social Services."

"So?" Kimberly digs up a bottle of bright red nail polish and repairs the color on the damaged fingernail.

"Just listen," Brenda says.

As the two girls talk, mousey little Emily glances back and forth between them as if she's watching a ping pong game.

"Heather told Lynda Miller that Danny had to go downtown for a dental appointment," Brenda explains. "He was supposed to meet his mom at her

20

office so she could give him a ride home, but she got stuck in a conference that ran late. Heather said Danny claimed that he needed to staple some school papers together and the stapler was empty. So he went through his mom's desk looking for a box of staples."

"He must have wanted to fill the stapler for her." Emily says. "Danny is always so thoughtful."

Kimberly and Brenda ignore her.

"He told Heather he found the file by accident, but she thinks he was snooping. Anyway, he was curious, so he took a peek."

"All right," Kimberly says. "What did he find out?"

"You have to swear not to tell. Both of you."

"I never swear," Emily says. "I'm a Christian."

Brenda doesn't groan, or roll her eyes, or slap her, or anything.

"Then promise," she tells her.

"Oh," Emily says brightly, "I can promise."

"Me too," Kimberly says. "Now talk."

Brenda drops her voice to a whisper, but she doesn't bother to glance around to see if anyone else is listening. Like me.

"Neeve Maynard is the guy those nurses found unconscious, sliced up, and completely naked behind the University Health Center on Halloween."

"No!" Kimberly exclaims. "That story made the national news, but they never gave his name."

"There's more," Brenda says. "For three days he didn't speak a single word that made sense. He was so incoherent the doctors thought he had brain damage. He didn't know how to write his name, how to feed himself, or even how to use the bathroom."

"Ewww, gross," Kimberly says.

"The police think he was the victim of a satanic ritual."

"What does Neeve say happened?" Emily asks. It's a good question, and it's the first time I've ever heard her say anything intelligent.

"He doesn't know," Brenda answers. "When he finally stopped babbling, he told the doctors he couldn't remember anything about his life before waking up in Mountain View Hospital. He thought his name was Neeve Maynard, but he wasn't sure. At first, he said he's sixteen years old, but then he said he had a vague memory of celebrating a birthday recently, so maybe he's seventeen. He doesn't know how he got on campus. He doesn't know who cut him up or why. The police figure he was brought here from out-of-state, but so far he doesn't match any of the missing person notices."

"That's freaky," says Kimberly.

"Who is he really?" asks Emily.

Brenda shakes her head. "No one knows. There's no birth certificate or Social Security number under the name of Neeve Maynard, not anywhere. They put him in foster care because he said he was in his teens, and they didn't think it was safe for him to be on his own. That's why they enrolled him in school too. He did okay on the I.Q. tests they gave him, even with gaps in his memory, so they made him a junior."

"How did the Taylors end up with him?" Kimberly asks.

"The caseworker moved one of the Taylors' other foster kids to a different home," Brenda answers, "specifically to open up a slot for him. Until the police find out who he is and what happened to him, the caseworker wants him to live with the Taylors because Mr. Taylor is a policeman. The Satanists might be looking for him so they can finish what they started."

Emily gasps and presses her hands over her heart.

I wonder if any of the information is accurate.

If so, I've finally found someone whose story is more tragic than mine. At least I know my situation was bad luck—wrong place, wrong time. An accident. I would have a hard time coping if I knew someone had hurt me on purpose and might be looking for me to hurt me some more.

When lunchtime comes around, I want to tell Juanita what I heard.

But what can I say? Let me tell you some gossip I heard about this gorgeous guy in my World History class?

No, I don't know him.

No, I don't know if it's true.

No, I don't trust the source.

Yes, I'm an idiot.

Juanita has her own agenda when she joins me in the cafeteria.

She looks as if she's about to burst a vein.

She sits down, and as she opens a container of orange juice, she says, "I decided to ask all my teachers how the school came to be named for Millard Fillmore, starting with Mr. Ullom this morning after English class. So far, not even one of them could tell me." She giggles uncontrollably. "I've never seen adult faces turn so many shades of red. Ms. Christopherson, my band teacher, got so flustered she knocked over the stand that held all of her sheet music."

I laugh with her.

"I'll have to try it on my teachers," I tell her. "But I'll bet Mr. Mitchell, my World History teacher, will know the answer."

We compare teachers, past and present, for the rest of lunch period.

We leave together, but then she turns right to go to A Wing, and I turn left and head for the nurse's office.

The halls are emptying fast, and I realize we talked through the first bell. When I get to B Wing, I pause just long enough for the nurse to give me my medication. I'm thinking about something funny Juanita said and smiling as I roll past the front office and the teachers' lounge.

I'm just about to C Wing when who should come out of the boys' restroom?

Kenneth Nelson.

Kenneth Nelson, Captain of the football team and All-State quarterback, with his swaggering gait, tough-guy confidence, and aura of entitlement.

He stops and gapes as if he doesn't believe I have the gall to be here.

Another guy, who is so enormous across the chest and shoulders that he's straining the seams of his letterman's jacket, is right behind him. I don't know his name.

Godzilla, maybe.

Kenneth Nelson steps right in front of me and plants his fists aggressively on his hips. His face twists into an ugly sneer.

"What are you smiling at, bitch?" he snarls at me. "You don't have any right to be happy. It's your fault she's dead."

The other guy moves up beside him, effectively blocking my way.

I'm really scared.

I don't know what they might do.

They're big enough to pick me up, wheelchair and all, and chuck me through a window.

I put the chair in reverse and start backing up.

Footsteps approach from behind me.

I pray it's not another football player.

"Miss Day," the principal, Mr. Haskell, calls, "how are things going for you?" He looks at the two guys blocking my path, and says, "Gentlemen, you're going to be late for your next class."

They take off.

Mr. Haskell must know the guys were bullying me, but he pretends nothing is wrong. He just goes on talking.

"I understand Mrs. Anderton gave you a pass to use the faculty elevator," he says, walking beside me as I start down the hall. "I'm glad she thought of it. Even if you don't have any classes on the second floor, every student needs to have access to the library."

He chats about trivialities all the way to World History.

He is careful to make sure I can't get in a word. Without saying it directly, he lets me know what his attitude would be if I made a complaint about Kenneth Nelson: *Intimidating Karissa? Nonsense. I was there. I didn't see anything inappropriate. Besides, I walked with her to her next class. If she felt bullied, why didn't she tell me?*

When we reach my classroom, Mr. Haskell accompanies me inside since I'm late. He gives Mr. Mitchell a nod. I'm sure it's so Mr. Mitchell won't have an excuse to ask me why I'm tardy.

As I take my place in the back, Neeve Maynard turns in his seat and stares at me like the rest of the class does. Unlike everyone else, though, he smiles at me just a little, like maybe he understands. His half-smile feels like part encouragement and part sympathy.

# Echoes: A Modern Fairytale

After trying so hard to find a way to get his attention, I finally have it, but when I attempt to smile back at him, tears spill down my cheeks.

Getting Neeve Maynard to like me is the least of my worries.

I fold my arms on the desktop and drop my head down on them.

I am alone, helpless, and afraid.

I don't know what to do.

I cry silently.

I'm a cripple in a wheelchair.

The most popular and powerful kids at school hate me.

The football team is out to get me.

And I'm not going to get any support from the administration.

I should've died.


For the next couple of days, I try to decide if I should tell my parents about Kenneth Nelson and the encounter in the hallway. Maybe I should also tell them about the threatening letters I received.

But I know there's nothing they can do.

The football team already has me in its sights.

When I was discharged from the rehab center, I had a home study tutor for a couple of weeks to help me catch up on my coursework. I liked it. I wanted to continue home study until the end of the school year so I could do my assignments at my own pace in my own room.

My folks said no.

Transferring to a different school might have made a difference if I had never come back to Millard Fillmore High. Maybe the football team would have forgotten all about me—out of sight, out of mind—if I'd just stayed away.

Now it's too late.

Going to the police would be as useless as telling my parents. Kenneth Nelson is too well known, too popular, too much of a local hero. I understand that colleges are tripping over each other trying to recruit him. He's just hasn't decided which offer to accept yet.

So what's left?

My folks can't afford to hire me a bodyguard.

About all they could do is to move far away, and they can't do that without jobs waiting for them.

Nothing can be done.

No one can help.

I'm on my own.

I'll just have to be more aware of the time between classes to make sure I'm not caught all by myself again. I'd better start being more cautious at home, too, and keep the doors locked whenever my parents are gone.

It's not hard to find out where someone lives. Heck, someone could have

24

followed me home from school already.

I start nervously chewing on my thumbnail. I force myself to stop.

If I'm not careful, I'll work myself into a real panic by thinking about what possibly might, maybe could, perhaps will, happen in the future.

I decide to think about the one person whose existence is more messed up than mine.

Neeve Maynard.

Assuming that even a fraction of what Brenda said is true, Neeve must be extraordinarily brave.

If I woke up with no memories except for my name, if I was injured and bleeding and surrounded by strangers, I'd start screaming and never stop. They'd have to lock me in a padded cell.

Yet here he is, going to high school like any other teenager.

Even though I pretty much hate my life right now, at least I'm living with my own family. I might not have friends here in the Rocky Mountains (it's too early to tell if Juanita will become one), but I have friends in Chicago. We text each other nearly every day.

Without his memories, Neeve doesn't even know if he has parents somewhere who are looking for him, parents who miss him and cry at night because they don't know where he is. He might have brothers and sisters and friends and neighbors all wondering what happened to him.

I don't know how he bears it.

# Chapter Five

As I roll through the halls and around campus, I keep an eye out for Neeve.

If I can't find an opportunity to talk to him in World History, maybe I can catch him before or after school. I'm sure I can think of an excuse to speak to him. If nothing else, I can thank him for his sympathetic smile on a day when I needed one. But I don't see him on the school grounds, in the hallways, or in the cafeteria. In fact, I never see him anywhere except in class, and he tends to come late and sprint out as quickly as possible.

I've started dreaming about him, although in actuality it's been nothing more than a vague sense of his presence on the fringes of my dreams, just like he's on the fringes of my thoughts when I'm awake, just like he's on the fringes of my life at school.

I realize I'm obsessing about him, but what else do I have to distract myself from reality? I can't think too far into the future without becoming frightened and depressed. If I asked my dad—which I'm never going to do— he would probably say this is a harmless diversion while I'm adjusting to my altered circumstances. Anyway, I hope that's what he'd say.

In the meantime, Juanita and I are becoming friends. We chat in homeroom and English and the cafeteria as if we've known each other forever.

Then without warning, one day when she joins me for lunch, Juanita brings two girls and a guy with her. My heart sinks. Is she going to dump me now that she's had time to get acquainted with other kids?

One girl is about Juanita's height, probably 5'7" (which is four inches taller than I am when I'm standing and a lot taller than I am when I'm sitting.) Her black hair (which is probably artificial) is streaked with pink and maroon stripes.

The other girl is closer to my height, 5'3". Her light brown hair is parted down the middle and curves around her face like a couple of parentheses. She is wearing square, purple-framed glasses that match the purple sweater she has on.

The boy reminds me of the cartoon character Charlie Brown. He has a round, pleasant face and nondescript hair. He's not too tall and is a bit stocky, but not fat.

I manufacture a smile and welcome them in the off chance that they might become my friends too.

"Karissa, this is Maren, Deedra, and John," Juanita says to me. "Maren and Deedra are in my Spanish class. John and I have band together. We're all newbies, so I figured we could hang out and support each other."

Maren (maroon and pink hair) sighs as she opens a brown bag and takes out a sandwich. "I thought in a college town there would be too many people coming and going for the high school to have cliques."

"Yeah," John says, spinning an apple on the table in front of him, "but I think it works the other way around. There is so much turnover that the full-timers stick together and exclude everyone else."

"So," I ask, wanting to get into the conversation so they can't ignore me, "did all of you move here because of the University?"

"My mom and I did," Deedra (purple glasses) says. "My parents got divorced last year, and my mother wants to finish her degree in elementary education. We came here because the tuition is reasonable and the cost of living is less than in Connecticut. My older sister got married a couple of years ago and moved to Texas, so it's just my mom and I."

John gives Deedra a sympathetic nod. "My parents just got divorced too." Then he glances around at the rest of us, as if he wants to make sure no one feels left out. "We moved here because this is where my mom grew up. We're staying with my grandparents for now. But there are five of us—my mother, two sisters, a brother, and I—and it's kind of crowded. My grandparents say they don't mind. They want Mom to go to college, but she says she doesn't know what to study. Right now, she works at Walmart."

We all automatically look at Maren.

"My dad's an electrician," she says, "but he wants to be a mechanical engineer. He got a job at the University in the physical plant." She grins brightly. "After he's worked there for six months, he'll get tuition at half price and a discount on his textbooks. His boss is really supportive. He's willing to adjust Dad's schedule if there are required classes that are only taught during work hours. Dad is very excited. He's wanted to go back to school for years. What about you two?" she asks Juanita and me.

So, they are just getting acquainted with Juanita too. Nice.

I already like these kids.

No one is focused on the wheelchair.

They're not pretending it doesn't exist, like some people do. They simply accept it the same way they accept Juanita's dimples, Maren's striped hair, Deedra's funny glasses, and John's stocky build.

"My mother starts graduate school next fall," Juanita answers. "I wanted to finish the school year in California, but my dad is an ER nurse. When Mom got accepted in the graduate program here, he applied for a job at Mountain View Hospital. They offered him a position, and he said he couldn't afford to turn it down. So here we are. My older brothers are all still in California."

The glances turn toward me. I smile, feeling pretty happy about the way this is going.

"My father is the new director of the University Student Counseling Center," I tell them. "He never really liked Chicago, so he jumped at the chance to come here. He grew up in Idaho and was glad to get back to the Rockies. My mom is a self-employed accountant. She didn't mind the change because—with video chats, emails, and faxes—most of her business is portable. I have two younger brothers who are already hooked on snowboarding."

"Hey," Juanita said, "I just realized something. We're all in Colorado now, and three of us came here from places that start with the letter C, too. California, Connecticut, and Chicago." She makes eye contact with Maren and John. "Either of you guys from Cleveland or China?"

"You're mixing cities, states, and countries," Maren says with a laugh.

"Does it matter?" Deedra asks. "It's an interesting coincidence."

"Coincidence starts with C too," Juanita points out.

"I used to live on Clover Leaf Circle," John says. "Does that count?"

"That's three Cs," I tell him. "Clover, Circle, and count."

"I think it's four," says Maren. "Circle has two Cs."

"I got the most Cs," John says. "Do I get a prize?"

We're all laughing.

It's silly.

It's stupid.

It's great.

When I came back to Millard Fillmore High School, I thought I would never laugh again.

The bell rings.

"Nice meeting you, Karissa," Maren says as she pushes back her chair and snatches up her books.

"Can we make this our regular table?" John asks.

"Sure," I say.

Juanita says it at the same time.

Deedra hooks her arm through a strap on her backpack. "See you tomorrow," she calls as she trots off.

"You're not mad that I invited them?" Juanita asks me as we leave the cafeteria together.

"No," I answer. "They're super."

"When we first came through the door and I saw your expression, I was afraid you'd be angry and ditch me."

"Don't pay any attention to my face," I tell her. "I washed it this morning and I can't do a thing with it."

It's an old joke, but she laughs anyway.

Another week is passing quickly.

I'm surprised at how different my mood is when I know I'm going to share the lunch period with friends.

When physical therapy with Randall Gregory sneaks up on me, I hardly notice, and even he isn't as bad as usual.

I feel strange.

I think I'm learning how to be happy again.


Then one Friday, when I get to World History after lunch, Mr. Mitchell is standing in the doorway of the classroom. He has a hat in his hand and holds it up in front of me.

"Take one, but don't show it to anyone until I tell you to."

I reach in and take out a slip of paper with a number on it.

I hear him give the same instructions to whoever is next in line.

When I pull up to my desk in the back of the room, I notice it was Neeve Maynard who came in behind me.

The bell rings as he takes his seat.

Mr. Mitchell begins class by announcing that we have a research paper to write, and it will be one-third of our semester grade. It's due the last day before spring break.

We all groan in unison.

"You can choose any topic related to one of the countries covered in your textbook except for the United States. I know most of you had U.S. History last year, and I don't want any recycled term papers. You can write about a single person, or you can write about art, industry, superstitions, religion, government, agriculture, warfare, or any part of daily life. I don't really care what your subject is.

"What I want is a strong thesis statement, supportive information, footnotes, and a thorough bibliography. You can use three resources from the Internet, but I want at least two from real books."

He picks up a book from his desk and holds it high.

"This is what a book looks like—for those of you who have forgotten." There are a few polite chuckles. "There is no length requirement, no specific number of words or pages. If you can cover your topic adequately in 500 words, good for you, but they'd better be a great 500 words.

"What I'm looking for is originality. I get tired of grading the same boring, dry research papers. I will give one A+ for the best written, most original, most informative article, and up to four As for the runners-up.

"Last year's A+ paper covered the lasting influence of William

Shakespeare. The paper was written completely in verse, including the footnotes. It was delightful and was selected to be the major piece in the school magazine."

Dramatic grumbles come from all sides of the room.

"I know it's a big assignment," he continues, "but you don't have to work alone. As you came in, you each drew a number from the hat. Students with the same number will team up and collaborate. Decide on your topic together then come up here and write it down, along with both of your names."

He holds up a clipboard.

"No two teams can choose the same subject, so it is first come first served. Now hold up your numbers and find your partners. You can have the rest of the period to talk among yourselves. If you can't think of a topic, feel free to thumb through the books at the back of the room for a little inspiration."

People begin sorting themselves out.

I hear a few whispers of "I'll trade you."

I hold up a card with "**11**" printed on it.

Neeve looks straight at me and holds up the matching number.

I feel as if all the air has been sucked out of the room.

My heart stops.

I can't breathe.

Then he smiles at me, and not a little half-smile like before. This is the real thing.

All the air rushes back into my lungs.

As his lips part and curl at the corners, his whole face lights up and his very white teeth actually sparkle. He is the most magnificent sight I've ever seen. Automatically, I smile back.

The aisles disappear as kids shove desks together so they can confer. Neeve works his way around them.

I can hardly believe it.

What are the chances that the last two numbers in the hat were both elevens? The odds must be astronomical.

It feels like magic.

But, I tell myself, every now and then a long shot comes in.

I'm so excited I'm embarrassed.

I don't want Neeve to notice, so I turn my chair around and scan the titles of Mr. Mitchell's books. I need time to pull myself together.

A book catches my eye, but of course it is too high for me to reach.

I stretch as far as I can, but I'm still three or four inches too low.

"May I get that for you?"

I glance up and up and up.

Neeve Maynard is really tall, well over six feet.

"Yes, thank you," I say. "The one about myths and legends."

He hands it to me.

"You like mythology?" he asks. His voice is soft and mellow and very appealing, like a Beethoven sonata.

"It intrigues me," I answer truthfully. "I can't help wondering if it isn't more history than legend. But if Perseus existed, what did he battle in order to create the myth of Medusa? How does a story develop about a woman with snakes on her head who can turn people into stone with a glance?"

"Maybe it's not a legend. Maybe he actually fought a Gorgon."

"That's the part that intrigues me. What if he did?"

He grins like he understands. His eyes are green, deep and mysterious like a pair of rare emeralds. A girl could get lost in those eyes.

"I'm Neeve Maynard. You must be Karissa Day, the wheelchair girl." The way he says it, it's a compliment.

I pat an armrest and say, "What was your first clue?"

He laughs. It's music, too, but it's more Andrew Lloyd Webber than Beethoven.

"Do you want to do our paper on Greek mythology?" He props his elbow on a shelf of the bookcase as he gazes down at me.

I'm impressed that he knows the story of Perseus was originally Greek, not Roman, and I tingle deep inside at his use of the word *our*.

I don't want him to have this power over me.

I decide to be contrary.

"I was thinking more like Odin, Thor, and Valhalla."

"I'm fond of Norse mythology too," he says, surprising me again. But what he says next about bowls me over. "I think it might be fun to write about the Brothers Grimm and their travels through Germany collecting folk stories."

"You read fairytales?" It pops out, and I sound like an imbecile, but I've never heard a guy over the age of six admit it.

"I guess I'm a little like you. I always wonder if some part of them isn't true." He pulls a chair around and sits. "Mythology or fairytales? Which do you prefer? Either would be interesting."

As I consider, I'm not thinking about which topic will be easier or more enjoyable to work on. I'm wondering what Neeve's reaction will be if I choose one subject over the other.

If I say I prefer mythology, he might think I'm too demanding and I'll insist on having things my own way. If I agree to fairytales, he might think I'm a pushover who'll be too passive to contribute.

I word my answer carefully.

"I like your idea better than mine," I say. "It's unusual enough that it probably hasn't been done very often."

"If ever," he says.

I nod in agreement. "And there are lots of different, creative approaches we could take. Before we decide, though, are there other topics you'd like to consider?"

"Not really," he says. "If you don't mind doing fairytales, it is my first choice."

I try to sound nonchalant, like it doesn't really matter to me one way or the other. "Fairytales it is then."

Actually, I'm delighted. The possibility of magic has always fascinated me, and I read fairytales, mythology, legends, and fantasy in huge quantities.

"I'll go sign us up," he says.

I watch him glide through the chaos.

His hair is very blond, like wheat just before it has fully ripened, and he wears it parted in the middle and gathered into a long tail held by an elastic band. The blue jeans and black t-shirt he's wearing show off how slender he is. But he's not skinny. He's lean with long legs and arms and narrow hips. His shoulders are broad, and muscles ripple beneath his clothing.

When Neeve gets to Mr. Mitchell's desk, he runs his finger down the list on the clipboard. He gives me a thumbs-up.

Then he adds our information.

I am elated.

We have a topic and over six weeks to work on it. I could faint.

When he returns, we agree to meet tomorrow to make our plans and divide up the research.

"I'll come to your house," he offers, "if that's all right with you."

"That's fine," I tell him. "Is 10:00 a good time?"

"Perfect."

I write down my address and cellphone number for him, hoping that he won't notice how badly my hand is trembling.

"I'll call you tonight to confirm," Neeve says. "I'm pretty sure a friend will drive me over. If I have to walk, we might need to adjust the time a little."

"If you need to walk," I say, "maybe we should meet in the middle somewhere." I glance down at my chair. "I have wheels."

"I wouldn't be comfortable with that," he says, frowning. "I'll see what I can arrange and call you."

The bell rings.

He smiles at me before he disappears out the door.

I'm in heaven.

World History is now officially my favorite class.

I float through the rest of the day.

I forget about Kenneth Nelson for whole minutes at a time.

Dad picks me up after school.

On the drive home, he tells me he has to go back to the University for an evening meeting, and Mom is running late with a client who has never heard of accounting software and whose ledgers are such a mess that figuring them out might become her life's work.

In the driveway, after he gets the wheelchair out for me, Dad hands me two twenty-dollar bills.

"You can order pizza," he says. He kisses my forehead and then waits until I've gone up the ramp and have opened the side door before he leaves.

After the pizza arrives, I take my share and go to my room.

This is the kind of evening I like.

I don't have much homework, my folks won't be home until late, and my brothers are already glued to the television in the basement. Plus, Neeve is going to call me.

What could be better?

Well, I tell myself, I could magically walk. That would be nice. Barring that, the evening looks pretty good.

I usually read a book or watch TV while I eat, but tonight nothing captures my attention.

I pull out my story, but I'm not in the mood. Instead I reach for my colored pencils so I can work on some thumbnail sketches. I need to decide which scenes I'm going to illustrate. It was a picture I drew in Chicago that inspired the story: a picture of a handsome fairy prince flying with a human girl in his arms.

Neeve calls.

"Karissa," he says, and I tingle just hearing him say my name. "My friend will drop me off at your place. Is 10:00 still a good time?"

"Yes," I answer.

"I'll see you in the morning then. Sleep well."

"Good night."

After he hangs up, I sit and stare into space.

I am drawn to Neeve by invisible forces that I don't understand. It's as if he's a magnet and I'm a bit of iron. I should be frightened that a total stranger exerts such an irresistible pull on me, but I'm not. I'm intrigued and excited and full of anticipation.

I hear the garage door open. I put away my story and open my Calculus textbook so I'll look busy. Whichever parent has come home will surely stop by to tell me good night.

# Chapter Six

Saturday morning, I wake up at 6:15.

Usually I'm not up before 9:00 on the weekends, sometimes not until 10:00, but Neeve is coming over today and I can't sleep.

I take a long shower, wash my hair, and shave my legs. I know that last part is stupid. I'll never wear shorts or mini-skirts again because of the scars, but I can't stand the grungy appearance of hairy legs. I have a plastic footstool that I prop my feet on. I have to lift my legs and arrange them with my hands in order to get them positioned right.

At 7:30 I'm blow-drying my hair. It's short and naturally curly, so all I have to do is fluff it with my fingers while I point the dryer at it a few times. I used to wear my hair long, but since the accident, that's not practical. It was always getting caught between my body and the back of the wheelchair, a very painful experience.

I'm putting the blow dryer away when Mom knocks on my bathroom door and then comes right in.

"I've got to go to the office," she says. "Mr. Keller found another mistake his bookkeeper made, and he's on the verge of a stroke. I don't know how long I'll be. Bennett is staying with Mike Williams until after the basketball game tonight. Phil Barker's mother is picking Jeremy up at 8:45 to take him to marching band practice, and then Jeremy is going over to Phil's house. Dad has a lunch meeting at the University. Will you be all right if you're home alone all day?"

"I won't be alone," I tell her. "Remember, that boy from my World History class is coming over so we can work on our research paper."

"Right. I forgot. There are sodas in the fridge and plenty of things for sandwiches or salads if you two get hungry. I've got to go now. Call me if you need me."

She's out the door before I can say goodbye.

I make my bed.

Before the accident, my room was generally a mess. I tossed my clothes on the floor and stacked books everywhere. If I missed the trashcan when I threw away a candy wrapper or a tissue, it was no big deal.

Things are different now.

When I could walk, I could dodge the mess.

Now if I leave something on the floor, it's likely to end up with tire tracks all over it.

Everything in my room—actually on the whole ground floor—has been arranged so I have access from the wheelchair. My bed is situated so I can reach it from either side. My books, CDs, and DVDs are all on low shelves in the bookcases. Decorative items like pictures and silk flowers and stuffed animals are up higher.

The laundry room is in a little niche off of the kitchen. My parents replaced the washer with a front loader, so I can continue doing my own laundry. Microwave and toaster are on a lowered counter. Cereal, bread, and soup are in bottom cabinets instead of cupboards.

When I first came home from the hospital, I thought my folks expected too much of me. If getting mangled in a car accident doesn't excuse you from chores, what does?

But now I appreciate every little thing I can do for myself.

If I'm going to be stuck in this chair for the rest of my life, and I'm always afraid that it's a possibility, I'm glad I won't have to depend on other people to take care of me. Even if I never walk again, I can go to college, live in my own apartment, find a real job, and build good friendships.

I can have everything I've always wanted.

I swallow hard. Well, maybe not everything.

As a cripple, I doubt I'll get married and have children.

But that doesn't mean I can't have a rewarding life.

Jane Austen never married, and I love her books, especially *Pride and Prejudice.* If you have a character like Mr. Darcy living inside your mind, being a spinster can't be too awful. (I like the word *spinster* better than the term *old maid.* It has more dignity.)

If I remember right, only one of the three Bronte sisters ever got married, and they have been popular novelists for nearly two hundred years. I'm ashamed to admit, however, that I'm not as fond of them as everyone else seems to be. I hated *Wuthering Heights.* Honestly, is there a single likable character in that whole book? Plus, I thought *Jane Eyre* was too depressing for words. I never got around to reading *Agnes Gray.* Maybe I'll put it on my summer reading list and see if it's as dreary as the other two.

The point is that those women found ways to have meaningful lives without husbands and children. (Unfortunately, none of them lived to reach old age. I hope there's not a corollary there.)

Oh well.

I still want writing to be my future livelihood.

I look at my clock radio. It's not even 9:00 yet.

I have over an hour until Neeve arrives.

If I could still walk, I'd probably pace restlessly through the house, but I don't think I'd get much satisfaction from rolling around in my wheelchair.

I take out my story and try to focus on it. Hopeless.

"Kari," my dad calls while knocking on my door.

I flip my story over. "Come in."

"Jeremy just left, and I have to go soon. Are you going to be all right?"

"I'll be fine."

"Tell me about this boy who's coming over."

Dad takes off his glasses, pulls a small blue microfiber cloth from his pocket, and begins to polish the lenses. Without his glasses in the way, his long, dark eyelashes are spectacular. I've always wished mine looked like his, but instead, I inherited Mom's stubby, almost invisibly pale, ones.

"I don't know him very well," I say. "He's in my World History class. Our teacher had us draw numbers from a hat to find our research partners. We've only talked a couple of times."

"No boyfriend-girlfriend stuff going on here?"

"Dad, look at me," I say. "No guy's going to want a girl who comes with this much baggage."

He puts his glasses back on and pushes them up his nose. "With or without the wheelchair, Kari, you're a beautiful young woman. What's the boy's name?"

"Neeve Maynard."

I can tell by the flash in Dad's eyes that he's heard the name before. He might actually have been on duty when Neeve was taken to the Emergency Room on Halloween night. Dad does some psychological testing, and sometimes intake evaluations, at Mountain View Hospital. He says he needs to keep up his clinical skills, but the fact is that he has always enjoyed doing the front-line work more than he has enjoyed being an administrator.

"Maybe I'll stick around long enough to meet him," Dad says.

"Fine with me," I tell him.

What else can I say?

Go away? I want to be alone with him?

I don't think so.

The minutes creep by.

I flip open my laptop and type in Brothers Grimm to get some idea of how much information is available.

I think there'll be enough.

The results are listed as over two million.

I don't bother looking at any of them. Instead, I roll into the kitchen to get a bowl of cereal.

# Chapter Seven

The doorbell rings.

I quickly drink the milk left in my bowl then pop it and the spoon into the dishwasher.

I wheel out to the living room as Dad reaches for the door.

I'm right behind him.

Neeve and Dad stare at each other for a moment.

"Dad, this is Neeve Maynard. Neeve, this is my father, Walter Day."

Dad extends his hand. Neeve takes it.

"Are we supposed to pretend we've never met?" Neeve asks.

Dad smiles slightly. "That's your choice."

"Too late now, I guess," Neeve says. "I never put it together. Day is a common last name."

"I would have warned you if I'd known," Dad tells him. "Karissa just told me you were coming a few minutes ago."

Neeve looks at me and then back at Dad. "Are you all right with this? My being here?"

"Is there a reason I shouldn't be?" asks Dad.

"No."

"All right." Dad leans over and kisses me on the forehead. "I've got to go. Good luck with the research."

After he leaves, there is an awkward silence.

Neeve speaks first. "That must have looked odd from your point of view. Do I need to explain?"

I shake my head. "It's none of my business."

"Thank you." He looks genuinely relieved.

"Come on in and sit down," I tell him.

"You have a nice home," he says, following me into the living room. "It has a very comfortable feel." He glances around. "How do you manage the stairs?"

Usually I don't like it when people ask about my disability, but there's something different about Neeve.

I'm not offended, and I'm not defensive.

*Why?* I wonder.

I guess I don't answer his question quickly enough.

He goes on. "It's like having an elephant in the room, Karissa."

"I've heard Dad use that expression," I say, "but I don't know what it means."

"It means, if there's an elephant in the room, it doesn't make any sense to pretend it's not there. Everyone can see it, so you might as well talk about it."

"Is the fact that you know my Dad like an elephant in the room?"

"Not really," Neeve answers. His mouth lifts up at the corners in a slight grin. "It's more like a rattle in a closet. You assume something is in there, but you won't know for sure until you've looked inside. Maybe I'll open that door for you someday. Not today."

*Fine*, I think to myself, *keep your old secrets*.

I'm tempted to say something sarcastic, something really rude. After all, my handicap—the most personal and devastating part of my life—is right out there in plain view. I suspect Neeve is struggling with problems as significant as mine, but I won't know what they are unless he tells me. It doesn't seem fair.

However, he's right. My chair is an elephant in the room.

"I don't do anything about the stairs," I say. "There's nothing up there that I need. While I was in the hospital, my parents moved my stuff down here."

"Is there a basement?" he asks.

"Yes, but it isn't finished. When we first moved in, there wasn't anything down there except the frames for the walls. My dad and my brothers hung the sheetrock to enclose one area. They painted it and got a carpet remnant for the floor. Jeremy and Bennett use it as a games room. I wouldn't be welcome down there even if I could still walk."

Neeve lowers himself onto our tan couch, sitting at an angle so he can drape his arm along the back.

"How old are your brothers?" Neeve asks.

"Jeremy's fourteen and Bennett's twelve."

A sunbeam backlights Neeve's hair, making it look like a halo around his head. His face is shadowed, and for a moment he looks totally alien, like something not of this world.

I think I gasp.

His brow crinkles briefly. Then he shifts position, and he is simply a good-looking teenage boy again.

"Have you given any thought to our project?" he asks.

"A little," I answer. "How about you?"

"A little. What have you come up with?"

"Well," I say.

Now that I have to put the idea into words, I'm afraid he'll think it's stupid. He watches me expectantly. I'm in a tough spot. I can sound like a moron by voicing a dumb idea, or I can look like a moron by not saying anything. I decide a verbal idiot is better than a silent one.

"Well," I repeat, "I was thinking it might be fun to write our paper like it was one of Grimm's fairytales. You know, start with 'Once upon a time there were two brothers,' or something like that. We'd need to come up with a storyline, though."

"I like it," Neeve says to my surprise. "Maybe the plot could deal with their search for a particular type of story."

"What kind?" I ask.

We're both quiet while we think. I learn something new about Neeve. He is completely comfortable in the silence, and he projects that calm to me so I'm comfortable too. I'm usually so nervous around guys that I babble incoherently in an effort to cover it up. Being with Neeve feels so natural that the nervousness never comes.

"How about having them search for a fairytale that actually includes fairies," he suggests.

"But there are lots—" I stop myself as I run stories through my mind. "Oh, I see what you mean! Cinderella's fairy godmother wasn't part of the original story. Instead, the ball lasted for three days, and birds brought her a different gown for each evening. There aren't any fairies in Sleeping Beauty, either."

"That's right," Neeve says. "The Brothers Grimm called them wise women, not fairies."

"Are there any fairytales that deal with fairies?"

"I don't think there are, not in the Brothers Grimm versions. Similar stories from other countries might include fairies."

"Then why are the stories by the Brothers Grimm called fairytales?"

"I don't know. The answer would be an interesting tidbit to include in our paper."

"I'll go get my laptop," I say. "We probably ought to make a list of things we need to research." I turn my chair around and head for my room.

I'm reaching for my laptop when Neeve speaks. I don't realize he's followed me until I hear his voice.

"You must really like to read," he says, looking at all my books.

I'm so startled I knock my story over and it flutters to the floor.

"I'll get those," Neeve offers.

Of course, he looks at them.

I feel like sinking through the floor. I don't ever show anyone my stupid stories or amateurish drawings.

He shuffles through the pages to make sure they're in order. He puts the drawing of the girl in the fairy's arms on top and studies it.

"I like this," he says. "You've got the wings exactly right."

I feel my face burning. I'm sure he's being sarcastic.

He thumbs through the pages again, pausing to study the pencil sketches. "These are very good."

"Don't patronize me," I snarl angrily. "I'm a cripple not an idiot." I grab at the papers, but he snatches them out of my reach.

"Why would I patronize you?" he snaps back at me. "Is that the kind of person you think I am?" He glares at me for a moment like he did at the boys who were talking about him in class. I'm actually a little frightened. "Maybe I'd better go. We can try this another day."

He drops my story on the desk and turns to leave.

My heart sinks down to my feet.

I really am an idiot.

"Wait," I cry. "I'm insecure about my art, that's all."

I stare at my hands, folding them together and laying them in my lap, trying to appear more composed than I feel.

"I look at what other kids our age can do," I explain, "the ones who've studied art since grade school, and I feel like I'm on the kindergarten level. It makes me defensive. I'm sorry."

I risk peering up at him, and his face is thoughtful. I can see the change in his expression when he decides not to be mad at me.

"I know what it's like to keep comparing yourself to other people," Neeve says. "It's a hard habit to break."

"Does that mean you'll stay?"

He gives me a wry grin. "Yes, I'll stay. And your pictures have given me a great idea. Instead of just writing a fairytale about the Brothers Grimm, why don't we illustrate it as if it were a children's book? I like to draw too. We can write the story and do the pictures together."

"I'll bet it's never been done before," I say, beaming up at him.

"I'd enjoy getting that A+," he says.

I hear a lot behind his words. What he really wants is to show up the creeps in our class—maybe in the whole student body—by having our story selected to go in the school magazine.

"How can we both work on the art?" I ask. "It seems to me that a picture is either done or not done."

"Don't be silly," Neeve says. "Drawing is a process, just like writing." He picks my story up again and crouches down beside me so we can both look at the illustrations.

"Look at these facial expressions," he says. "They're exquisite. The boy looks like he's got an armful of problems, not just a pretty girl. She looks as if someone has smacked her between the eyes with a hammer, completely shaking up her sense of reality. I can't do things like that. I'm good at drawing buildings and scenery. Sometimes I do silhouettes of people in action poses, fighting or running or jumping or even dancing. But I don't do faces very well, certainly nothing as subtle as this."

"You really think they're good?"

"They're better than good. Come on, let's go back into the living room and do some planning."

I get my laptop and follow him in a daze.

He still has my story in his hand. "Do you mind if I take this home with me to read? I'll give it back to you Monday morning."

"It's just a rough draft," I say. "I'm still working on it."

"That's all right," he says. "The pictures make me curious about the story. Please." His eyes seem to go from emerald to a green that's so dark it's almost black. "Please."

I drown in the depth of his gaze.

I surrender.

"Just don't forget to bring it to class."

"I won't."

Actually, I have the whole thing on my computer, not just the story but also the pictures. Every time I finish a sketch, I scan it so I can play around with layout and colors on the graphics program.

When Neeve leaves at 3:00, I'm good and tired of the Brothers Grimm, both of them, but I'm enchanted with Neeve.

He's not just another gorgeous guy.

He's smart, and witty, and clever, and talented.

I hope I can keep up.


Monday morning, for the first time since we moved here, I am happy about going to school.

As we turn off the main road, I tell myself not to expect too much.

I won't see Neeve until World History class.

Still, I can't help being excited.

As usual, after Mom parks, she pushes the button on her key fob, the hatchback opens, and she gets out of the van.

I hear a melodic voice say, "Let me get that for you, Mrs. Day."

When the wheelchair comes into view, it is Neeve's hand that guides it, not Mom's.

Mom follows behind him. She gives me a thumbs-up and says silently, "Way to go, girl."

Without asking for my permission, Neeve slips one arm behind my back and the other under my thighs. He lifts me out of the van as if I weigh no more than a ragdoll.

He sets me in the chair.

I can tell Mom is conflicted.

She is delighted to have this gorgeous guy paying attention to me, but his picking me up is a little too intimate for her.

She looks like a fish gasping for breath.

Her mouth pops open as if she wants to say something like, "Take your hands off my daughter." But she knows she can't say it without sounding dumb, so her mouth closes. Then it pops open again when she thinks of something else, but she rejects it too, and her mouth snaps shut.

"Mom," I say, hoping to stop the guppy impersonations before anyone notices, "this is Neeve Maynard. He's in World History with me."

Mom pulls herself together. "I'm pleased to meet you, Neeve."

He smiles at her. "I could have picked you out in a crowd. You and Karissa have the same beautiful eyes." He grabs my backpack from the van and hands it to me.

Mom switches from fish-mouthed to bug-eyed.

The strange thing is that Neeve doesn't sound phony or schmoozing. The words glide from his mouth with the ease and skill that one would expect from an ambassador. This kind of cool poise is not often seen in high school boys.

"See you later, Mom." I give her a little wave as I start up the ramp.

Neeve calls, "It was nice to meet you, Mrs. Day."

Mom is still standing there, entranced, when I glance back at her while Neeve opens the door for me.

"Where's your homeroom?" Neeve asks, walking beside me.

We get some startled looks from kids we pass.

"A-5," I tell him. "During first period, I have Mr. Ullom for English."

"Is he as good as everyone says?"

"I like him. His tells a lot of jokes. On Fridays he starts class by reading us a poem. He says he's determined to show the boys that there's nothing silly or sissy about good poetry."

"What about the girls?" Neeve asks me. "Doesn't he care if all of you enjoy it?"

"I guess he just assumes that most girls already do."

"Is he right? Are you fond of poetry?"

"Very much," I say. "I have several collections of famous poems, plus the complete works of Byron, Kipling, and Frost."

"Do you also write it?" he asks.

"No," I say with a rueful laugh. "I've tried. I just don't have the knack."

"I like to write poetry," he says, surprising me as much as when he suggested fairytales for our paper. "It's one of the ways I cope when I'm unhappy. I don't know if I have any great talent, but I enjoy doing it regardless."

"Can I read some?" I ask. "Or are the poems too personal?"

"They're pretty personal, but you let me read your story. I guess it's only fair that I let you read my poetry. I don't carry any of it with me, so you might need to remind me to bring you a sample."

He pulls my story out of his backpack and hands it to me.

"By the way," he says, "I really enjoyed this. In fact, I was thinking maybe we could end our paper with it—as an example of how the Brothers Grimm have influenced modern fantasy."

"Really?"

"Yes. Maybe we can talk about it Friday evening."

"Friday evening?"

"Yes, when we go out."

We've reached my homeroom by now, and we pull over to the side so we don't block traffic.

"When we what?" I sputter.

"When we go out. Isn't that what kids our age do? Go out on dates? Or don't you want to?"

"I—uh, I'd like to go out with you," I say, "but I'm not what you can call low maintenance." I smack the armrest of my chair. "This takes a van to haul around."

"Then I'm lucky I have a friend who owns a van."

"With a wheelchair hoist?"

"I'm sure Brenlyn and I can manage. And I'm sure he can figure out how to secure the chair so it doesn't bang around the back of the van while we're moving. He's very good with mechanical things."

"So we'll double date with your friend Brenlyn?"

Considering how appealing I find Neeve, considering how strongly I'm drawn to him, having someone else around is not a bad idea.

Much safer.

Neeve's face goes blank for a moment.

Then he looks amused.

"Yes," he says, "we'll double date with Brenlyn. How about dinner and a movie?"

Whoa. That's awfully expensive for a kid in foster care.

"All right," I say, "as long as it's Dutch treat."

Again that blank expression followed by something else, but not amusement this time.

"You want to pay your own way?" He sounds offended.

"Of course, it's only—"

He glares at me with his eyebrows pinched together so they're almost touching.

"I wouldn't invite you if I couldn't afford it," he says, sounding angry. "If you ever ask me out, we can argue about who pays for what. But when I ask you, I'll handle the cost."

I don't know what to say.

I'm glad when the first bell rings.

I want to wheel away, but he moves in front of me.

"Friday night? Yes or no?" he demands.

"Yes," I say, frustrated. I start around him, but he steps aside.

"Good. I'll see you in World History." He ambles off whistling softly.

I'm left wondering what in the world just happened between us.

Two guys pause in the doorway of my classroom.

One of them glances down at me. "Was that Neeve Maynard?"

"Yes," I tell him, surprised that someone in my class has finally spoken to me.

"He's kind of hard to miss," his friend says.

"I see him shooting hoops during lunch sometimes," says the first guy. "I wonder why I've never noticed him in the halls before."

# Chapter Eight

I float through my morning classes in a daze.

I don't know what to think about Neeve. His mood swings are a little scary, but they also add to his mystique.

I can hardly believe he wants to date me.

Okay, maybe I'm getting ahead of myself.

He's invited me on a first date. There might never be a second. Even so, I can hardly believe we're going out once. He is undoubtedly the best looking guy in the whole school, possibly the smartest too.

Yet, he asked me out.

Wouldn't Kimberly and her cronies just die if they knew?

When I enter the cafeteria for lunch, Juanita and John are already sitting at our table. They both wave.

I head cautiously for the hot-foods line.

Kids are rushing every which way, pushing and colliding and trying to catch up with friends.

I'm always terrified I'll run over someone.

"Hey, Karissa," Deedra says. Her glasses today are red and white in a swirly pattern, like a candy cane. She's wearing a red long-sleeved blouse with white jeans. When I first met her, Deedra's glasses were purple, but usually she wears simple wire-frames. I've never known anyone who owned three pairs of glasses before.

There are two kids between us in line. Deedra lets them pass her.

"Did you have a nice weekend?" she asks me.

"I did." I think of Saturday with Neeve. "How about you?"

"Awful," she says. "My mom's sister flew in from Las Vegas Friday evening. It's the first time they've been together since my folks got divorced. If my aunt had come alone, it would have been bad enough, but she brought my thirteen-year-old cousin, Sheila, with her."

"Don't you like them?" I ask her.

"They're all right in small doses," she says. "But they talk all the time and they never listen." She goes into a nasal voice, which she alternates with her own. *"So how are you, Deedra?*—I'm—*You should have seen the mess at the airport. The terminal is so inadequate. Have you ever flown into Las Vegas?*—Yes, remember—*It was a nightmare, wasn't it? Well, wasn't it?*—I didn't think—*Well, you would hate it now, wouldn't she, Sheila? It's so crowded, as if the streets aren't bad enough. Traffic in Vegas is just terrible. I'd say get rid of the tourists except we need their money. And talking about money, what do you think of the current economic situation? Blah, blah, blah. Yadah, yadah, yadah."*

I pick up a bowl of vegetable soup and almost spill it all over my tray, I'm laughing so hard. Luckily, I just slosh a little bit over the side. I mop it up with a couple of napkins before I grab some crackers and then a bottle of apple juice.

"It's enough to drive me crazy," Deedra says, "and if you think my aunt sounds bad, you ought to hear my cousin jabber. I don't know why Aunt Marlene brought Sheila along. After all, she ought to be in school." She sighs dramatically. "I don't suppose you'd like a guest for the night?"

"Sure, I'd love it."

"Oh," Deedra says, blushing, as we move to get in line at the cash register. "I didn't mean to invite myself over. I was just joking."

"Well, I'm not," I tell her. "Neither of my parents will be home until late. Dad is covering for someone at the hospital's psychiatric ward, and Mom will be in her office helping clients who ran into accounting problems over the weekend. My brothers and I call Mondays our Independence Day."

Deedra gets this almost pitifully hopeful look on her face. She steps up to the register, opens her purse, and pulls out a couple of bills. "Would your parents let you have a sleepover on a school night?"

"Sure, since this is the first time. If we stay up all night and are late for school tomorrow, they'll say *no* the next time. That's the way they work. What about your mom? What would she say?"

"Ordinarily she'd probably say *no*," Deedra answers, taking her change. She picks up her tray and moves aside. "But I think she might make an exception this once. I have bunk beds in my room, so my cousin Sheila sleeps in there with me, except she doesn't sleep. She just talks and talks and talks. It's probably because her mother never listens to her. I haven't had a decent night's sleep since they arrived."

The woman at the register rings up my total.

When we get to our table, Maren has joined Juanita and John.

"Why don't you call your mother," I suggest, "and see what she says?"

"She'll ask if you've cleared it with your parents first. Since we're new in town, she might even want to talk to your mother."

"I'll call Mom, but I know what she'll say."

"What are you two plotting?" John asks.

Deedra sits down as I get out my cellphone. She starts explaining about her aunt and cousin.

Mom doesn't even say hello.

"What's wrong, Karissa?"

"Nothing," I tell her. "I just wondered if you'd mind if I have a friend sleep over tonight."

"A girl friend?" she asks.

"Of course." She must be having flashbacks of Neeve lifting me out of the van. But really! Does she think I'd ask for permission to have a guy spend an overnighter with me?

"Is there a reason you want a sleepover on a school night?" Mom asks.

"My friend, Deedra, and her mother have had company for a couple of days. With all the chatting and socializing, Deedra is short on sleep. I offered her a quiet place to catch up."

"Do you think she'll be okay on an air mattress?" Mom has an aunt who is a chatterbox. She can sympathize.

"Sure. An air mattress doesn't talk all night."

"All right. You'll need to pull something together for dinner. I imagine the boys will call dibs on the frozen pizza."

"We'll manage."

Deedra hands me a note. It reads *Tell her my mom might call her. Lydia Swanson.* "Mom, Deedra and her mother are new in town. Mrs. Swanson might call you to confirm. Her name is Lydia. Lydia Swanson."

"That's fine. I'll vouch for you."

"Thanks."

"Karissa, I'm glad you're making friends."

"Me too. Talk to you later."

I offer my phone to Deedra, but she pulls out her own.

As predicted, her mother asks for Mom's name and phone number.

It's all arranged before the bell rings. As soon as Deedra's mother finishes her last class at the University, she'll go home, pack a few things, and then drop them off at the front office.

Deedra and I agree to meet there as soon as school lets out.

I feel almost like a normal girl.

Kenneth Nelson and his buddies left the cafeteria with Coach Bederman as soon as they finished eating, so I can let my happiness show.

When I get to World History, Neeve is waiting by the door.

He gives me a quizzical look and then grins. "You're not mad about the Dutch date anymore."

"I wasn't mad this morning, not really."

His blending of Dutch treat and double date sounds strange. I would think he was trying to be funny if both terms hadn't seemed to puzzle him earlier. Maybe the gaps in his memory include certain idioms.

"My dad says I'm a rescuer," I tell him. "I guess I was trying to take responsibility for your finances. I apologize."

"It's all right." He follows me into class, still talking. "Do you want to get together this evening? We could study or just hang out."

The usual classroom babble stops.

I don't know if it's because Neeve is paying attention to the cripple or because the cripple is talking to the guy in foster care. I don't answer him until I'm in my place at the back of the room.

He pulls around an empty chair and sits close to me.

Kids turn in their seats to watch.

"I wish I could," I say quietly, self-consciously, because of all the attention we're getting, "but I've got company coming over."

I have mixed feelings about turning him down. Half of me is overjoyed that he wants to see me, and I regret having to say *no*. The other half is glad that I have plans so he doesn't think he's my only friend.

He drops his voice lower too. "A boy?" he asks with a frown.

He looks jealous.

I would jump up and down with excitement if I could stand.

"No, a girl. She needs a quiet place to crash for the night."

"How about tomorrow?" There's a challenge in his voice.

I answer with a challenge in mine. "Okay. Why don't you come over for dinner? We can work on our paper afterward."

He pretends to consider it, but I can tell by his expression that the decision is already made. "What time?"

"We usually eat around 6:30. Why don't you come over at 5:00 and help me cook?"

"You can cook?"

"Yeah, I can."

He drops his head and stares at the floor a moment.

When he looks up again, he says, "I don't mean to sound rude, but you need to know that I can't eat red meat, pork, or fried foods. They make me physically ill. Am I still invited?"

"Fish?" I ask. "Chicken?"

The bell rings.

"They're both fine," he says and goes to take his regular seat.

He looks back at me. I mouth the words: *You're still invited.*

The rest of the day drifts by.

I go to class.

I stay in crowds, watching out for Kenneth Nelson.

Deedra meets me at the office, where she picks up the bag her mother left for her. We're waiting outside in front of the school when Dad comes to pick us up.

He drops us off at the house then goes back to work.

Deedra and I have fun.

She thinks my bedroom in the den and my private bathroom are really cool. She is particularly fascinated with the shower. She tries the moveable seat half a dozen times, pulling it out, sitting down, working the lever, and riding it back into place.

"This should be standard equipment in every shower," she says.

We watch a DVD in my bedroom while we eat meatloaf left over from Sunday's dinner and boxed macaroni and cheese.

At a slow part in the movie, I tell her, "Your glasses are really cute. Did you break the other ones?"

Deedra pulls them off, like she has to check which ones she's wearing, and then slips them back on.

"My dad's an optometrist. A couple of years ago, he decided that new glasses are the ideal gift for me. I have glasses for Easter, Christmas, Fourth of July, summer, fall, winter, and spring. Just wait till you see the ones for Halloween. They're orange and black and have little white ghosts all over. I don't know where he finds the frames."

She shakes her head and shrugs. "My vision is stable, so the glasses sort of pile up. Every now and then, when I feel like being extreme, I'll pull out a pair that matches something I'm wearing."

After the movie, since we're responsible teenagers, we spend an hour or so doing homework while we snack on ice cream and cookies.

At 9:00 Jeremy knocks on my bedroom door. "Mom called and asked me to set up an air mattress for you. Where do you want it?"

"In front of the bookcases," I tell him. "That'll leave me an aisle for the wheelchair."

He plugs in the air pump.

I wheel out to the small linen closet in the hall and get sheets, blankets, and a pillow. There's a regular linen closet upstairs, but since I can't get to it, Mom lets me keep bed and bathroom supplies down here. This was probably a broom closet originally. Dad put in the shelves.

I feel bad that I can't make up the bed for my guest like a real hostess, but Deedra seems to enjoy doing it herself.

She plops on the mattress and bounces a couple of times before she settles down. "This is great," she says. "It's more comfortable than my mattress at home. Are they expensive?"

"I don't think so," I tell her. "You can get them at Walmart or Target."

"Super."

I let Deedra have the first turn in the bathroom.

By the time I've washed my face, brushed my teeth, undressed, and pulled on a nightgown, she is fast asleep.

I go into the kitchen to leave my parents a note.

A pad of paper is kept on the counter just for this purpose. It's a family rule that everyone checks it as soon as they come home.

I write: *I invited Neeve Maynard over for dinner tomorrow. He's coming at 5:00 to help me cook. We'll eat at 6:30. I took salmon steaks out of the freezer to thaw.*

I usually don't go to bed this early, so I fish my story out of my backpack. I look at the picture I drew of the fairy prince flying with the human girl in his arms. In my story, Jaydon (the fairy) has just saved Lark from being captured by trolls. Now he is taking her to the palace to meet the queen. As part of the narrative I explain that, as Jaydon flies, he and Lark shrink and shrink until they are no bigger than a peanut. I decide the next illustration should be of the fairy palace, which rests in the elbow of an ancient oak tree.

I draw until almost 10:30.

My parents will be home any minute now.

Reluctantly I put the story away.

Finishing my picture will have to wait until tomorrow.

No, I think, it'll have to wait a couple of days.

I smile as I turn out the light.

Neeve is coming to dinner tomorrow.

I pull myself into bed and prepare to have lovely dreams.

# Chapter Nine

All day I'm excited for school to end so I can go home and prepare for Neeve's visit. I'm not able to concentrate on anything else. Luckily, I have no tests, and none of the teachers call on me.

When the final bell rings, I dump my books in my locker and head outside. Deedra waves to me on her way to the bus. A little while later, so does Juanita.

Half an hour goes by, and I'm still waiting in front of the school.

My cellphone rings.

"Hey, Dad, where are you?"

"Kari, honey, I've been in a fender-bender. The car in front of me got t-boned by a car that tried to turn left against the light. I skidded into them. The car's not damaged, but I'm still filling out the police forms. I'll be there as quickly as I can."

"All right. If I'm not waiting at the curb, it'll be because I got cold and went back inside. I'll watch for you."

I'm just about to turn around and head for the wheelchair ramp when my way is blocked.

"Well, well," Kenneth Nelson says, "look who's out here all by her lonesome."

The guy who was with him before is there again.

I start to back up.

I bump into something.

I glance over my shoulder and see three more lettermen behind me.

"What shall we do with her?" Kenneth asks his buddies.

"We could tie her to that chair and drop her in the lake," the guy standing beside Kenneth says. He raises his right hand, arcs in through the air, and drops it rapidly toward the ground. "She ought to sink like a rock."

All the guys laugh.

My eyes dart around. Surely someone will come out of the school soon. There are a few cars left in the parking lot.

51

I wish I hadn't already put my cellphone in my pocket. I'm afraid to reach for it now. I don't want to give the guys an excuse to touch me, which they might do if they tried to grab my phone. As long as they're just spouting off, I can hope that something or someone will come along and distract them or frighten them away.

If they go so far as to put their hands on me, they might feel committed to some kind of action. I wish there weren't so many of them. They could easily slip into mob mentality, their bravado spurring each other on to more and more reckless behaviors.

"Dropping her in the lake," Kenneth says, "sounds like letting her off too easy. I'm sure we can think of something else, something that's more fun and takes a little longer."

"Should I go get my car?" one of the guys asks from behind me. "We can't do much with her out here in public."

I know I have no hope if they force me into a car.

"My dad will be here any moment," I state as emphatically as I can. "You'd better get away from me."

Kenneth makes a big show of looking up and down the street. "He's not going to make it in time." He hooks his thumb toward the parking lot, and his friend sprints away.

I'm preparing to scream when I hear a musical voice calling my name.

"Hey, Karissa," Neeve says, "You left your textbook on your desk in World History." He walks up and hands it to me. "It looks like your father is running late. A friend of mine will be here in a minute. Can we give you a ride home?"

I swallow and try to keep my voice steady. "I'd like that, thank you."

Kenneth Nelson and his friends step back. Kenneth winks at me and says, "Catch you later, wheelchair girl." When his buddy pulls up in a faded red Mustang, the guys pile in. They burn rubber out of there.

I can't stop tears from welling up in my eyes. "Is your friend really on his way?" I ask.

"Yes," Neeve says. "I wouldn't lie to you."

"Except about my book," I say. I know I didn't leave it on my desk. Even if I had, Neeve was through the door and out of the room before anyone else.

I hand the book back to him.

His brows pinch together in a frown.

"That's yours," he says.

I flip it open and see my name.

I'm sure I put the book in my backpack after class and then in my locker. I had already decided not to do any homework tonight except with Neeve. I'm confused.

I look at the book again and thumb through the first few pages. There's Jim Logan's name written inside a heart. I did that my first day here. I was feeling sad because I never got to go out with him in Chicago. Funny, I haven't thought about him since before the accident.

A dark blue van pulls up at the curb.

"Here's Brenlyn," Neeve says. "Do you want to call your father and let him know you have a ride?"

I sweep my hand across my cheeks to wipe them dry before I reach into my jacket pocket and pull out my cellphone.

"Dad," I say when he answers, "a friend of Neeve's is here with his van. They've offered to take me home."

"That's great," he says. "We'll have to come up with alternate plans for you so you don't end up stranded again. If I ever get away from this damned mess, I need to shoot back to the University for a while. I'll see you at dinner."

"Okay. Bye." I look up a Neeve. "He got caught in a small accident."

The van is an older model and has a front bench instead of bucket seats. Neeve picks me up, sets me on the bench, and then scoots me over until I'm sitting in the middle. He goes around back to help load my wheelchair. I hear clinking and clanking as things are rearranged. A few minutes later, Neeve and his friend climb in on either side of me.

"Karissa, this is Brenlyn. Bren, this is Karissa."

"I'm please to meet you," I say. "I appreciate the ride."

"Honored," he mumbles. It's an odd thing to say, and he looks uncomfortable having said it. I turn to Neeve questioningly.

He has an amused expression on his face. He doesn't explain. Instead, he reaches over and fastens my seat belt before he puts on his own.

Brenlyn starts up the engine. He drives without saying anything else, all the way to my house. He must be the friend who drove Neeve over on Saturday. He knows the way without asking for directions.

When we arrive, Neeve and Brenlyn get my wheelchair out of the back of the van, and Neeve picks me up and sets me in it.

"Thank you for the ride, Brenlyn," I say.

"You're welcome, miss," he replies awkwardly.

"Thanks, Bren," Neeve says. He nods his head, and it reminds me a little of how royalty dismisses a servant. Then he grins and the moment passes.

Brenlyn grins too. "Call me when you're ready to leave."

"I will."

As Brenlyn drives off, Neeve says to me, "I hope you don't mind if I stay. It seems silly to go home for an hour just to come back."

"No problem."

I ride up the ramp, unlock the side door, and lock it again as soon as we're both inside. I hang my jacket on a coat tree that Mom insists on having in a corner of the kitchen. She says it is too much to expect us kids to go all the way to the hall closet to put away our coats. (That's Mom being sarcastic.)

53

Neeve hooks his jacket on top of mine.

"Make yourself comfortable," I tell him. "I'll be back in a few minutes."

"Do you mind if I introduce myself to your brothers in their game room?"

"You can as far as I'm concerned, but I can't guarantee that they're down there." I point to the basement stairs.

"I'll check. The older is Jeremy and the younger is Bennett, right?"

"Good memory," I say. I leave him and go to my room.

I don't use much in the way of cosmetics, but tears still left tracks down my cheeks. I wash my face, re-do my makeup, especially around the eyes, and fluff out my hair.

I go back to the kitchen and turn on the oven so it can preheat. After I take a lemon cake mix and a bottle of vegetable oil out of a cabinet, I get a carton of eggs from the refrigerator. Bowls, handheld electric mixer, and cake pans are all on the same low shelf. When I have everything on the counter, I spray two 8" round cake pans with vegetable oil.

"Is there anything I can do to help?" Neeve asks. He doesn't startle me because I've been listening for his footsteps coming up from the basement. I didn't hear him, but the door at the bottom of the stairs squeaks, and I heard that.

"There's nothing in lemon cake that you can't eat, is there?" I crack eggs and dump them on top of the mix in the bowl.

"No, I'm delighted to say. I'm very fond of cake. In actuality, I fancy all desserts. I have quite a sweet tooth."

I smile. I like listening to him talk. Sometimes he reminds me of a nineteenth century novel.

"Did you meet my brothers?"

"I did. You were wrong, however, when you told me they wouldn't welcome you downstairs even if you could walk. They would like to show you what they've done with the room. You're the eldest and they look up to you. I told them if you were agreeable, I'd carry you down after dinner."

I don't say anything until after the cake is in the oven and the timer is set.

"We'll see," I say finally. I like the idea of him holding me, but I can hardly imagine what my parents will think if he gets into the habit of picking me up and carrying me places.

"What can I do to help?" he asks again.

"How are you at making salads?"

"Fruit or vegetable?" he asks.

"You can cook?" I exclaim.

"Actually," he says, teasingly, "I usually don't cook salads."

I groan and roll my eyes.

He laughs his musical laugh.

"Look in the refrigerator and decide for yourself," I tell him.

He takes out lettuce, carrots, radishes, and green onions. He sets them on the counter, thinks a moment, and then adds mushrooms and a cucumber to the pile. "If you invite me back sometime, I'll stop at the grocery store and get the ingredients for my favorite fruit salad."

The cutting board and colander hang from hooks on the wall and knives are in the slots of a wooden block on the counter. He helps himself. He separates leaves of lettuce, drops them into the colander and rinses them off. After he pats them dry, he piles them on a double layer of paper towels. He rummages in a drawer until he finds a peeler then starts to work on the carrots.

I watch for a few seconds and shake my head in amazement.

"I haven't decided exactly what to have with the broiled salmon," I tell him. "I can roast potatoes and steam some broccoli, or—I don't suppose you like creamed peas and potatoes."

"I do," he says, "and I think they go particularly well with salmon."

He is good with a knife. He chops and slices and dices like a professional chef.

It's too early to put things on to cook, but I get everything ready. I wash small red potatoes, cut them into quarters, drop them into a saucepan, and then cover them with water. I make the frosting for the cake. I put the dirty dishes and flatware in the dishwasher.

By the time the cake comes out of the oven, there's nothing left to do until it's time to turn the heat on under the potatoes, make the white sauce, cook the peas, and put the salmon under the broiler.

I go into the living room and Neeve follows me.

"We have an elephant in the room again," Neeve says.

I glance up, startled.

"I can't pretend I don't know those guys were frightening you. What did they say?"

Instantly, all the fear comes back.

Tears start down my cheeks again.

"Tell me what's going on, Karissa. Maybe I can help."

He can't, I know that, but I need to talk to someone.

I was so scared.

I dread going to school tomorrow.

I'm afraid to stay home by myself.

I don't know what to do.

Neeve crouches down beside me and takes my hand. "Please tell me."

I don't say anything.

After gently tugging my hand from his, I wheel into my bedroom.

He follows.

I pull the shoebox from the bottom shelf of the bookcase. I toss aside my old stories and dump the letters onto my bed.

# Chapter Ten

Neeve picks up an envelope and takes out a letter that's composed of words cut out of magazines, just like in the movies.

I can read it from where I am.

## *You* RE next BITCH!

Under the message is a picture of a bloody corpse taken from a slasher-movie advertisement. A football sticker is in the bottom right corner.

Neeve looks at me with disbelief or disgust.

I can't tell which, maybe both.

He opens another.

It is a pamphlet from the mortuary that handled Josie Peters' funeral. Written across it in red magic marker are the words:

### We're dying to serve you.

Neeve returns it to the envelope, throws it down, and picks up the next one. It's longer, a whole paragraph. I can't read the small print from my position, but I know what it says. I have them all memorized.

```
She was the closest thing to
an angel this school had.
She should have been at
cheerleading practice instead
of with a loser like you.
If you had left her alone,
she wouldn't have been there
and she'd still be alive.
It should have been you.
```

Neeve sits down on my bed to read the next one.

He doesn't say anything until he's read them all. It doesn't take long. Most of them are short, just a few hateful words.

He puts the letters back in the shoebox and hands it to me.

"What happened that day?" he asks. His voice is rough, hoarse.

I don't know when I started crying so hard, maybe when I realized that he was getting angry—not at me, but for me.

I have a difficult time forcing the words out.

"I'd only been going to this school a few weeks," I explain. "In English we were supposed to read *A Tale of Two Cities*. I hadn't read it before, and I didn't own it. Mr. Ullom said the number of copies in the school library was limited but there was a used books store just a few blocks away, and they had several. The weather was nice, so I decided to walk over to the store, buy a copy, and then take a public transit bus home."

I reach for a tissue to mop my face.

"I thought I would remember the directions he gave, so I didn't bother to write them down. When I started walking, though, I realized I wasn't quite sure which way to go. I was headed back into the building to ask him, when this girl came out. On impulse I asked her if she could tell me where the store was.

"She was really nice. She said she had to run home because her little sister had locked herself out of the house. She said it wasn't much out of her way and she'd drop me off.

"We'd only gone a block when some university student who was late for class sped around a corner on his race to campus. He clipped the back of her car and sent us spinning into a tree. The impact was on the driver's side, and it bent us down the middle like the letter **U**. The crash was so loud they heard it at school. Dozens of kids got there before the police and the ambulance."

I'm really sobbing now. I'm not sure I can enunciate clearly enough for him to understand me.

"The girl, Josie Peters, was killed. The car had bucket seats and mine was thrown off its tracks. I was halfway in the backseat. I guess that saved my life. Kenneth Nelson, the captain of the football team, was one of the kids who got there before the authorities. He tried to get to Josie, but he couldn't reach her. He watched her die. They were going to get married after graduation so they could go to college together."

Neeve's voice is as hard as steel. "That explains all of the footballs. Why the hell hasn't someone done something?"

I stare at the floor and don't answer.

Neeve jumps to his feet.

"Your parents don't know?" he shouts at me. "You haven't shown these letters to them?"

"Shhh, the boys will hear you."

57

"Do you have a death wish?" He is angry and not holding anything back. "They could have kidnapped and killed you today. Do you feel so guilty that you want them to hurt you?"

I bury my face in my hands.

In a moment I hear the water running in my bathroom. Neeve comes back with a cool washcloth. He presses it against the back of my neck. When I move my hands, he gently washes my face.

"I'm sorry I yelled at you," he says. He looks over at the alarm clock on my bed stand. "You said we'd eat at 6:30. Are your parents planning on being home by then?"

I nod, hiccupping and gulping and trying to get control of myself.

"I'll go finish dinner. You figure out what to do about the way you look. If I was your father and came home to find you with your face all splotchy and your eyes swollen from crying, I'd take a horsewhip to the visiting boy— no questions asked."

"He's not like that," I say. My throat is so tight from crying that I can hardly speak.

"Nevertheless, he would do something. Maybe he'd just toss me out. It would be better if we avoided the whole situation. Which plates should I use to set the table?"

"That's Bennett's job this week," I say. "He'll come up and do it as soon as he hears the garage door open."

"That gives us a little time." He frowns at me and shakes his head. "Is there a reason you don't want your parents to know about the letters?"

"Yes. Please don't tell them."

"I won't, at least not until after you and I have talked."

He turns and strides away.

I go into the bathroom and look in the mirror. To say I look awful would be a compliment.

It takes almost half an hour of alternating hot and cold water on my face to return my complexion to normal. I use eye drops to get rid of the red, and then I do my makeup for the third time today.

When I roll into the kitchen, the potatoes are cooking, the salmon steaks are under the broiler, the white sauce is thickening, and homemade vinaigrette is in the salad dressing shaker. The cake has been taken from the cooling racks and frosted.

I gawk.

Neeve gives me a self-satisfied smirk. "I don't get much of a chance to cook at the Taylors. I find it relaxing."

"You are phenomenal," I blurt out. Immediately I feel myself blush.

"Ah," Neeve says, "that looks good. You needed some color."

"Did you leave anything for me to do?" I pretend to be peevish. "After all, I invited you to dinner, not the other way around."

"The peas and potatoes need to be finished," he says.

"You've done it all except pouring on the white sauce."

"So I have," he says, grinning at me. "I'll let you cook for me another time."

The garage door opens.

"Show time," Neeve says so softly I almost don't hear him.

"This tastes wonderful, Kari," Dad says after we sit down at the table and he's had a chance to sample everything.

"Neeve did most of it," I say. "He likes to cook and doesn't get the opportunity very often."

Mom gives Jeremy and Bennett an ah-ha look. "You see, there are other boys who cook." Mom turns to Neeve to explain. "I have to fight a war every time I want one of the boys to help me in the kitchen."

Neeve is sitting next to me, across from my brothers. He glances from one to the other. "Surely you guys intend to live on your own someday."

"I'll have a girlfriend or a wife cook for me," Jeremy announces smugly while he takes his second helping of peas and potatoes.

"What if she gets sick," Neeve asks, "or leaves you?"

"That's what take-out is for," Bennett tells him.

Neeve chuckles and shakes his head. "Pizza three times a day sounds horrible to me, but maybe you could stand it for a while." He nibbles at his salad. Despite his size, he is not a big eater, not like my brothers.

"I want to thank you for bringing Karissa home," Dad says. "I didn't think the police were ever going to let me leave that accident."

"I'm glad we could do it. In fact," Neeve pauses a moment before he goes on, "I was thinking we might as well bring her home every day."

I stare at him, my fork suspended in the air.

"I wouldn't want to put you out," Dad says, "or your friend. It's his van, right?"

"Yes, but he picks me up after school so I can help him in his shop. Your house is on the way. It wouldn't be any trouble to drop Karissa off. I'm sure it would make things easier for you, not having to worry about her transportation."

I see the conflict on Dad's face. It's clear he would appreciate not having to interrupt his workday.

"What does your friend do?" Mom asks.

"He fixes things," Neeve says, "mostly clocks and watches and jewelry, but also small appliances, and sometimes toys. Especially those," he closes his eyes and crinkles his brow, "those . . . you know, cars and planes and boats. They come with a box and a . . . " He makes a rectangular shape with his hands, then pinching his thumb and forefinger together, he indicates a long skinny something coming off the top.

"Remote-controlled cars," Bennett yells as if he's come up with the winning answer on a game show, "with a control box and antenna."

Neeve snaps his fingers. "That's it. Thanks, Ben."

Bennett beams. No one calls him Ben, but I can tell it makes him feel good, older and more mature. I have a feeling we'll all be calling him Ben from now on.

"Is that what you do?" Jeremy asks. "Fix things with him?"

"No," Neeve says. "He has a contract to paint miniature lead soldiers in authentic period uniforms for collectors. That's what I do. They take patience, steady hands, good eyes, and no great talent. He has pictures for me to copy. It frees him up to work on other things. When he has a good week, he pays me a little so I have extra spending money. But mostly he pays me by driving me wherever I need to go since I don't have a driver's license or a car."

No birth certificate, no social security card, no I.D. at all until he finds out who he is. Poor guy.

Neeve turns to face Dad. "Honestly, Dr. Day, bringing Karissa home would not be inconvenient in the least."

I know what's bothering Dad. He has a hard time asking for favors. He thinks he should be able to do anything and be everything himself.

"Maybe I could pay him for the gas," I suggest. "That way he wouldn't feel like we were taking advantage of him, and I wouldn't feel like a charity case."

It's the right thing to say, I can tell.

"That is an excellent idea," Dad says. "Of course, Neeve, I wouldn't expect you to make a commitment for your friend. He would have to agree."

"I'd call him right now and check," Neeve says, "but he's on a house call tonight."

"House call?" Dad repeats.

Neeve nods. "Someone's grandfather clock isn't working, and it's too awkward to bring into the shop. Why don't you let us take Karissa home tomorrow? She and Brenlyn can work out the details then."

"All right," Dad says. He clearly wants to be convinced.

Everyone has finished eating, and Mom gets up to clear the table.

Out of the blue, Jeremy asks Neeve, "Say, which do you think is more important for a guy, to play sports or to play a musical instrument?"

Fire spurts out of Mom's ears and smoke pours from her nose and mouth—okay, not really, but almost.

This is a long-time argument between her and Jeremy.

If we didn't have company, they'd start screaming at each other.

Neeve can't help but feel the tension in the room, but he answers anyway. "Sports are good for young men because they teach discipline, teamwork, how to take directions, and when to lead and when to follow."

Mom is just about ready to explode.

Jeremy looks like he wants to leap up and give Neeve a high-five.

"However," Neeve continues smoothly, "unless you want to become a professional athlete and have the dedication and the talent to do so, you'll lose interest as you grow older and more important things demand your attention. On the other hand, a well-mastered musical instrument can be a friend and a comfort for life."

Jeremy glares as if he's been betrayed.

Neeve doesn't seem bothered by it. "What instrument do you play?"

"Clarinet," Jeremy grumbles in a sulk.

"Ah," Neeve says, "I love the sound of a clarinet."

Jeremy juts out his chin aggressively. "Do you play?"

"As a matter of fact, I do."

"Yeah, right," Jeremy snarls. Then he jumps up, dashes from the room, and in a moment returns with his clarinet. "Here, show me how it's done."

Mom looks at me with her eyebrows raised questioningly. I shrug to let her know that I have no idea what to expect. She sits back down.

Neeve takes the clarinet and turns it around in his hands a few times, as if he's getting acquainted with it or something. I wonder if it bothers him to use Jeremy's mouthpiece. I kind of expect him to wipe it off with his napkin or something, but he doesn't.

He scoots his chair back a little and puts the clarinet to his lips.

I don't know the name of the tune he plays, but it makes me yearn for spring days, gentle breezes, insects buzzing through the air, and water trickling over stones.

My emotions are so stirred up I almost get tears in my eyes.

# Chapter Eleven

Jeremy stares with his mouth dangling open. "How long have you taken lessons?"

"I don't remember anymore." Neeve hands the clarinet back. "I played the flute first, though."

Ben jumps up. (That shows the power of Neeve's personality. I'm already thinking of Bennett as Ben.) "May I?" he asks me.

"It's upstairs," I say.

Neeve catches on immediately. "You play the flute?"

"No," I say. "I tried in junior high, but I don't have a drop of musical talent. The boys got it all."

When Bennett returns with my flute, he has his trumpet with him too.

Neeve takes the flute and plays something Irish or Scottish. It makes me want to dance. In fact, it's such a happy melody that I don't experience the crushing depression I usually feel when I fear I will never dance again.

Then Neeve takes the trumpet and makes it cry.

I usually think of the trumpet as having a military call-to-arms and march-off-to-battle kind of sound—except when I listen to the old Louis Armstrong tunes on YouTube. He could turn the trumpet into a soft, break-your-heart, sing-a-love-song type of instrument.

So can Neeve.

"What else do you play?" I ask. Someone this talented can't be limited to woodwinds and brass.

He shrugs. "Almost anything, I think."

In a moment, Bennett is back with Mom's guitar and violin.

Neeve's eyes light up.

The flute might have been his first instrument, but strings are his passion. It shows in every line of his face.

He accepts the guitar first, strums, plucks the strings while adjusting the pegs to get the tune right, and then goes into a Mexican mariachi number that sounds like he's a whole band all by himself.

When he picks up the violin, though, it is with the sensual touch of a lover. The moment he draws the bow across the strings, I stop breathing.

All the loves, hates, joys, and sorrows of life blend into the flowing notes he coaxes from the violin's heart. The melody soars and plunges, weeps and laughs. When he stops, I don't care if I never hear another note of music.

Nothing could compare with that.

Neeve's face is exalted, as if he has been gazing into heaven.

He returns the violin to its case.

Mom whispers, "That's the way the violin is supposed to be played." She gets up, puts her arms around Neeve's shoulders, and kisses the top of his head. "Thank you."

Neeve's eyes fly open, and his mouth shapes a silent *oh*. It occurs to me that he might not remember the last time someone hugged him.

Mom begins briskly stacking plates and gathering flatware.

She pokes Jeremy, and he pokes Bennett.

The three of them clear the table.

Dad looks at Neeve with concern. Finally, he asks, "Could I speak with you privately for a few minutes?"

Neeve is still high from the music, or maybe it's from the unexpectedness of Mom's embrace. I don't know which. But I can tell it takes real effort for him to pull himself back to the moment.

"I know what you want," he tells Dad. "You want to know how much of my memory has come back."

Dad nods. "Let's go into another room."

"If you don't mind your family knowing the truth," Neeve says, "I would just as soon tell them. I'm going to be around here quite a bit for the next several weeks while Karissa and I work on our report. After that," his eyes meet mine, and my heart speeds up until it is setting world records, "if Karissa will let me, I'd still like to come around. It'll be easier on me if I don't have to pretend."

"It's your decision," Dad says.

Mom comes in carrying the lemon cake on a tray that also holds a knife, cake server, napkins, and forks.

Jeremy has the dessert plates.

Bennett brings in the coffee pot and a pitcher of milk.

Slices of cake are passed around.

Mom and Dad have coffee. All of us kids opt for milk.

Appreciative comments are made after people begin to eat.

"Are you going to be a professional musician?" Bennett asks. "Have your own band or something?"

"I doubt it," Neeve says. "I don't know."

"There must be some reason you can play all those instruments," Jeremy says in a hostile tone. I can tell he's still irritated that Neeve didn't side with him on the sports issue. He wants to play football, but he doesn't have the physique for it. He's stick thin. Mom won't sign the permission slip, and if Mom won't, Dad won't.

"I suppose there is," Neeve says, "but I don't remember what."

Jeremy's face goes red. Now he's really getting angry.

"I don't mean to sound evasive," Neeve says. "I have holes in my memory." He gets to his feet slowly. He turns around and pulls up his shirt to expose his back.

I think we all gasp at the same time.

I can't help it. I reach up and trace two pale pink marks in the small of his back. I feel his muscles tremble beneath my touch.

Brenda's brother, the one in Neeve's P.E. class, was right when he said the lines are in a pattern.

I recognize the shapes. They're hieroglyphics or runes.

I don't know what they say, but I know someone has carved a message into Neeve's flesh.

The scars higher up aren't ovals. They're more like triangles with rounded edges. It looks as if someone cut around the shoulder blades, then flayed off all the skin inside the outline. The pain must have been excruciating. With raw patches that large, I should think the doctors would do skin grafts, but the shoulder blades have the same, glossy pink cast as the other scars.

"Holy crud," Jeremy says. "Were you in a car accident like Karissa?"

"No," Neeve answers. "Someone chose to do this to me." His voice sounds emotionless on the surface, but underneath there is such a fury that I would be terrified if it was aimed at me.

He tucks his shirt back in. "I wanted you to know so you'd understand why I have trouble remembering sometimes. Like when I couldn't think of what those remote-controlled cars are called. Or like now, when I don't know why I play so many instruments. I'm not trying to be secretive, and I'm not a druggie or anything like that. I just don't remember."

"Who did it?" Bennett asks.

"I don't know," Neeve answers. "I only get brief flashes of what happened."

"It's Post Traumatic Stress Disorder," Dad says. "Sometimes full recollection is never recovered."

"I'm not sure I want it to be," Neeve says.

"How much memory have you gotten back?" Dad asks.

"I'm not sure," Neeve says. "I seem to do fairly well with general information, like literature, history, and mathematics. In terms of personal knowledge, it's a blank wall until I'm reminded of something somehow. Like when Karissa asked me if I knew how to cook. All of a sudden, I remembered not only that I could, but also that I enjoy it.

"Before Jeremy asked me if I could play the clarinet, I wasn't aware of playing any kind of instrument. Holding the clarinet reminded me of the flute, but it wasn't until Karissa asked me what else I could play that I remembered other musical instruments."

"What about your family?" Mom asks.

Neeve just shakes his head and shrugs.

Mom and Dad let it go.

I do too for the moment, but I'm getting familiar enough with Neeve's expressions to know something is not right. He's not as upset about the family issue as he is about other things. That doesn't seem logical. Finding your family would be the most important goal for a person who has lost his memory, wouldn't it?

When Neeve's cellphone rings, we all jump.

"Excuse me," he says. He wanders around the bar that separates the dining room from the kitchen and ends up over by the sink with his back to us. "Hello." He listens a moment. "That's all right." A pause while he listens some more. "Sure," he says. He follows it with, "Say, would you mind if we drive Karissa home after school from now on? She would contribute to the cost of gas, which would help you, and her folks wouldn't have to interrupt their workdays to get her, which would help them." Long pause. "Thanks, Bren. I'll meet you out front."

He breaks the connection and turns around.

"Brenlyn is on his way to get me. He has a pickup to make, and he needs me to help him with some awkward and heavy lifting. He said he would be delighted to drop Karissa off after school. He doesn't feel right about receiving money for it, since it's on our way, but he said he would accept a couple of dollars every now and then if you insist."

He takes his coat off the rack.

"It was nice getting to know all of you." He shakes hands with Dad and the boys, and then he kisses Mom's hand. It seems completely natural. "Thank you for having me over."

Although he doesn't touch me, his eyes say wonderful things. "I'm sorry we won't get to work on our paper, Karissa. I'll see you at school tomorrow."

"I'll walk you to the front door," I say, "the walking part being a figure of speech."

I can't believe I just made a joke about being a cripple.

What is Neeve doing to me?

When we get to the door, Neeve bends down, and for a moment, I think he's going to kiss me goodbye.

Instead, he whispers in my ear, "I'll be waiting for you in front of the school tomorrow. We need to talk about those letters. See if you can't get there a little early."

He opens the front door, and I see Brenlyn's blue van already parked in the driveway.

After they drive off, I go back to the dining room. I know Dad will want us to process the experience with Neeve. Sometimes I wish my dad were a plumber or a lawyer or a businessman or a cowboy—anything but a shrink.

Dad starts out by asking, "How much do you know about Neeve Maynard, Kari?"

"Not much," I say. "I know he's in foster care with a family named Taylor. He's a good student. He doesn't hang out with any particular crowd at school. He writes poetry and likes to draw." I shrug, a little surprised at the disparity between what I feel and what I know about him. "He enjoys mythology and fairytales. We're just getting acquainted."

"He's the guy they found on Halloween, isn't he, Dad?" Jeremy asks.

Dad doesn't answer.

His silence means *yes*, but he can't talk about it because he got his information in his professional capacity. Neeve showing us his back doesn't release Dad from the obligations of confidentiality.

So I answer the question for him. "I've heard rumors at school that he is, but I don't know if they're true."

"What if he is?" Dad asks Jeremy. "Would it make a difference in the way you treat him the next time he comes over?"

"Heck, no," Jeremy says. "I was just curious."

"What about you, Ben?" Dad says. I smile. Neeve even has Dad shortening Bennett's name.

"I like him," Bennett answers. "He came downstairs to meet me and Jeremy when he first got here. He thought we did a great job on the game room. He wanted to bring Karissa down and show her."

"He seems like a nice boy," Mom comments, "but lonely and eager for acceptance. I think that's why he wanted us to understand about his circumstances. Even though he didn't share much, it took courage for him to tell us what little he did—and to show us the awful scars on his back."

"I agree," Dad says, "and we need to regard that information as a sacred trust. What Neeve told us was extremely personal, and it's important that we respect his privacy. That means we don't talk about him casually. We don't participate in gossip. When he comes back, we don't pester him with questions. We let him tell us what he wants us to know, when he wants us to know it. Can we all agree to that?"

We can and we do.

"When I go for my trumpet lesson next week," Bennett says, "I'd sure like to tell Mrs. Shumaker that Karissa's new boyfriend plays at least five different instruments."

"He's not my boyfriend," I state, maybe a bit too quickly. Then I add nonchalantly, "But I do have a date with him on Friday."

After the dishes are done and I go to my room, I can't relax.

Too much has happened today.

I put on my favorite bedtime CD. It's *The Gospel Music of the Statler Brothers*. Weird, huh? I'm not particularly religious, but my Grandma Baker was. She loved the Statler Brothers. She used to play their music on an old cassette player when she babysat us kids. This double CD was the last gift she gave me before she died.

I make it through the first three songs then turn the player off.

I pull myself out of bed and back into my wheelchair.

I get "Lark and the Secret Doorway" out of my backpack and start reading. Lark and Jaydon had just arrived at the fairy palace, which was hidden behind some leaves on an old oak tree.

# Chapter Twelve

Neeve is leaning on the Millard Fillmore sign out in front of the school when we drive up the next morning. He waves as he walks toward us.

"He's acting a bit like a boyfriend," Mom says as she pulls on the emergency brake.

"I don't think so," I say, but the mere possibility makes my heart thump erratically. "He's just being kind to the wheelchair girl."

"You need to take a closer look," Mom says in her most serious mother-to-daughter voice. "If you don't want things developing in that direction, you need to slow them down right now."

Neeve doesn't come over to my door. He goes to Mom's and waits until she lowers the window.

"I'll get the chair, Mrs. Day," he tells her.

"Thank you," she says. She pushes the button to the hatchback.

A moment later, he brings the wheelchair around to my side. My door is already open. As before, he lifts me up and sets me in place. He grabs my backpack.

"You and your friend are still going to take her home after school?" Mom asks, as if things could change dramatically in ten hours.

Well, I guess they could. My life fell apart in a matter of minutes.

"Yes," Neeve says. "You don't need to worry."

"Okay. You two have a good day."

"Bye, Mom." I watch her pull away, not quite ready to face Neeve. He doesn't wait.

"The more I think about those letters," he says in an undertone, "the angrier I get. Added to the scene I interrupted yesterday, I believe those football players pose a genuine threat to your life."

Well, duh!

That's why I'm scared.

I think it but I don't say it.

"What do you suggest?" I can't disguise the frustration in my voice. I've spent so much time thinking about this. "If I show the letters to my parents, all that will happen is that they'll end up feeling as frightened and as helpless as I do. If I show the letters to the police, they might admit someone is trying to scare me, but they won't do anything. Legally, I don't think they can unless the football players actually hurt me.

"Here at school, Mr. Haskell has already let me know what his attitude is. He saw Kenneth Nelson and one of his buddies bullying me in the hall, and all he did was tell them to go to class. Then he walked me to World History, talking all the time, making sure I couldn't tell him what happened."

"That was the day you came to class in tears?" Neeve asks.

"I wasn't in tears," I tell him, "until you smiled at me."

He sounds confused when he says, "I made you cry?"

"It was only because I was already feeling bad." I want to explain to him, but I'm not sure he'll understand. "When you smiled at me, it made me feel like I wasn't quite alone, even though I knew I was, really. That's what made me cry."

He cups my chin with his hand and tilts my head up. Then he bends down so he can look me straight in the eyes. "You don't have to face this by yourself. Count on me, if no one else."

He makes my heart flutter with his big green eyes staring at me so seriously.

I appreciate his offer of support, but he can't be with me all of the time.

If Kenneth Nelson and his buddies want to snatch me from school, someday they will. There were five of them yesterday. The next time there might be more.

Maybe Neeve could take Kenneth Nelson down in a fair fight. I don't know what kind of experience he has with boxing or wrestling or martial arts. But even if he has a black belt in karate, he can't handle a dozen football players by himself. They'd just tackle him and dogpile him until he couldn't move. Then Kenneth Nelson would do whatever he wanted with me.

I don't dare say any of this to Neeve.

I might not have a whole lot of experience with guys, but I know they can be sensitive and resentful if they think their masculinity has been called into question.

So I say the only thing I can think of: "Thank you."

Neeve walks beside me as I wheel up the ramp.

At the top, he opens the door for me. "I don't understand why Kenneth Nelson is taking his anger out on you instead of using his energy to mourn."

"When my Grandma Baker died last year," I tell him, "Dad said there are five stages to grieving. If I remember them right, they're denial, bargaining, anger, depression, and acceptance. Most people go through the whole process and end up reconciled to the loss. But it's possible to get stuck somewhere and not move on. I guess Kenneth Nelson is stuck on anger."

"Even if that makes sense," Neeve mutters, "it doesn't help us protect you from him."

"Meeting me in the mornings and taking me home in the afternoons will help a lot. During the rest of the day, I can stay in crowds. I don't think he'll try anything when other people are around."

"You're probably right," Neeve concedes with a quick nod. "He's basically a coward. He and his friends had me outnumbered yesterday, and they backed off even before Brenlyn arrived."

His tone is derisive.

He implies that he could have handled all of them by himself if he put forth a little effort, but with Brenlyn's help he wouldn't even have had to raise a sweat.

I don't know if he's confident, cocky, or insane.

He escorts me to homeroom.

After English, I go to the gymnasium to check in with Mrs. Scott before heading for the library.

I see Neeve outside walking toward the track.

After I return to the main building and take the elevator to the second floor, I see Neeve turning the corner into the 2A wing.

How did he get ahead of me?

Since the first time I noticed Neeve in World History, I've tried to spot him in the halls or the cafeteria, and I never have.

Not once.

Until today.

Now, I see him everywhere I go.

He doesn't meet me after classes or join me and my friends for lunch, but whenever I glance up or look around, there he is.

Sometimes he drifts up beside me as if we just happened to be going the same direction.

Sometimes I see him lounging in a corner or standing beside the drinking fountain as I roll by.

Sometimes we pass each other going in opposite directions.

It's beginning to freak me out.

How does he know where I'll be?

He has never asked me what my schedule is.

I've never told him I check in with the nurse during the lunch period to get my medication. I've never told him I go to the library after Mrs. Scott marks the attendance sheet in P.E.

Nevertheless, he is always nearby.

If our classes are so close together, why didn't I ever see him in the halls before now? I think about asking him to explain it to me on the way to or from school, but somehow we always end up talking about something else.

When Mom takes me to physical therapy, I'm so preoccupied that I automatically do whatever I'm told, and I don't even notice any pain.

Abby Madison, my favorite therapist, is ecstatic.

She says I'm making progress.


Friday morning when I wake up, I have a severe case of the jitters.

I am going on a date with Neeve tonight.

I think I'll be sick.

I didn't go out very often in Chicago. I went to a few dances, and every now and then some guy took me to a movie. I never dated anyone special, never a guy that I really liked.

I'm not sure how I'm supposed to act.

When I get to school and Neeve lifts me out of the van, suddenly I'm embarrassed.

I'm tongue-tied when he walks me to homeroom.

If I'm this big a mess now, how will I ever survive the night?

When I get to the library, I can't study.

Kimberly, Brenda, and Emily come in as usual and snub me.

Who cares? I already know more about Neeve than they ever will. I don't want to listen to their gossip anymore.

I need to detach from reality for a while.

I get my story from my backpack.

The words stare at me from the pages.

Finally I force myself to concentrate. Jaydon just introduced Lark to his mother, the queen.

The bell rings and about gives me a heart attack.

After my pulse slows to normal, I gather my papers together and stash them in my backpack. I head for Calculus.

Somehow I make it through the day without having a complete melt down, but by the last bell I'm a nervous wreck. I guess Neeve senses my agitation on the drive home. He and Brenlyn talk about work issues the whole way.

"See you at 6:30," he says as I open the side door to the house.

"See you then," I squeak.

Immediately I start to get ready for our date.

I take a shower.

Although I showered in the morning, I've heard that nervous perspiration is the most noticeable and most offensive body odor, and I don't want to take any chances.

I put on double deodorant and slather lotion over every square inch of skin that I can reach.

I decide to wear a nice pair of black slacks and a pink cashmere sweater instead of my usual jeans and t-shirt. I spend half an hour fluffing out my hair instead of a mere minute or two. I put on my makeup with care and then spritz a little perfume on my wrists and neck.

When I'm all ready, I wait in the living room.

I practice breathing, just to make sure I won't forget how. My parents think up excuses to come in every few minutes to check on me.

The doorbell rings at exactly 6:30.

Somehow my parents appear out of nowhere and answer it.

Neeve looks wonderful.

Rather than pulling his hair back and binding it with an elastic band, he wears it loose. It fans out over his shoulders and glimmers like liquid gold. He is wearing a pale blue dress shirt, open at the neck, over a darker blue tee, a tan sports coat, and stonewashed jeans. Despite the chilly temperature, he doesn't have on an overcoat.

I'd be content to spend the evening just looking at him.

"How long is the movie?" Dad asks Neeve.

"I'm not sure," Neeve answers. "I think it'll be over around midnight. We should be back here by 12:30."

"Well," Mom says, bending down to give me a quick kiss on the cheek, "have a good time."

When we get to Mama Mia's Meals, the Italian restaurant Brenlyn suggests, Neeve decides there is no sense in getting out the wheelchair for such a short distance.

He carries me inside, ignoring the startled looks of the other customers.

After we're shown to a booth, he sets me on the bench, helps me take off my coat, folds it carefully, and puts it on the seat between me and the wall.

He gently slides me over so there is enough room for him to sit down beside me. I am acutely aware of how close his body is to mine, almost touching at the shoulders.

Brenlyn sits across the table from me, and I take a good long look at him. He is easily as tall as Neeve. His hair is long and blond too, although it is more honey-colored, like mine. His eyes are aquamarine. There is something about his face that is familiar, but I can't place it.

Talitha, Brenlyn's date, is across the table from Neeve. She could easily be a supermodel. She is only a few inches shorter than Brenlyn, and she has a body to die for—long legs, small waist, and full breasts. Her hair is light red, what people call strawberry blond. It hangs to her waist, but if it weren't so curly it would probably reach the backs of her knees. She smiles easily, showing lots of teeth like a movie star. I would be jealous if she went to my school and we were rivals, but she's so far out of my league that all I can do is try not to gawk.

"Do you work?" I ask her while we're making small talk, waiting to be served.

"Yes," she says in a voice so musical that she almost sounds as if she's singing. "Before I moved here, I grew exotic flowers. I cross-pollinated to produce unusual colorization and to develop new fragrances."

"You're a botanist?"

Her face goes blank as if she's never heard the word before, and I have a startling epiphany.

The reason Brenlyn's features look so familiar—and Talitha's also—is because they are so similar to Neeve's. At the very least, their ancestors came from the same region of the world, maybe Norway or Sweden. I would guess it was recently too, because all three of them stumble over words and phrases that the average grade-schooler knows.

Talitha interrupts my thoughts by answering my question. "Botanists are interested in the science of plants. I think horticulturist would be a more accurate term for what I did. I grew plants to sell, not to study."

Her comment shoots down my theory of recent immigration.

The average grade-schooler might have learned the word botanist from The Science Channel, but not horticulturist. That comes from an advanced vocabulary.

"Of course, now," she continues, "I help Brenlyn in his shop. Growing flowers has become more of a hobby than a job."

After the waitress brings our orders, we chitchat about the food and the weather and our favorite flowers.

All the time we're talking, my mind is spinning around the implications of Neeve and his friends coincidentally being from the same country of origin. Then it occurs to me that maybe that's why Brenlyn hired Neeve in the first place, because he was drawn to someone who seemed familiar.

"How did you and Neeve meet?" I ask Brenlyn. He doesn't say much, and I'm trying to pull him into the conversation.

He looks at Neeve, and it's Neeve who answers.

"I was walking over to the mall," Neeve says, "and I saw Brenlyn struggling to lift a big rototiller out of his van. I offered to help him carry it into his shop. After that, I wandered around looking at things. I was particularly interested in the miniatures. I asked him if he needed any help."

"He told me he would work for free," Brenlyn says, "if I would give him a ride to and from school. However, his work is worth much more than that. I pay him what I can, plus I'm his taxicab anytime he needs me."

As I listen to Neeve and Brenlyn, I notice Talitha's reaction. She is surprised by the story, and she appears uncomfortable with it. Almost as soon as I make that observation, however, her facial expression changes from tense to relaxed, as if she realizes she hasn't been reacting appropriately.

Suddenly, I am annoyed.

Why would Neeve and Brenlyn make something up?

I'm nothing to them, nothing worth a lie.

There are so many pauses, so many blank looks, so many not-quite-right reactions that I don't know what to think.

73

I pinch off a corner of garlic bread and pop it into my mouth. I chew thoughtfully. Maybe Mother was right, maybe I need to slow things down until I know Neeve better.

When we leave the restaurant parking lot, a car parked at the curb turns on its lights and pulls out behind us. Another car appears to follow closely behind it. I only notice because, from where I'm sitting in the back seat, I can see the headlights reflected in the side mirror.

I've watched enough television mysteries to pay attention when the car behind us changes lanes when we do and makes all the same turns. I'm relieved that it drives on by when we get to the mall where the movie complex is.

Neeve offers to carry me in, but I insist on taking my wheelchair. The movie he selected, a new fantasy epic called *The Spire*, is nearly three hours long.

If I have to use the restroom, I need to be mobile.

Besides, the parking lot is crowded and we have to park in the very back. That's a little too far for a guy to haul one hundred and fifteen pounds of girl.

In the theater, a couple of rows at the rear are indented so a wheelchair fits at the end. I expect to stay in mine, but Neeve lifts me out and sets me down in a regular seat. The armrest between his seat and mine is moveable, and he pushes it up and out of the way so he is sitting right against me.

Then he takes my hand.

All thoughts of slowing things down dissolve.

I would never have guessed that holding hands could be so sensual. The touch of Neeve's palm against mine is as stimulating as if he kissed me. I think. I would be willing to test it to find out for sure.

The lights dim and the previews begin.

Pictures flash across the screen.

Music blares from loudspeakers overhead.

All I can focus on is Neeve.

He smells of fresh air, pine trees, and wild flowers. I don't know if the scent comes from bath soap, shampoo, or aftershave, but it's a completely masculine fragrance despite its sweetness.

The warmth I feel from his body is comforting, like cuddling with one of my Grandma Baker's quilts. I feel safe for the first time since I started getting hate mail in the hospital.

The movie begins.

Watching it with Neeve and his friends is fascinating.

My dad says that nothing defines you more accurately than what you find funny.

Neeve and his two friends laugh at exactly the same times, but they don't always coincide with the rest of the audience. I'm sure Dad could draw deep and revealing conclusions from observing them.

Me? I just enjoy the sound.

They laugh in three-part harmony. Talitha is the soprano. Neeve is the tenor. Brenlyn is the bass. (When I join in, I'm the alto. Then we could be a choral group.)

It's twenty minutes short of midnight when the movie finishes, and we're all feeling kind of high on adrenaline. The picture was full of suspense, magic, deception, humor, fighting, and a touch of romance.

I don't want to go home yet.

Neeve told my parents I'd be home by 12:30, so we have time for a short excursion.

When we get into the van, I say, "Hey, Brenlyn, how about showing me your workshop? It's around here, isn't it?"

"Not very far," he answers. "What do you think, Neeve?"

"Is the floor too cluttered for the wheelchair?"

"No. I was out making calls most of the day, so it's just like we left it last night."

"You sure you want to see it?" Neeve asks me. "It's nothing special."

"Hey!" Brenlyn exclaims.

Neeve laughs. "Sorry, Bren. Of course it's special to you. I just don't want her to be disappointed."

"I have zero expectations," I say. "I'm just curious."

"All right," Neeve says. "If you don't mind, Bren, let's show her."

We join the line of cars waiting for the light to change so we can turn left out of the mall parking lot.

There is quite a bit of traffic on the main road, and I wonder if the University or the high school from Shawon or a neighboring town has had some kind of sporting event, or maybe a dance.

When we finally reach the front of the line, Brenlyn turns left on the yellow light.

Within seconds, cars are zipping around us on all sides.

My breath catches in my throat.

I close my eyes and concentrate on inhaling and exhaling in a smooth, steady rhythm instead of gasping and hyperventilating.

Since the accident, I'm a nervous passenger regardless of who is driving—and it wouldn't make any difference if I were riding in an armored car or a tank instead of a van.

I'm thankful when we leave the congested thoroughfare and enter an old neighborhood full of small, square houses.

A couple of cars follow our example, maybe thinking we know an alternate route, or maybe they simply live around here.

The homes are mostly dark.

Only an occasional light is visible through drawn curtains.

We pass a delicatessen. Next to it is a beauty parlor. There aren't many streetlamps, and the only reason I recognize the businesses is because they both have security lights mounted above their doors.

Halfway farther down the block, we pull into the driveway of a simple red brick dwelling.

Painted on the front window are the words: QUICK FIX. Underneath, it reads: "If you can break it, I can fix it."

Neeve and Brenlyn haul out my wheelchair.

As Neeve lifts me from the van, Brenlyn goes to unlock the front door. Talitha goes with him, her arm hooked in his.

I don't know why, but I almost expected there to be no shop.

Neeve and his friends seem too exotic to do anything as mundane as work. I wouldn't have been surprised if Brenlyn had suddenly remembered that he left the key to the shop in his other coat or made some other lame excuse for not bringing me here.

Surprise!

Not only is there a shop, but it is also handicapped accessible.

# Chapter Thirteen

I roll up the ramp, and when I get to the top, Brenlyn holds the door for me.

The room I enter is small, less than half the width of the house. There are two counters with a walkway between them. The longer counter, the one on the right, holds a cash register, a telephone, and a desk organizer with pencils, pens, and notepads. The front of the counter is glassed in and displays a variety of knickknacks for sale.

On the shorter counter are an electric coffee maker, disposable cups, powdered creamer, and little packets of sugar.

A low, oval table covered with magazines is centered in front of the picture window. There are two chairs on each side of it.

The whole setup looks like something out of a 1950s movie—back when customers were friends and proprietors provided extras along with good service.

It's no wonder Brenlyn can't always afford to pay Neeve. If he has very many people coming in and out, they could drive him into the poor house just with the cost of coffee.

I follow Brenlyn between the counters and down a hallway. On the left, we pass a spacious bedroom. Through the open door I glimpse a chest of drawers, a desk, a rocking chair, and a queen-sized bed. Next there are two doors that are closed, maybe a bathroom and a closet. On the right is a good-sized kitchen. Besides the regular fixtures and appliances, there is a drop-leaf table with two chairs. Across from them is a television and DVD player on a stand.

I guess Brenlyn lives here.

Then I'm in a room that runs across the entire back of the house.

Now this is a workshop!

I wheel around, looking at this and that.

The walls are covered with shelves that are piled high with pieces of lumber, sections of pipe, spools of wire, and balls of twine, as well as jars containing nails, nuts and bolts, screws, springs, and gears in a thousand sizes. There are a gazillion different kinds of tools.

On a rack near the entry hall are items with numbered tags attached to them. There's a porcelain doll, a toaster, two matching lamps, an old VHS player, a birdhouse, a couple of clocks, an antique radio, a sewing machine, an upright vacuum cleaner, and a bunch of toys.

I assume some objects are waiting to be fixed, and others, having been repaired, waiting to be picked up.

One section of shelves on the left is filled with plaster casts for making ceramics. In the far corner is a kiln, and next to it, is a deep utility sink.

Along the rear wall, between a window and the backdoor, is a bookcase devoted to miniatures. But not just lead soldiers. There are whole villages of ceramic cottages, churches, and schools, plus the people who go with them.

A group of Santa Clauses are clustered beside half a dozen Easter bunnies, an assortment of Halloween ghouls, and a heavenly host of angels. Some of the articles have been painted and some have not.

There are also two lovely Swiss chalet dollhouses with delicate wooden furniture to go inside.

"We sell the finished items in the store," Talitha says.

The interior floor space holds two worktables, each with a gooseneck lighted magnifier clamped to the edge. Half a dozen stools are scattered here and there.

The larger table is nicked and scarred. The only things on it are the inner workings and outer casing of a gold pocket watch, which are spread out on a white cloth. The smaller table holds little jars of paint in every color imaginable and a handful of paintbrushes that sprout from an old coffee can.

"Is this your work area?" I ask Neeve, pointing at the smaller table.

"Yes." He shows me the miniature soldiers he's been working on. He does a dozen at a time. First he paints all of the skin, then all of the colors the uniforms have in common, then all of the unique colors, and finally the details—and the details are unbelievable. I hold a finished soldier under the magnifier, and I can see designs on the buttons and pupils in the eyes.

"Do you make the miniatures?" I ask Brenlyn.

"Not all of them," he answers. "I do the ceramics, and I build the dollhouses and furniture, but I have suppliers for the soldiers."

"It's getting late," Neeve says, glancing at his watch. "I think we'd better go."

"Okay." I take another quick tour around the room. "But I want to come back sometime when I can examine everything."

"All right," Neeve says, "another time."

He and I go out the front door and wait beside the van while Brenlyn locks up.

I hear some scraping and crackling from the bushes.

Connie A. Walker

Someone's dog or cat is rummaging through the underbrush I assume.

The next rustling sounds are louder, made by something big.

As I peer in the direction of the noise, football players rush out of the shadows too fast for me to count.

Some of them carry baseball bats.

All of them smell of beer and marijuana.

The stench is overpowering, nauseating.

Then I spot Kenneth Nelson.

His eyes are wild, and he stares at me with open hatred.

In slow motion he reaches inside his coat pocket. When he pulls his hand out, he is holding something. It catches the light from the streetlamp as he points it at me.

It's a gun.

My mouth falls open.

He shoots me.

The bullet sets my stomach on fire like a flamethrower.

I scream.

Automatically, I clutch at the wound, trying to stop the bleeding. Blood oozes out between my fingers anyway.

My dad says that in this country there are two main theories about what happens when you die.

Some people believe you travel through a bright tunnel where relatives who have passed on welcome you into paradise. That's the religious point of view.

Others believe you only see bright lights because your brain is suffering oxygen deprivation and is firing off neurons at random. They say when you die it's all over. That's the scientific point of view.

Different countries with different religions have different beliefs.

When I was in the car accident with Josie Peters, I never lost consciousness. I felt all the pain and all the passage of time and all of the terror of wondering if the paramedics would ever get me out.

I didn't see a bright tunnel or flashing lights.

This time it is different.

I begin to hallucinate.

I see Neeve, Brenlyn, and Talitha grow into giants and tower over the football players.

Brenlyn and Talitha are outlined in a warm, white radiance.

Neeve glows a cold, dull red. His face is dark, alien, and horrible.

The three of them go berserk.

Neeve grabs the gun from Kenneth Nelson and crushes it in one hand. Then he swings his fist, and with a single blow, he sends Kenneth Nelson spinning into the wheelchair ramp, fifteen feet away.

Brenlyn and Talitha hit, punch, and kick wherever it will do the most good.

A lot of shouting and cursing goes on.

A bulky letterman sneaks up behind Neeve.

I try to call out a warning, but my breath merely wheezes between my teeth.

The bat whistles through the air and slams into Neeve's spine. If the bat had been made of wood instead of aluminum, it would have shattered.

Neeve doesn't go down.

He doesn't even stumble.

He whirls around, wrenches the bat free, and then smashes the guy across the gut with it. The letterman soars through the air like a fly ball to the infield.

I watch for lights to snap on inside the nearby houses. They don't.

Surely the neighbors can hear the commotion.

Where are the gawkers?

Where are the morbid curiosity seekers?

Why aren't there any sirens?

Kenneth Nelson struggles to stand up. He makes it to his knees and then freezes like a statue while he watches his hulking teammates being thrashed by two guys and a girl.

Within minutes, athletes are strewn all over Brenlyn's front yard like so much litter after a sporting event.

Growling and baring his teeth like a wild animal, Neeve jerks Kenneth Nelson upright. He wraps his long fingers around Kenneth's neck.

Brenlyn is on Neeve in a flash. "Stop," he yells. "Let him go."

Kenneth Nelson's face turns red, then purple.

Brenlyn clasps his hands together and brings them down like a sledgehammer on Neeve's arms.

"Let him go!" he shouts. "You can't kill him. If you contaminate yourself further, there will be no hope."

Neeve howls in fury.

Swinging behind Neeve, Brenlyn slides his arms under Neeve's armpits and links his hands at the back of Neeve's neck. He applies pressure.

Neeve's head tips forward. His fingers loosen.

Talitha grabs Kenneth Nelson. He makes a gurgling sound then slips from her hands and hits the ground.

Neeve's face is contorted with anger. Twice he twists, trying to break free, but Brenlyn doesn't let go. Regardless, Neeve manages to land a couple of kicks to Kenneth Nelson's midsection before Talitha yanks the football player out of range.

All the while, Neeve shouts a string of strange syllables. I get the feeling that he's swearing in a foreign language.

Finally, Neeve stops struggling.

His breath is loud and uneven. He stands with his eyes closed while his whole body trembles. I can tell he is battling himself, trying to rein in his rage.

After what feels like a century, he shivers and all the fight goes out of him. He sort of slumps forward and Brenlyn catches him.

"I'm all right now, Bren," he says quietly. "Thank you."

Brenlyn mumbles something as he releases Neeve, but I can't hear the words.

Standing with his head held high, Neeve closes his eyes. His chest expands as he inhales deeply. He exhales. He does it again. Once. Twice. Three times.

He looks tranquil and in total control of himself.

He bends his arms and brings his fists together, knuckles to knuckles, at shoulder height. His fingers tighten as if he's grasping something invisible.

He yanks his hands apart and rips a hole in the night.

Through the gap, I see daylight, blue sky, green hills, and a unicorn grazing in a patch of pink flowers.

"Take Karissa through to the field," Neeve says to Talitha. "Then go get Haydon and my mother."

Talitha lifts the wheelchair with me in it, approaches the opening, and steps into another world. She sets the chair in the grass, sprouts wings through her blouse, and flies away.

It looks so real.

In my delirium, I wonder if I've conjured Talitha into an angel or a fairy. She's beautiful and glorious and spiritually transcending.

She makes me believe in heaven.

I sigh.

My breath rattles in my chest.

I raise a hand to my forehead to see if I'm developing a fever, but I'm so sticky with blood that I can't tell.

Even though the sun is shining, the brightness of day fades as if dark clouds are rolling across the sky.

My peripheral vision collapses inward, turning the edges of the world brown, leaving only a bright spot in the middle. Is this the tunnel of light people see?

I'll find out soon enough.

I'm dying.

After the car accident I was terrified.

For some reason, this time I'm not afraid.

The unicorn saunters over and lies down at my feet. It's smaller than I imagined one would be. It's nowhere near horse-sized. Maybe it's goat-sized. I've never seen a live goat. Now, I never will.

It rests its head on my knees and touches my left hand with the tip of its silver horn.

I use the last of my strength to lift my right hand so I can stoke its head.

I leave a dark red smear down its white neck.

I let my eyelids droop closed. I stop struggling to live.

I am light, weightless.

The unicorn's horn pricks my hand like a needle.

My soul is pulled back into my body.

"No," I gasp.

*It is not your time,* I hear in my head. *I'll help you until the healer comes. My name is Stryker.*

"Please," I whisper, "I can't do this to my family again. A funeral is cheaper than a hospital stay. And the sadness will pass, instead of lasting forever, like it will if my parents have to deal with a cripple for the rest of their lives."

*Your future is full of dreams and hopes and loves waiting to be discovered.* The unicorn gently blows its warm, sweet breath into my face. *Be calm and find peace. Help is almost here.*

I do feel calmer, with less pain, but it's still hard to breathe.

Neeve and Brenlyn have pulled all the football players, including Kenneth Nelson, through the rip in space. I can see a crude seam where the pieces of nothing have been overlapped.

I feel my life drifting away again.

I am very tired.

I don't want to hurt anymore.

This time, the prick to my hand is less like a needle and more like a butcher knife.

The unicorn frowns at me.

My lips curl up at the corners. Before I know it, I'm smiling.

How many people get to have a unicorn scowl at them before they die?

I love it. It's a good final moment.

I let go of my earthly ties.

My spirit rises above my body. I look down at the wheelchair girl, and I'm glad that it's not me anymore.

*Your Highness,* I hear the unicorn call out, *I can't hold her. She's fighting me.*

"I'll be right there, Stryker," Neeve says. In a moment, he comes over and kneels beside me.

He takes my blood-encrusted hand and lifts it toward his face. By the time his lips touch my palm, my hand is clean, as if someone has washed the blood away. His kiss jump-starts my heart, pulling me back into the here and now.

His deep green eyes search mine. "I want to tell you a story, Karissa. Will you stay with me and listen?"

"Yes," I whisper.

"Promise me." His voice has a commanding power. Even if I were uninjured, I would not have had the strength to protest.

"I promise." I doubt I'll be able to keep my word, but there's no sense worrying Neeve about something that can't be helped.

He kisses my hand again then holds it next to his heart.

"Once upon a time," he says, "a young boy looked into a magical pool and asked to see his future. The face of a lovely young girl appeared on the surface of the water. Although the boy was but a youngster, he instantly fell in love with her.

"As he grew up, he searched for her everywhere—among the rich and among the poor, in cities and on farms, in places of learning and places of entertainment—but he found no sign of her. As he neared adulthood, he became discouraged.

"He went back to the pool and asked where else he should look. A voice came from the water and told the boy that his future bride was far beyond the ends of the world. To find her, he would have to pay a great price in pain and sorrow. The voice wouldn't tell him what the price would be, but it warned him that even after he found the girl, their happiness was not assured.

"Together, they would have to go on a quest to recover what the boy lost when he paid the price. If they succeeded, they could spend their lives together. If not, they would be separated forever.

"The boy was the seventh of eight brothers, and he saw this quest as not only an opportunity to find his ladylove but also a chance to prove that he was no longer a boy, but a man.

"The boy went to his father and described his visions and laid out his plans, expecting to receive his father's blessing. Instead, his father forbade him to go, saying he was too young for such an undertaking.

"The boy grew angry. Why should he have to wait just because his father still thought of him as a child?

"He went a third time to the magic pool, this time to learn how best to elude his father's authority.

"The voice told him if he left home at this time he would be captured by his father's enemies and hurt almost beyond bearing in both his body and his spirit.

"Rather than frightening the boy into being cautious, the warning made him more determined.

"Before he could change his mind, he grabbed some food and clothing, shoved them into a pack, threw the bag over his shoulder, and set out in the dead of night. At the last moment, he thought to leave a note for his mother so she wouldn't grieve when she found him gone.

"He traveled for three days.

"As foretold, his father's enemies caught him. The cruel things they did to his body damaged the part of his soul that bound him to goodness and light.

"The next day, the boy was found by a search party that his father had sent. Because of the severity of his wounds and the damage to his soul, the boy should have been executed on the spot. If he were allowed to live, he would grow to embrace darkness and become as evil, violent, and hate-filled as those men who had hurt him.

"But the leader of the search party was filled with pity and would not deliver the death blow. Instead, he sent for the boy's family.

"How they wept when they saw him! And he wept with them, knowing he was responsible for their pain as well as his own. He knew what they must do, and he was prepared to die although he regretted never having found the girl.

"But his mother would not allow him to be killed. She said she would open a walkway between worlds so he could be taken to a place where he could heal and fight the darkness growing in his soul. The only problem was that someone would have to carry him, for he was too weak to go on his own.

"Who would volunteer for such a task? It was possible that the evil inside the boy might infect whoever touched him.

"His father could not take the boy because he had great responsibilities at home and to the community. The boy's mother could not go because she did not have the physical strength to carry his weakened body. Although the boy had several siblings, his parents would not even consider letting one of them go with him. They would be too susceptible to the evil.

"The leader of the search party had brought his eldest son with him, and that young man offered to carry the boy through the veil. The young man was of strong character and pure heart. Because he and the boy were not related by blood, he would not be easily contaminated by the growing darkness the way a member of the family would be. He was certain the evil could not touch him.

"But it might mean exile for them both.

"If the boy could not conquer the darkness, he would be unable to reopen the doorway between worlds so they could return home. His friend did not have the power.

"However, if the boy reclaimed the light, he would not only be able to return the young man to their world, but himself also. He would be able to go home, whole and happy, to his family.

"So the boy's mother opened a passage to a different land, a land where the people had forgotten how to use magic. In fact most of them didn't even believe in its existence. There, where magic had lain dormant for centuries, the darkness would develop much slower inside the boy, and that would increase his chances of conquering it.

"So the young man carried the boy through the veil."

My eyes drift closed, but I still listen to Neeve's story. His words seem to glue me together somehow. I think even the bleeding has stopped.

"The boy was taken into the home of a kind family, and his physical injuries healed.

"His friend found work that he was good at and enjoyed.

"Every day the boy battled the darkness. Every day he met with his friend, who listened to him, counseled him, and acted as his conscience.

"Then one day the boy saw the girl. She was there in that strange land and just as lovely as she had been in his visions. But she too had been hurt in her body and spirit."

Neeve pauses.

He doesn't say anything for such a long time that I finally ask him, "Then what happened?"

He kisses my fingers before he continues.

"The boy and the girl became friends.

"Together they went on a quest to recover what the boy had lost when he paid the price for finding her. As they faced adversity side by side, as they shared failures and successes, the girl grew to love the boy as much as he loved her.

"Then one glorious day, they found the lost item. When they touched it, they were both filled with light. They returned to the boy's home in triumph.

"They were married in two worlds. They traveled back and forth through the veil so their children could grow up and be comfortable in both lands. They lived together in love and devotion and happiness forever and ever."

Even though my eyelids each weigh about a hundred pounds, I force them up. "The Brothers Grimm would have enjoyed that," I say, "if only you had thrown in an ogre or two."

He smiles at me tenderly.

I hear a fluttering sound in the air and look up.

Talitha has returned with an old man and a beautiful lady.

They are angels.

The old man's wings are like transparent gold. The lady's have a lustrous blue sheen like pale pearls glowing in moonlight.

# Chapter Fourteen

"Mother," Neeve says to the beautiful lady.

She is tall, slender, and regal.

Her delicate, shimmering gown looks as if it's made of sunbeams and spider webs. Her porcelain face is framed by heavy blond ringlets, held back by a gold circlet that is adorned with a single emerald, the color of her and Neeve's eyes.

There is such longing on their faces that I expect them to fly into each other's arms.

They don't even touch.

"This is the girl in your sketches?" the queen asks.

Queen? Why would I think *queen*?

Then I tell myself it makes perfect sense.

I'm hallucinating and creating a world of fantasy while I die, so of course I would make Neeve's mother the queen, just like Jaydon's mother in my story about Lark and the secret doorway.

"Yes," Neeve answers. "Her name is Karissa Day."

The old man glances at me and then takes a quick survey of the football players.

"The girl first," Neeve tells him.

"What happened to her?" the old man asks.

"She was shot with a metal projectile," Neeve says. "I got her through the veil as quickly as I could, but she is barely hanging on."

The old man touches my forehead softly. "You'll have to hold her here and keep her still while I pull it out. She's so close to passing over I don't dare put her to sleep. What about the young men?"

"They attacked us," Brenlyn answers. "We fought back."

"That explains the damage," the old man mutters.

While they talk, Neeve lifts me out of my chair and then sits down in it with me on his lap. I want to protest, to tell him the seat is full of my blood and he'll ruin his jeans, but I don't have the strength.

He arranges me so I'm lying across him. My head lolls sideways against his shoulder. He supports me with one arm, which he clamps around me like a vise. His other arm is a steel band across my thighs.

"Kari," he whispers the name only my dad calls me. "Try to hold still. This will hurt, but just for a second."

The old man gently moves my hand from the wound in my stomach and replaces it with his own.

I feel pressure building up inside me.

It's like being shot all over again.

I scream, or maybe I whimper.

The bullet pops out, and the old man catches it.

"Thank you, Hayden," Neeve says. "Can you repair her now?"

"I think so," he says. "Talitha, will you go and pick me a handful of gainberries?" She nods and takes off. Then he asks Neeve, "Can you maintain the hold on her until Talitha gets back?"

"Yes," Neeve answers.

He releases his iron-like grip across my thighs and gently places his hand on my chest, right above my heart. I get a sensation similar to when the unicorn pulled my consciousness back into my body, but this is a hundred times stronger.

I become warmer and more substantial.

For the first time since I saw the gun in Kenneth Nelson's hand, I think I might survive.

The old man says, "I'll tend to the worst of the young men while we wait for Talitha."

"Do just enough to remove the threat of death," Neeve instructs. "I need them distracted from Karissa. Pain is a good distraction."

"What do you want me to do about their memories?"

Neeve considers for a moment.

"Alcohol is forbidden to the young people of their world," he says finally, "and they've been drinking a lot of it. If you conceal the part about Brenlyn's shop and the fight, Bren and I can go back and arrange their automobiles to look as if they crashed into each other. That will account for their injuries and will get them into trouble on many levels. It doesn't matter if their memories of the accident are vague. Human memories are flighty anyway."

"What about Karissa's memory?" the queen asks.

Neeve runs his fingers down the side of my face, tracing my hairline.

I feel tingles all through my body.

He places his hand over my heart again.

"We can't tamper with her mind," Neeve says. "She's heard the whispering of echoes all her life. She already half believes. She writes stories and draws pictures in an effort to understand. If we do anything to her memory, she might lose the ability to listen in the future."

"Maybe a dream?" the queen suggests.

"No," Neeve asserts. "She'll find a way to explain it to herself until she's ready to hear the truth."

Talitha returns with her hands cupped around something that glows with a crimson light between her fingers.

"You need to set her down now," the old man, Hayden, says.

Neeve gets up out of my chair and places me on the grass.

There are no bloodstains on his clothing.

Hayden mumbles a few words, crushes a berry between thumb and forefinger, and dribbles the juice into my mouth.

It explodes along my senses.

My body convulses and then goes stiff.

I try to make sense of what I'm experiencing.

I taste music and hear color. A sweet/tart flavor and a tangy aroma swirl through my arms and legs, through my organs and bones. Unimaginable sensations, from pleasant little tickles to sharp jabs of pain, engulf me.

"What is it?" I exclaim with more forcefulness than I thought I had left inside of me. I gasp as a sting pierces my core. It is followed by a satiny, soft caress across my skin.

"It is a berry," Hayden says. "It provides whatever your body needs at the moment. In your case, it will help replace the blood you've lost and speed up the healing process."

"Sounds like magic," I whisper.

Hayden pats my hand. "That's because it is, my dear."

He crushes a second berry and drips more liquid into my mouth.

The phenomenal sensory bursts are just as vivid as they were the first time.

Neeve kneels beside me. "Kari, Brenlyn and I have got to leave for a little while. Hayden will take care of you."

"No," I cry, half begging, half demanding. "My folks will panic if I'm more than a few minutes late. You need to take me to the hospital and then call my parents."

"I'll have you home by half past midnight, just as I promised."

"Half past midnight on what day?" I ask.

I feel tears slipping down my cheeks. I don't want to repeat the worry and financial burden my family went through after the car accident, but even that would be better than having me disappear for days or weeks or months.

How long does it take to recover from a gunshot wound?

"Don't worry, Karissa," Neeve whispers in my ear. "You're in a fairytale. Anything can happen in a fairytale."

He leans over and places his warm, firm lips on my forehead.

A gush of ecstasy floods me.

Then he takes my hand and kisses the palm.

My heartbeat is firmer.

My respiration is stronger.

I wonder how much magic there is in his lips.

He stands.

I can't take my eyes off him.

It isn't just because he's inhumanly handsome, which he is. My reaction goes deeper than that. There is an undercurrent of magnetism that pulls my heart toward him, as if that's where my heart belongs, as if I'm being pulled home. I didn't know it was possible to be drawn to someone like this.

I ask myself, *Am I'm falling madly in love with him, or am I merely obsessed with his exotic strangeness?*

Either reaction should frighten me.

I barely know him.

I suppose it's a moot point. (I just learned that term in Mr. Ullom's English class. It means *unimportant* or *debatable.*)

How I feel about Neeve is irrelevant if I'm going to die tonight.

"I've got to leave," Neeve says to the queen. "The darkness has been intensifying ever since I came back through the veil."

"I know," she says with a tremor in her voice. "I wish I could hold you in my arms."

Her hand drifts upward but stops a few inches from his cheek.

Neeve's face goes through a terrible transition, showing the depth of his yearning and sorrow and loneliness and, I think, self-loathing. It is awful to watch.

"I played the violin for her family," he says. "Her mother hugged me and kissed my hair when I finished. It felt so much like you I thought my heart would break."

Sadness tugs unfamiliar lines into the queen's perfectly smooth brow. "I never thought I'd envy a human."

"I'm sure Karissa's mother heard the echoes when she was a young girl," Neeve says. "That's why she recognized them in the song I played."

"Your Highness," the old man says, clearly addressing the son and not the mother.

"I'm just Neeve, now. You know that, Hayden."

Hayden shakes his head and continues. "What about her legs?"

I hold my breath.

Can this magical healer fix me so I can walk again?

Neeve turns away. His neck muscles tense. His hands clench into fists.

I hear him mutter beneath his breath, "Nothing. She has to find her own way back."

I'm stunned.

Does Neeve want me to stay a cripple? I want to kick and scream and shout (especially kick, because that would mean I can use my legs). But this is a dream, I remind myself. I can't blame Neeve for what happens in my dreams.

He spins around. "Bren, we've got to go."

Then he freezes, staring up at the sky.

I twist my head and follow his gaze.

Flying toward us is the largest angelic being I've seen so far.

I glance back at Neeve.

He looks as if he might shatter into a million pieces.

"Father," he says quietly.

I am awestruck.

If I had never seen a king portrayed in a movie or described in a book, I would still have labeled Neeve's father *The King*. Every inch of his towering height and majestic breadth, every stitch in his dark green brocade suit, every grey strand in his rich brown hair and pointed beard, every line on his handsome, weathered face shouts Absolute Ruler.

He lands next to his wife.

Neeve falls to his knees and bows his head.

The king says, "None of that, Neeve." His voice is strong and authoritative, but it is also full of compassion and caring. "Stand up. You're still my son."

Remaining on his knees, Neeve looks up. "I'm sorry, Father."

There is something ritualistic in his words.

"For sending for your mother and not for me?" the king asks with his eyebrows raised. "Surely you know that you can't set foot in my realm without having me notice eventually, even if I'm preoccupied with matters of State."

"I didn't think you'd want to see me."

"You thought wrong." The king turns to his wife. "Really, Alaina Mae, why didn't *you* send for me?"

"Justus, dear," she answers, smiling lovingly while she strokes his arm, "I knew you would come if you wanted. Who am I to dictate to the king?"

"You're my wife, and you don't seem to have any trouble dictating to me in private." There is affection behind his words, even if they sound a bit sharp. He extends his hand to Neeve. "Stand up."

Neeve obeys but without taking the hand. "I wasn't apologizing for sending for Mother and not for you," he says, his voice turning bitter. "It was for being a stupid, foolish child."

"I know that," his father answers. I get the impression that Neeve's father knows everything in the universe that's worth knowing.

"There are three major ways to learn life's lessons, Neeve. You can listen to the wisdom of your elders. You can watch the actions of other people and observe the consequences. Or you can plunge headlong into life and make your own mistakes. The third way is often the most painful, but it also has the most lasting impact."

The king gazes at me a moment.

The pain is almost gone.

I wonder if this is a positive sign. I've heard that right before people drown or freeze to death, they feel good, like everything is going to be all right. I don't know if people who've been shot go through the same thing.

The king asks Neeve, "Is there a reason you brought her here instead of taking her to the healers in her own world?"

"Yes," Neeve answers tightly, as if he's trying not to be irritated about having his judgment questioned. "I was afraid she would die before I got her to them. Also, her father is a wise man, a mender of broken minds, what they call a psychologist.

"When I was taken to their hospital to have my—" his voice breaks and he closes his eyes for a moment before continuing "—to have my injuries tended, my physical pain and emotional anguish were so acute that I couldn't remember how to speak in foreign tongues. The doctor sent for Karissa's father. He met with me several times, chatting patiently about little daily things until I remembered how to talk."

Neeve's tone grows harsher now. "He knows I'm damaged, although he doesn't understand how much or why. It is only because Karissa is also suffering from physical and emotional pain that he risks letting her be with me, hoping that somehow we'll find a way to help each other. If I brought her back to him injured, he wouldn't trust me in the future."

His voice gets louder, defiant. "Even if I didn't need her to listen to the echoes for me, I would not let anything separate us. I've waited too long, sacrificed too much, to let her go now."

King Justus reaches out to touch Neeve, to offer comfort I think, but Neeve backs away.

The king takes a step forward and grasps Neeve by the shoulders.

"I've had a long, rough life," he says. "If I haven't been corrupted yet, I'm damned well not going to be corrupted by touching my own son." Then he wraps his arms around Neeve, and Neeve just crumples against him, hugging his father with his head buried against his shoulder.

Tears trickle out of the corners of my eyes. I brush them away without thinking and am surprised to discover I can raise my arms.

I look at Neeve's mother, remembering her hesitancy to touch him earlier, and she's crying too.

"Alaina Mae," the king says over Neeve's shoulder, "you had better go back to the palace. The darkness is thickening. As his mother, and as young as you are, you'll be particularly susceptible."

"I know. I can feel it." The queen tarries for a moment. "Neeve, dear, hurry so you can come home."

"I'm trying, Mother," he says.

Then the queen kneels in the grass and puts her lips close to my ear. "Please help my son. Please bring him back to us." She kisses my forehead, and a shock goes through me like an electrical charge.

The queen stands and touches her fingertips to her lips. She blows Neeve a kiss. Then her delicate blue butterfly wings spread out behind her and she flies away.

The silence is broken when Hayden, the healer, points to the football players and tells Neeve, "You'd better go prepare the scene for these. They will start to regain consciousness soon."

Neeve pushes away from his father.

The king tips his head at the roughly torn piece of space. "You did a sloppy job on that."

Neeve shrugs. "I was in a hurry."

"So I see." The king strokes Neeve's cheek. "I know you have difficult times ahead, but never forget that your mother and I love you. We want you back."

"I'll do my best." Neeve throws his arms around his father for one more, quick embrace.

The king spreads his wings. They remind me of a monarch butterfly, which seems appropriate I suppose, but the yellow-orange is brighter and the brown is deeper.

"You'll fix that," he says, aiming his pointy beard at the tear.

It's a statement, not a question.

"Yes," Neeve says, "as soon as I take Karissa back through."

Nodding, the king lifts into the air and heads in the direction his wife has gone.

"We won't be long," Neeve tells me.

He takes hold of the ragged edges of reality and reopens the slit onto Brenlyn's driveway. He heaves a football player over each shoulder and passes through. Brenlyn and Talitha follow him, their arms full of bulky bodies, also.

The unicorn lies down in the grass beside me, and I run my fingers through its silky mane. The bloody smear I made earlier is gone.

*That feels nice,* it says, laying its head on my stomach, carefully avoiding the wound. Its head weighs next to nothing.

"Thank you," I tell it, "for not letting me die."

*You're welcome.* It lifts its head. *Hayden, old man, are you getting senile? Pay attention to your patient. She needs a bit more healing. You won't want to keep His Highness waiting when he returns.*

"I was just about to take care of that, Stryker," Hayden mutters defensively. "You always enjoy having a chance to boss me around."

*That's true,* the unicorn says, *but it is also true that the girl is not quite healed and His Highness is bound to be impatient.*

92

"Open your mouth, dear," Hayden says to me, holding three of the red berries in his hand. "You're strong enough to chew these now, and they're more powerful when taken whole."

I follow his orders, but with trepidation. Considering what the juice alone did to me, I'm worried about the effects of the complete fruit.

As soon as I bite down, I am transported far beyond the heavens.

Everything around me is made of light.

The brightness throbs with spikes of molten gold and icy blue. I am filled with the splendor of creation and the wonder of life. My senses are a kaleidoscope of unearthly sounds, tastes, smells, sights, and feelings.

The universe spins around me, and I hear planets and stars and gigantic nebulas singing to me.

I have no idea how long I'm transfixed.

Time loses meaning.

I am only vaguely aware when Neeve returns.

"She looks almost back to normal." His voice blends dreamily with the other sounds in my mind.

"You need to clean her up and repair her clothing," Hayden says.

Even though I'm high on magical berries, I have enough awareness to be embarrassed by Hayden's suggestion. What does he expect Neeve to do? Give me a bath while mending the bullet hole in my sweater? Oh, and don't forget soaking out all of the blood.

Whatever the old man has in mind, Neeve does nothing but finger back my hair and straighten my jacket across my shoulders.

Hayden calls Brenlyn over. "Will you take care of the chair?"

"Of course," Brenlyn mumbles.

After a few minutes, Neeve picks me up and sets me back in my wheelchair, which looks as if it just came from the factory.

"Thank you, Hayden," Neeve says. "I noticed that you took care of the bruises my fingers made around the neck of Kenneth Nelson."

"I thought they would be inconsistent with the accident you were staging."

"You were right, of course," Neeve says. Then he calls out to the unicorn, "Thank you for your help, too, Stryker."

*My pleasure, Your Highness. It was good to see you again.*

The next thing I know, Neeve picks up my wheelchair and carries me through the opening in space, back into nighttime.

I watch him carefully match up the sides of the jagged hole and then run his finger down the seam. It disappears.

All of a sudden I'm dizzy, as if I've been spinning around in circles.

I have the oddest images in my head.

I feel as if I'm waking from a particularly vivid and exhausting dream.

Neeve is crouched down beside my chair.

"How are you doing?" he asks.

93

"I—uhm—I don't know," I say, feeling muddled. "Did I pass out or something?"

"Or something," Neeve says as he stands up. "I think I kept you out too late. It's been a long evening, probably too long for a first date. We need to get you home."

He picks me up and sets me in the van and climbs in after me. Brenlyn and Talitha take my chair around back.

Quickly I review the evening: dinner at Mama Mia's Meals, the movie, and the tour of Brenlyn's workshop. Maybe it was a little too much. I haven't been out at night since the car accident. No, not since we left Chicago.

Neeve puts his arm around me and I lean into him.

"I don't want to go home," I whisper.

"It's after midnight," Neeve says, nuzzling my hair with his chin. "You need to sleep. I'll call you in the morning so we can decide when to work on our report."

# Chapter Fifteen

I pry my eyes open Saturday morning.

My mind is in a fog.

All night I had strange dreams. I became Lark in my story, and Neeve became Jaydon. I was surrounded by images and sensations that I've never experienced in real life and that I've never imagined in my fantasies. Part of the time I was elated. Part of the time I was terrified.

I feel as if I've been awake all night, but I couldn't have dreamed without sleeping.

Only with great effort do I haul myself out of bed and into my chair.

I gather clean clothes and head for the bathroom.

I'm in the shower, soaping my body when I feel a new pucker of skin on my abdomen. I can't get a good enough look at it, so I rinse off quickly, towel myself dry, and slide into my chair naked. There's a full-length mirror on the back of the door, and I roll up to it as close as I can.

Two inches above my navel is a small, round, pink indentation that wasn't there before. Since the accident, I've spent hours examining every single scar on my body. I know each one intimately.

As I glare at this new addition, the memories of Kenneth Nelson, the gun, the bullet, the pain—it all comes whirling back.

But it couldn't have been real.

No one heals from a gunshot wound over night. Do they?

I can't think.

My head spins all the way around like the girl in *The Exorcist*.

It isn't until I start to shiver that it occurs to me to get dressed.

This is never an easy chore, but I'd rather struggle and do it myself than have someone do it for me.

I slip my panties over my feet and pull them up as high as my knees. I lift my legs with my hands, one at a time, and tug on the waistband to guide them up my thighs. I raise my hips by leaning over the arms of my chair, alternating sides, until the panties are in place. I do the same thing with my sweatpants. I almost always wear sweatpants on the weekend since they're easier to get into than jeans. I have no problems with the bra and t-shirt.

It's all casual and comfy.

After all, who cares what I wear? There aren't any guys hanging around, checking me out anymore. Except Neeve.

Neeve?

Last night in my dreams, Neeve was a prince, a prince with parents who could fly.

I shake my head like maybe I can shake some sense into it.

I reach under my shirt. The new scar is still there.

Oh, what the heck!

If I'm delusional enough to think Neeve has parents with wings, I am certainly delusional enough to think I have a new scar.

Maybe I'm still in the hospital after the accident and am experiencing a pain-induced delirium. That would explain everything.

My stomach grumbles, and I realize I'm hungry.

That argues for reality not fantasy.

I've eaten food in my dreams before, usually my Grandma Baker's lemon cookies, but I've never felt hunger. And my stomach has never made rude noises.

Perhaps I've lost my mind and Dad has institutionalized me. If so, when they figure out which antipsychotic medication to give me, I'll regain my sanity.

In the meantime, I might as well pretend everything is all right.

I get out the blow dryer to do my hair. That keeps me occupied for a couple of minutes.

My cellphone rings.

I almost create a new door out of the bathroom, trying to get to it.

I look at the caller I.D. It's Neeve.

I'll be calm. I'll be cool. I won't rave like a lunatic.

"Hello?" I say.

"Good morning," Neeve says, sounding completely normal. "Did you sleep well?"

I lose it.

My voice comes out a hoarse bark. "I got shot last night?"

Dead silence.

Then I hear him breathing, so I know he hasn't hit the *end call* button.

Several minutes pass.

Barely whispering, he asks, "How much do you remember?"

If I had been standing, I would have fallen to the floor. As it is, I sort of sag against the back of my chair. It's my turn to drag out the silence.

Finally, I whisper back, "Is it true?"

Another pause, but shorter this time. "May I come over so we can talk?"

"Everyone is home today," I tell him. "We won't have any privacy." I take a moment to think. "We can go over to the library when it opens. It's only a couple of blocks from here. Maybe one of the study rooms will be free. Or, if you prefer, there's a Starbucks across the street from it."

"Okay, I'll be right there."

I exhale noisily. "Aren't you at home? How long will it take you to get here?"

"No time at all. I can get there as fast as walking from one room to another."

I picture Neeve tearing a new hole in space. I shiver and shove the image from my mind. "I haven't eaten yet," I say. "Have you?"

"No."

"You might as well come over and have breakfast."

"What about your family?" he asks.

"I told my folks we were going to work on our research paper today. They won't mind if I feed you first."

"I'd feel more comfortable if you asked."

"Okay." I open my door and head for the kitchen.

Mom is measuring pancake mix and dumping it into a bowl.

"Hey, Mom," I say. "Neeve's in the neighborhood and wants to know if it's too early for him to come over."

"Ask him if he likes blueberry pancakes," she says.

Ordinarily, Mom doesn't like to cook. If you want to give her a gift she'll really enjoy, take her out to dinner. The one exception is breakfast. She loves fixing pancakes, crepes, waffles, French toast, cinnamon rolls, and a dozen kinds of muffins. Sometimes she makes donuts or apple fritters. I'll bet she knows how to cook eggs a hundred different ways.

"Oh," she says before I can ask Neeve about the pancakes, "ask him if he prefers bacon or sausage."

This one I can answer on my own.

"He can't eat beef or pork," I tell her. "That's why I made salmon the night he came to dinner. The only meats he can eat are poultry and fish."

"Hmm," she mumbles to herself, "turkey sausage tastes pretty good, and it's healthier too." She makes a notation on her grocery list. Then she says to me, "How about blueberry pancakes and vegetarian kitchen sink omelets?"

I check with Neeve.

"He likes blueberry pancakes," I tell Mom. "He's curious about the omelet."

"When will he be here?" she asks.

Neeve answers in my ear. "Go to the door. I'll be on your porch."

If I hadn't remembered what I went through last night, I wouldn't have believed him. Today, I'm willing to believe just about anything.

I open the front door.

He's standing there, waiting.

Saturday breakfast with the whole family is a rarity. Usually the only morning we're all sure to be home at the same time is Sunday.

Still, here we are.

As we gather around the table, I'm surprised that Neeve and I are acting so normal.

It helps that after the polite comments of "Gee, that looks great," and "This smells good enough to eat," Dad pinches his eyebrows together and gives Bennett a stern look.

As Bennett forks a couple of pancakes onto his plate, he blurts, "Neeve, I hope you won't be angry, but I told my trumpet teacher about how good you are on all those different instruments. Dad says I should've asked you if it was all right."

Before Neeve can respond, Jeremy plunges in. "I told my band teacher, too. But honestly I wasn't gossiping about you. It was more like validation, you know? It was like saying, 'Here's this really cool guy, and he can play any instrument so well that it rips your heart out, so maybe all the work is worth it.' My band teacher was *way* impressed. He'd like to meet you."

"My trumpet teacher wanted to know if maybe you'd play at our next recital. She always has a guest performer to balance out the program because some of the kids are pretty bad."

Everyone stares at Neeve.

He looks uncomfortable for just a moment. Then he throws back his head and laughs—really, really laughs—until his whole body shakes.

It's not the reaction any of us expect, especially not Dad.

We don't understand what's so funny, but we can't help smiling at him.

"I'm sorry for laughing, Ben," Neeve says after he catches his breath. He grins very wide. "When you started with 'I hope you won't be angry' I expected something terrible like—" he stumbles around for words "—like maybe you put my picture on the Internet with a 'Wanted Dead or Alive' poster as a joke and ended up with fifty thousand bounty hunters offering to take the job. I wasn't prepared for you to apologize for bragging about me to your teacher." He includes Jeremy with a glance. "I didn't know anyone apologized for paying someone a compliment."

He chuckles a bit more before he settles down.

Then he addresses Dad. "I appreciate your kindness in wanting to shield me. I think, though, that it might be to my advantage to demonstrate my musical talents in public. Perhaps it would make me appear less defective in the eyes of the community."

If those words had come out of my mouth, I would've sounded like the village idiot or a posturing phony. They sound completely natural coming from Neeve. I wonder if he's a bit of a hypnotist, along with being a musician, a poet, an artist, and a guy who rips holes in reality.

Up until Bennett started apologizing, we had been passing food around the table. Then things stalled while we waited to see how Neeve would react to the boys talking about him behind his back.

Now the flow of food gets going again.

When Mom makes pancakes, she always gives us the option of several kinds of toppings. Today we have maple syrup, blueberry syrup, whipped cream, and fruit (blueberries, strawberries, and peaches, all from the freezer).

A platter holds two large omelets, each cut into thirds.

When it reaches Neeve, he asks Mom, "What is a vegetarian kitchen sink omelet?"

Mom gets a tickled look on her face, like she always does when she has the opportunity to explain. "It's an omelet you make by putting everything you have into it except the kitchen sink. Of course, if it's vegetarian, you don't include meat. These have onions, red bell peppers, celery, broccoli, bean sprouts, pecans, and cheese."

"They never turn out the same way twice," Bennett says, "but they always taste good."

Neeve slides a section onto his plate. He holds it up a second so he can inhale the aroma.

"Hmm," he mumbles. "Smells delicious."

After that, we sort of all dig in.

Table talk is reduced to an occasional mumble between bites.

It is after we finish eating that Mom shocks us.

She gets up, goes over to the China closet, and takes her violin from the bottom drawer. She doesn't keep it there, so I know something odd is going on.

She removes Neeve's plate and sets the violin down on the table in front of him.

"I can't play it anymore," she says, flexing fingers that have gotten knobby in the joints with arthritis. "I wasn't ever able to make it sing the way you can. It deserves to be played right. I want you to have it."

We're all stunned. Mom loves that violin.

Neeve looks up at her with longing in his eyes.

"I want to accept it," he says very softly, "but I don't know if the Taylors will let me, or even if I should. It would only take one of my foster brothers losing his temper, and this wonderful instrument could be smashed into kindling. Things of value don't last too long in foster care. There's too much frustration and pent-up anger in the air."

"You could probably keep it in the orchestra room at school," Jeremy suggests.

"If I were taking orchestra," Neeve says, "but I'm not."

"Is there a reason you can't take orchestra?" Dad asks. "You're certainly good enough."

"It never occurred to me to sign up for it," Neeve answers. "I didn't remember I could play anything until the night Jeremy offered me his clarinet. Now it's too late. We're over a month into the new semester." Neeve strokes the case. "Maybe I could just play it here."

"No," Mom says. "It belongs with you. There's got to be a way for you to keep it." Her mouth gets this really determined expression. She taps her lips with her fingertips. She can be wonderfully stubborn. I'll bet she was a terror as a kid.

"Orchestra at school," she says, "seems like a good solution. Do you have a free period in your schedule?"

"Actually, I have two. The principal was hesitant about loading me down too much. Because of the memory problems, he wasn't sure where to place me."

"So," Mom continues, "it is merely a matter of letting them see how talented you are. Would you be offended if I called the school and asked the orchestra teacher to let you audition?"

"No," Neeve says slowly, thoughtfully, "if you think it's appropriate."

Dad catches on to what Neeve is implying faster than Mom does.

"The request really should come from the Taylors," Dad says. "They are his foster parents."

"All right," Mom says, "I'll just call them and invite them over for dinner." She's thinking fast now. You can almost hear the cogs in her brain turning. "After dinner we'll have some entertainment provided by the boys and Neeve. Once the Taylors hear Neeve play, I'll tell them I'd like to give him the violin. They can help us decide what to do about it." She glances at my brothers. "What do you think, guys? Will you prepare something to play at a family recital?"

"It's all right by me," Bennett says.

Jeremy nods. "Sure."

"Neeve?" Mom asks.

"Yes," he says, smiling like an angel. Then he turns to me. "Karissa, will you accompany me on the flute?"

I give him a withering glare. "I told you I don't have any musical talent. The boys got it all."

"I know that's what you said, but I don't quite believe it. Will you try if I choose something that isn't too hard? It can't be a family recital without you."

I fall right into his bottomless green eyes. Again. A tiny portion of my mind wonders if I will actually ever have free will when I am with Neeve.

"Okay," I agree before I can stop myself.

# Chapter Sixteen

I get so distracted that I forget why Neeve came over in the first place. It isn't until he asks me if we shouldn't head over to the library that I remember.

Mom, never a procrastinator, doesn't let us leave until after Neeve has given her the Taylors' telephone number.

I grab my laptop and shove it into my big sectional purse. After Neeve and I pull on our coats, I give him my backpack to carry. He slings one strap over his shoulder. Even though researching the Brothers Grimm is the furthest thing from our minds, we look like a couple of kids who're going to the library to study.

Once we're outside, Neeve repeats the question he asked me earlier. "How much do you remember about last night?"

"No way," I tell him. "I haven't had a psychologist for a father without learning a few things. If I tell you what I remember, you'll only explain those parts to me. I want to know everything. First of all, who are you really?"

I expect him to stall, to try to keep what he reveals to me at a minimum. Instead, he answers.

"I am Neeve Maynard Trudimahn, seventh son of His Royal Majesty, King Justus IV of Auravale, born to his second wife, Queen Alaina Mae of Ranstania, the fourth child and first son of that union."

I go into shock. Couldn't he have just said something like *I'm a prince from another dimension* and leave it at that? It still would've been hard enough to handle. But all that other stuff? It makes it sound so official!

I stammer a little when I tell him, "Say it again."

He repeats it word for word.

I try to wrap my head around it. I decide to ignore the king and queen portion, the part that means he's a prince, and just figure out his place among the siblings.

"So in English," I say, trying to get it clear, "that means your father had six sons with his first wife. Then he married your mother, and she had three girls before you, right?"

"Mostly," Neeve says. "That's leaving out the daughters my father had with his first wife and the children my mother has had since I was born."

"I don't get it," I say. "If you're describing your family, why leave out your older sisters and younger siblings? Girls don't count where you come from?"

"Daughters," Neeve says, "can't inherit the crown as long as there are living sons, and sons born after me do not affect my status in the succession. That I am the seventh son means that I am seventh in line for the throne. In actuality, my father had six sons and eleven daughters by his first wife, then three daughters, me, another daughter, and another son by my mother."

"Holy crud," I say. I do some quick addition in my head. "Your dad has twenty-three children?"

Neeve chuckles. "It's not like we've all been rattling around the palace at the same time. We're spread out over many decades. Considering how long my father has lived, twenty-three is not a large number. He is quite old by your standards."

"And you?" I ask. "How old are you?"

He scrunches up his face as if he's searching his brain for a good answer.

It doesn't seem like such a difficult question to me.

Finally, he says, "Time isn't a constant where I come from, the way it is here. It's flexible. That makes it hard to convert our years into yours. Let's just say I'm older than a child but not yet an adult, like you."

"And," I say, "you come from a world that's just on the other side of—of—of our night?" I know it sounds lame, but I don't know how else to phrase it.

"Not exactly," he says. "Anywhere," he points to the ground at our feet, "is just on the other side of everywhere," he sweeps his hand toward the horizon, "if you know how to open the right doors."

Okay.

That's worse than trying to cope with the king and queen part.

My head might explode.

When I pictured him opening up the space between the Taylors' house and ours, I was sort of being facetious, regardless of the fact that I'd seen him rip open a passage between worlds last night.

I mean, really!

Sometimes you can *know* something and still not *believe* it!

Maybe I'll have to ignore the part about opening passages, too.

When we get to the library, I figure it's all right for me to put my brain on hold for a few minutes.

We go up to the lady at the front desk.

"Is there a study room free?" I ask her.

Although they like to reserve those rooms for large groups on Saturdays, and therefore don't usually allow two people to monopolize that much space,

I realize right away that this woman is going to give us a room, not because one is available, but because I'm the wheelchair girl.

Her eyes are full of pity. She knows fate has been cruel to me, and she hopes I'm not bitter. Surely I realize life isn't fair. Blah, blah, blah. She doesn't have to say it out loud. She looks it.

She makes a couple of taps on her keyboard and then studies the computer screen for a minute. "Room number three is open for the next two hours. Is that long enough, honey?"

I smile pathetically. "If that's all you can offer us, we'll have to make it do." I let her see I'm being brave.

"Well," she says, not wanting to be insensitive to the needs of the disabled, "I'll see what else I can arrange."

"Thank you. You're so kind."

I practically simper, I'm so grateful.

Not.

I hate pity.

The study room is a long rectangle, and running down the middle is a twelve-foot table. Cheap, molded chairs are crowded everywhere. Sections of newspaper have been left scattered on the tabletop. They spill over onto a couple of chairs.

"You are absolutely shameless," Neeve says as he closes the door. He hands me my backpack and then begins stacking chairs in the corner to get them out of the way.

"I can't help it," I say with a touch of bitterness. I park the wheelchair at the head of the table and gather up newspapers. I refold the sections neatly and place them on a corner of the table. "She was just aching to demonstrate how understanding and supportive she is when dealing with the handicapped."

I plunk my backpack on top of the newspapers then pull out a couple of folders and my world history book. I get my laptop from my purse and flip it open. We need to look like we belong here, just in case someone peers through the little window in the door.

"I'm sure," I say, continuing to complain, "she'll tell her family and friends all about it, how she had to bend the rules for the poor little cripple. People like her make me want to barf."

"You're right about her," Neeve says, placing a chair at my left side and sitting down. "She was being patronizing. But how did you know? Mind reading isn't a human talent."

"I know, but reading body language is an ability that can be learned. It's an important skill to have if your dad's a shrink."

"Shrink?" Neeve repeats with his eyebrows pinched together for a moment. "Oh, you mean a psychologist."

I have a new and startling insight.

"Holy crud!" I cry out. "Mind reading isn't a human trait, but it is a non-human one? Like you and Brenlyn and Talitha?" I feel my face start to burn as past experiences begin to make sense. "And your parents? Your mom and dad heard everything I was thinking?"

"They could have, of course," Neeve answers nonchalantly, "but it's considered impolite to eavesdrop. Why else would we use oral speech at all? Going into someone's mind is an intimate experience. You need to be invited."

"Except you read my mind every time I use a term that you're not familiar with. So do Brenlyn and Talitha, don't they?"

"That's not the same thing. When you speak, you project all kinds of images and meanings and associations along with your words. We just tap into those."

As I'm trying to figure out the shade of difference between mind reading and tapping into projected images, I must get a peculiar look on my face, skeptical or mistrustful or something.

Neeve reacts defensively. "Under no circumstances would any of us force ourselves into your mind. That would be as bad as a physical assault."

Whoa! I tell myself.

Lots of emotion here!

Backpedal, girl.

"I believe you," I say quickly. "I didn't mean to imply that I felt violated. I was just surprised."

He props his elbows on the table and drops his head into his hands. I watch him take deep breaths.

I cup my hand around his arm. "I'm sorry, Neeve. This is all new to me. I didn't mean to be insulting."

He lifts his head, looking sad and weary. "I'm the one who should apologize, Karissa. The anger comes from the darkness, which is always nearest the surface when I allow myself to have strong feelings, either positive or negative. Right now, I feel very close to you because you know about me and you're still here. The only way to keep the darkness completely contained is not to feel anything, to make myself go numb."

"I don't want you to go numb," I say softly. "I want you to feel close to me."

He takes my hand in both of his and gazes at me with his big emerald eyes.

My heart pounds against my ribs so hard I think it might break free and fall at his feet.

"I wish I understood what's going on," I tell him. "You really haven't explained anything to me yet."

"Yes I have." He buries his face in his hands again. "The fairytale I told you last night is my story. I'm here trying to conquer the darkness that is growing inside of me. Brenlyn is the young man who brought me through the doorway my mother opened. Talitha was Brenlyn's betrothed, and she followed him. Now she is his wife."

"And me?" It pops out of my mouth without warning.

He lifts his head and smiles at me with such a tender expression that I almost gasp out loud.

"Yours is the face I saw on the waters, the face I left my father's home to find."

Intellectually, I knew that was it.

Emotionally, I wasn't prepared to hear it.

My eyes fill with tears.

I'm not sure why. Maybe because Neeve was willing to risk so much, has in fact suffered so much, to find me. Maybe because I've considered myself hopelessly flawed and inadequate since the accident, believing no guy would want me unless I could walk. Maybe because Neeve acts like he could love me even if I'm stuck in a wheelchair for the rest of my life.

The tears spill over and snake down my cheeks.

"Please don't cry," Neeve says. "I'm sorry. Do you want me to leave?"

I pull a tissue from a packet in my purse.

"Don't be silly," I say. "I'm just weepy because I haven't had time to process everything that's happened in the past twenty-four hours."

I close my eyes and try to organize my thoughts. Looking at Neeve is so distracting that I'm not sure I can explain what I'm feeling without sounding stupid or melodramatic.

I begin slowly.

"The evening started out with a dream date: a nice dinner, an exciting movie, and a visit to a fascinating workshop. I was having a wonderful time. Then, suddenly and without warning, I was shot and almost killed by the most popular guy at school.

"After that, I was taken to another world where I talked to a unicorn and watched people fly. I went on a magic-berry high that took me up to heaven and scrambled all my senses. Plus I learned the guy I like is a prince who can crush guns with one hand, throw football players around like rubber balls with the other, and then calmly rip holes in space."

He grins wryly at me, raises his eyebrows, and nods his head. "I suppose it was a little much." Then his expression sobers. "Somewhere toward the end of that list of grievances did I hear you say something about a guy you like?"

I drop my eyes and can feel my face flushing. "Yes."

"Thank you," he says softly. "I was prepared for you to reject me since I am damaged and am fighting a battle inside myself that I might lose."

"Here in my world," I tell him, "everyone has the potential for both good and evil. We fight battles with ourselves all of the time. Sometimes we win.

Sometimes we lose."

"Good and evil aren't as black and white here as they are where I come from. So much of your world is in shades of gray."

"Is the difference because of the magic? You said in your story that we don't know how to use magic anymore, so it's gone dormant."

"For someone who was holding onto life by a thread, you have amazing recall." My hands are clasped together on the tabletop, and he runs a finger across them. "Although magic hasn't disappeared here, lack of usage has made it weak. Luckily it's not completely inert yet. Otherwise, I wouldn't be able to open doorways like I did last night."

I give him a quizzical look. "Oh," I say teasingly, "was that jagged slash in reality the way you open a door?"

He laughs dryly. "I already got chastened by my father for making a mess of it. You don't need to remind me."

His mentioning his father gives me a twinge of discomfort.

"Neeve," I say, "you remember your family. Is there really anything wrong with your memory?"

His expression grows troubled. "Yes, there is. Brenlyn has helped me recall a great deal, but there are still many gaps, things I can't quite remember from my earlier life. Also, I should know much more about your world than I do.

"Part of the standard education for the royal family includes information, both current and historical, about the worlds closest to our own. I've taken Earth Studies, but it's all so sketchy in my mind. I read and I listen carefully. Sometimes, I can pull things into focus. Sometimes, everything sounds garbled.

"Part of the confusion comes from the constant pain in my body, and part of it is from the evil growing in my soul. The darkness tries to make me forget my ties to the light, to what I love, to my memories, to what brings me joy."

While he talks, I watch his face.

His features are so angelic, so heartbreakingly handsome, that it's hard to believe there is an epic battle being waged inside of him. But after Kenneth Nelson shot me, I saw the fury, the hatred, the hunger to hurt, the desire to destroy.

If the dark part of Neeve wins and he's stuck in our world without a conscience, his immense physical strength and access to magical powers could transform him into a monster from humanity's worst nightmares.

If he went on an angry rampage, he could cause unimaginable calamities.

What kind of defenses could we poor humans muster to confront him?

Last night he tossed Kenneth Nelson and his cohorts around like toys. He crushed a gun in one hand. A baseball bat slamming across his back didn't even make him stumble.

Humanity would be helpless against that kind of might.

I wonder if even Brenlyn and Talitha together would be strong enough to stop him, to confine him, to kill him if necessary.

I begin to tremble as I recognize the staggering possibilities.

Neeve places his hand gently over mine.

I jerk back.

"Please don't be frightened, Karissa," he says. "I am fighting as hard as I can. I'll die before I allow it to overpower me."

I glare at him accusingly. "You said you wouldn't read my mind without being invited."

"I can sense your fear without reading your mind." He glances around, and when he speaks again, his voice is filled with sorrow. "In this quiet room in the safety of the library, what do you have to be afraid of besides me?"

"I don't want to fear you," I tell him.

"I don't want to be feared," he responds. "But what can I say? What can I do to reassure you?"

"Just talk to me. Tell me what you left out of your story."

"What do you want to know? Ask. I swear I'll answer as honestly and completely as I can."

# Chapter Seventeen

I consider how best to proceed.

One time, after Dad and I watched a cop show on television, he described the art of interrogation to me. He said sometimes they get it right in the movies and on television, and sometimes they don't.

Apparently the tactics depend on whether the goal is information or intimidation.

If the interviewer wants information, he or she starts out with easy questions with simple answers, ones that are not emotionally charged and that, sometimes, are not even relevant. The interrogator tries to build rapport and to establish trust. Only after the person is relaxed and is used to answering whatever is asked does the interviewer move on to the difficult questions.

So, applying that to my current situation, what do I want to know that has an easy answer?

Neeve has already admitted that he can read my thoughts, or at least tap into my projections. So anything related to that should be okay.

"Tell me," I say, "about the day Kenneth Nelson and his buddies were threatening me outside of the school. All of a sudden you were there with my world history book in your hand. How?"

Neeve doesn't reply immediately.

I wait calmly because he has already promised to answer.

"Let me make sure I understand the question," he says. "You want to know how I knew you needed help and how I got there when I did."

"Exactly," I say.

He gazes down at the table. He breathes hard for a few seconds, like he's really expending a lot of energy thinking. Then he begins to talk.

"If I went into your mind without permission, it would be like planting a listening device in your house so I could spy on you. Invading your privacy like that would be wrong. But if I was outside working in my yard, and you were inside your house talking with your windows open, I might hear what you said even though I wasn't doing anything to make it happen."

He frowns and shakes his head a little, like he's not pleased with his explanation.

I try to encourage him by giving him a little smile.

He smiles back.

It's as if we're both acknowledging that we're in unfamiliar territory and are doing our best.

"When I recognized you for the first time, I opened myself up to you completely. It's sort of like going outside to listen for your voice."

He grimaces and taps his fingers on the table.

"No, it's more like turning on a radio and waiting to see if you'll come on the air to broadcast." He gazes at me solemnly. "Can you appreciate the difference between the action of going into someone's mind and the inaction of just being available to listen if they speak?"

I'm not sure.

It seems like a very fine line, but I nod because I want him to continue.

He exhales a gentle sigh.

"I was in the van with Brenlyn, and I could feel terror building up inside of you. You were broadcasting loudly. I told him to return to the school, and then I opened a doorway from the van to you. It only took a second to assess the situation. I opened another door, this one to your locker, got your textbook so I could intervene in a way that hopefully wouldn't lead to violence, and then I stepped back through. The rest you observed yourself."

Okay.

I'm not sure that was an easy question after all. Anyway the answer seems complicated. I'll have to process it later.

Move on to something else.

I ask the first thing that pops into my head.

"Did you do something so we ended up as partners for our research paper?"

"Yes," he says, grinning at me. "I manipulated things so only you and I could pick up the elevens."

"How?" I ask.

He shrugs, and I can almost hear him thinking something like: In for a penny, in for a pound. Throw caution to the wind. Sink or swim. Now or never. Or some other platitude that indicates that this is a big step, and he's not convinced that I will react well.

"I enchanted them so they would slip out of the wrong fingers."

It's the first time he's made a direct reference to doing magic himself. He stares at me like he's waiting for my disbelief.

"That would work." I force my voice to sound matter-of-fact. "But how did you know we'd be drawing numbers that day?"

"Although you are the only person I listen for, you're not the only one I hear. Mr. Mitchell is a particularly loud thinker. All week, he toyed with different ideas about how the class could get their partners—everything from assigning us at random to having us play blind man's bluff. I made sure I got to class early enough to hear what he finally decided so I could guarantee that you and I ended up together."

"But you got there after I did."

"When I listened to Mr. Mitchell's plans, I wasn't actually in the classroom. I opened the passageway just a crack so I could peer in. I waited for you to arrive before I stepped through."

"You open magical doors in a building full of kids and no one ever notices?"

"It's not hard to make sure no one pays attention. Very few people observe what's going on around them."

That's another one to think about later.

Are there any more easy questions?

"You said Talitha followed Brenlyn. I guess that means she knows how to open doors like you, right?"

"No," Neeve says. "The ability to open walkways between worlds is a royal gift. Talitha asked my younger sister to help her. I imagine Shiane foresaw something in my future—or Brenlyn's and Talitha's—that convinced her to agree. Besides, she is at that age when girls become fascinated with love and romance and great emotional sacrifices."

"Preteen," I mutter under my breath. "Or early teens." Then my mind latches onto what he said earlier. "What do you mean foresaw? Is your sister a prophet? A seer?"

"Shiane has mage-level talents."

When Neeve says Shiane's name, a small, sweet smile curls up the corners of his lips. She is obviously special to him.

"What I did to guarantee that you and I would become research partners is a simple trick compared to what mages can do. When Shiane is fourteen years old, she will begin formal training in sorcery. Already she has demonstrated remarkable abilities. Foresight is just one of them. By the time she reaches adulthood she'll be able to do things you can't even imagine."

I almost get distracted and ask him to tell me about sorcery, but I catch myself. I don't want the conversation to stray too far afield. I get us back on target. "So, after Brenlyn brought you here, Talitha decided to follow him and turned to Shiane for help."

"That's right. And it has turned out to be a blessing for Brenlyn." Neeve's voice is suddenly self-mocking and embittered. "Some days, the darkness pummels me like fists, and I fall into deep, black depressions. Other days, it gnaws at me like teeth, and I fly into red-hot rages. Those are the times when I draw on Brenlyn's strength the most. I don't know how he bore the burden before Talitha joined him. She is a cool oasis in the desert for him. She revitalizes him, so he can continue to help me."

He puts his elbows on the table and clamps his hands around his head. "They don't even resent me or hate me for creating this misery in their lives." He tips his face up so that he can look at me from beneath his eyebrows. "Can you imagine the debt I owe them? If I reclaim the light, I'll spend the rest of my years looking for ways to repay them."

Gently I stroke his arm from wrist to elbow. His skin is silky to the touch, but I can feel the hard muscles underneath.

"They must love you very much," I say.

He jerks upright.

His eyes focus on something far away, something I can't see.

"Although I brought this nightmare onto myself," he whispers, "they have chosen to be with me, to support me, to help me fight my way clear. Why should they have volunteered for this? I have nothing to offer them in exchange. Right now, I can't do anything for them that equals what they're doing for me. If I'm overpowered by the dark, I won't even be able to send them back home."

His eyes meet mine, and they are filled with wonder and with tears. "They must love me very much."

"Yes," I say.

"Even Talitha," he continues, the awe still filling him. "She could be with Brenlyn without ever seeing me. But she helps me too. Sometimes, while I'm working, she sings to me, songs about home and family and love and kindness. Then I feel the light growing stronger."

"They know you're worth it."

"And you, Karissa? Am I worth it to you?"

"Oh yes," I tell him.

Taking my hands in both of his, he looks at me with such devotion that I can hardly bear the weight of it.

"I have loved you since before I was Shiane's age," he tells me. "When I began searching for you, my friends were still focused on learning how to hunt and fish and fight. I don't think they even realized there was a significant difference between boys and girls.

"I wanted to lay the world at your feet. I thought I had so much to offer you. I was smart, honorable, not bad looking, and would eventually have been well educated. Although I would never inherit the throne, I would still have had wealth and property and a position of importance.

"Now I have less than nothing. When my uncle captured me, he took everything from me, even my future."

"Your uncle! Your uncle was the one who tortured you?"

"Yes." Remembered pain and anger and humiliation flash behind Neeve's eyes. "It was my father's bastard, elder half-brother."

When Neeve first uses the word *bastard*, I think he is calling his uncle a vulgar name. Then I realize he is merely describing a situation of birth.

"Why would he do that to you?"

"It wasn't me personally," he says.

He pauses and stands.

"Excuse me a moment. I didn't sleep much last night."

He stretches, extending his arms overhead with his fingers nearly touching the ceiling. His six-pack abs are clearly defined underneath his knit shirt.

For a moment I concentrate on nothing more than inhaling and exhaling smoothly, desperately hoping to avoid panting and drooling.

He drops forward and, keeping his legs completely straight, places his hands flat on the floor.

I've never seen anyone who could actually do that except on The Fitness Channel.

He doesn't sit back down in the chair.

He hooks his butt on the end of the table and extends his long legs out so his feet are past the rear wheels of my chair.

He takes my hand and rubs his thumb across my fingers.

"My uncle would have been happy to grab any of my father's children. I was just unlucky enough to be the one he found." His brow crinkles with thought. "When Uncle Maldon finished torturing me, he left me where my father's men would be sure to find me. He would get no satisfaction from hurting one of us unless he could gloat about it to my father."

"Why does he hate your dad? If your uncle is angry because he was born illegitimate, it seems to me he should be mad at your grandfather."

"Or my great-grandfather," Neeve says. "Justus II was a hard man. He would not give my grandfather permission to marry Maldon's mother, nor to declare the birth as legitimate. In fact, Justus II threatened to denounce my grandfather as a traitor to the Crown if he didn't marry the woman selected for him.

"By the time Grandfather inherited the throne, he had been married to my grandmother for many years. She was a good and faithful wife, and he grew to love her. Besides bearing my father, she gave birth to six other sons and five daughters. My grandfather would never have insulted her by legitimizing Maldon at that late date, setting him above the children of his marriage. Maldon believes my father usurped his rightful place on the throne."

"That's crazy," I say. "All the decisions having to do with Maldon, his mother, and their rights were made before your grandparents married, before your father was born."

"That's too logical a concept for someone who has willingly given himself over to the dark. Maldon has no conscience. He worships power and considers his holy offerings to be greed, anger, hatred, and violence. When you look at Maldon, you see what evil looks like when it takes on a body."

A tremor shakes Neeve like a fierce chill.

Anguish twists his features.

He sits there panting as if he's just finished running a marathon.

Sliding back onto his chair, he folds his arms on the tabletop and drops his head down on them, hiding his face from me.

"Oh, Loving Universe," I hear him whisper, "please don't let me turn out like him. Please lead me back to the light."

It takes me a moment to realize he's praying.

I reach over and stroke his hair. "You could never become like him. There's too much goodness in you."

"You don't understand, Karissa." Neeve's voice crackles with emotion. "I'm a ship floundering in a storm. I've been tossed against the rocks, my hull is breached, and I'm taking on water. I don't know if I can weather it out. No matter how hard I try to stay afloat, I'm sinking."

"Brenlyn, Talitha, and I won't let you. We'll bail for you as long as you need us to."

"I wish it were that easy, but Maldon destroyed my connection to the light and I'm sailing blind. You and Brenlyn and Talitha are candles in the night, and I appreciate you more than you can know, but I'm not sure you're enough to guide me to shore."

He buries his face against his arms again.

All of a sudden, I am sick of the whole nautical metaphor.

We're talking around the real issue, whatever it is, and I'm irritated.

I want cold, hard facts.

I want to know what we're up against.

"You swore that you'd answer my questions, no matter what I asked. Right?" There is steel in my voice, and he glances up at me, startled.

"Yes." He wipes his eyes as he sits up straight in his chair. That hint of tears almost makes me back down, but I keep going.

"Then I want to know what your uncle did to you, everything, and exactly what it means in terms of the light and the dark, and your future, and my future, and any future we might have together."

He looks as if I just bashed him across the head with a lead pipe. The color drains right out of his face. I've never seen that happen before. It's painful to watch someone go that pale that fast.

His eyes are wide and ghostly.

His lips move, but no sound comes from his mouth.

He tries again.

I feel my resolve begin to soften.

Dad says timing is everything when working with Post Traumatic Stress Disorder. Perhaps I shouldn't press Neeve to tell me more than he's ready to share.

His haunted look and silent mouthing make me uncomfortable. Maybe I'm no more ready to hear the truth than he is to tell it.

Yet, I can't risk having a relationship with him as long as this mysterious unknown hangs over him. I'm struggling with my own demons. I need to know how much garbage he's carrying around with him before I become so emotionally entangled that I can't break free.

Maybe when I know what happened, I'll go into overwhelm, have nightmares, and become traumatized myself.

But it's like when you pass a car accident on the side of the road. You know it might be terrible, you know it might make you sick, but you have to look anyway. You know if you don't, whatever you imagine will almost certainly be worse than the truth and it will stick with you forever. You'll always wonder what happened, how bad it was, and who was involved.

While Neeve is searching for words to answer my questions, I review what I already know, combining what I remember from the news broadcasts with the gossip I heard in the library.

His wrists and ankles had been bound.

His feet were blistered and torn.

Symbols had been carved into his flesh.

His shoulder blades were flayed raw.

I envision his bare back in my mind.

I see the scars.

The horrifying truth hits me like a physical blow.

I throw my arms around him and gather him to me.

"Oh, Neeve," I cry while tears stream down my cheeks, "he cut off your wings."

# Chapter Eighteen

I can't pretend to understand the implications of what happened to Neeve, but I know I've correctly verbalized what he couldn't. I know because he clings to me, burrows his face against my chest, and sobs.

My mother says there is nothing in the world more gut-wrenching than watching a strong man break down.

That's the way I feel about Neeve. He rips my heart in two.

I hug him and pat his back and kiss the top of his head, the way I used to with Jeremy and Bennett when they were little and got hurt.

Neeve cries so long and so hard, I wonder if he's mourned at all since being forced to leave his family last October. So many losses at one time: his parents, his siblings, his home, his friends, his world, and his wings, which were somehow his connection to divine light.

I don't know what to say to comfort him.

He told me that when Talitha sang to him it made him feel better. I softly start to croon "Brahms's Lullaby."

> "Lullaby and goodnight,
> "With roses bedight,
> "With lilies o'er spread
> "Is baby's wee bed."

He quivers in my arms and settles down a bit.

> "Lay thee down now and rest,
> "May thy slumber be blessed.
> "Lay thee down now and rest,
> "May thy slumber be blessed."

I hum the second verse because I can't remember the words, and then I sing the first verse again.

Neeve stops crying.

After another minute, he sits up. I'm sure it's a relief to his muscles. It couldn't have been comfortable, sitting in his chair and sprawling over the arm of mine while I held him.

"I'm sorry," he whispers.

All in all, he looks pretty good. His complexion doesn't go splotchy the way mine does when I cry. Of course his eyes are red, his cheeks are wet, and his nose is runny.

He produces a white linen handkerchief from somewhere and uses it to dry his face and wipe his nose. Then he rests his hands on top of the table.

"You can't imagine," he says with his voice quaking, "what an obscenity it was for Maldon to do that to me. Our—our—," he has to pause and swallow before he can force himself to continue, "our wings are actually a part of our soul, the part that lets us soar, that lifts us up to the light. With that part missing, we become earth-bound, left with few defenses against those forces that dwell in darkness.

"When people like my uncle dedicate themselves to evil, their wings atrophy. They shrivel and grow weak and fuse into place until they can no longer be extended. People like that become what in your mythology you might call dark elves."

I don't know if I should ask questions or just let him talk. But I'm afraid if I don't ask what I want to know now, I'll forget later.

"I saw Talitha's wings go right through her blouse. How is that possible? There weren't any slits or tears in the fabric."

Neeve takes my hand and kisses the palm. It's the first time he's done that in this world. His lips are warm and soft, and although I know this sounds crazy, I taste the sweetness of strawberries where his mouth touches my skin.

"Because our wings are part of our souls, they don't have substance the same way our bodies do. They are only partially in the physical world."

"Then how could your uncle cut them off?" I speak without thinking, and I'm horrified at myself. I clamp my hand over my mouth. I hold my breath, waiting for Neeve to explode, or to start crying again, or to call me an insensitive moron (or worse), which I would certainly deserve.

He does none of those things.

He looks almost overcome with anguish, but I think he realizes that I don't mean to add to his pain. I just want to understand.

"Our wings aren't totally insubstantial. They change in solidity to meet specific needs. To fly in celebration of life, they only need to materialize a little. Our joy helps lift us into the air. However, in dire circumstances they become more substantial. Your father would say they prepare us for the *fight or flight* response."

Neeve's face pales again as memories swamp him.

I'm about ready to tell him that he doesn't need to explain if talking about

116

it hurts too much, but then he goes on.

He really is outstandingly brave.

"At first my uncle merely had his henchmen try to intimidate me. They formed a circle around me and shoved me back and forth, spinning me and tripping me. Occasionally one of them would smack me with the back of his hand or the flat of a sword.

"All the while, my uncle watched and laughed and urged them on. I knew I could endure that.

"Even when he stripped off my clothing and whipped me, I wasn't terribly afraid, even though it was certainly painful. I was sure that when he decided I had suffered enough, he would send me back to my father. So I thought about my mother and about my friends. I thought about you and how happy we would be together when I found you. In my mind I wrote a piece of music for you, the piece I played on the violin for your family that night.

"It wasn't until he strapped me face down on a table and started applying hot metal rods to the bottoms of my feet that I began to panic. That was when I realized he was trying to force my wings to extend. There was only one reason for him to do that.

"I fought against the ropes with all my might. Of course the fear only made my wings materialize faster. As they solidified, he took his dagger and cut a message to my father in my skin. As he inscribed each symbol, he told me what it was. My horror and revulsion were all that was needed to force my wings completely into the physical world."

My voice comes out a hoarse whisper. "What did he write?"

Neeve closes his eyes and bites his lower lip.

After a few minutes, he says, "It's a vulgarism. I'm not sure I can force myself to say the words in your presence, even though they have no significance here."

I take his hand in mine, and before I know what I'm doing, I kiss his palm.

His eyes fly open and he stares at me.

All of a sudden it occurs to me that I know nothing whatsoever about Neeve's culture. Belatedly I consider the possibility that palm kissing might have a meaning I don't understand.

"Did I do something wrong?" I ask nervously.

He gives me that tender smile, the one I'm beginning to think of as my own special look.

"No," he says. "I realize your customs are different from mine."

"But it means something specific in your world, doesn't it?"

"It is a pledge," he says, kissing my palm again, "a promise of eternal love. Maybe someday you'll be able to give it to me the way I give it to you."

I look at him and see the reflection of my face in his deep green eyes. Suddenly I sense new meaning to the traditional marriage vows.

When most young couples hear *love, honor and cherish for better or for worse, for richer or for poorer, in sickness and in health,* they probably think: "None of those bad things will ever happen to us. We'll get to love, honor, and cherish each other for better, for richer, and in health."

Later when reality sets in, they end up angry and disappointed because the worse and the poorer and the sickness parts happen, and they're not prepared to deal with them.

For Neeve and me, though, ignoring the negative isn't an option.

We're already living in the worst.

We're both damaged physically: he's missing his wings and I'm missing my legs. We're both flawed emotionally: he is full of rage and hatred and expanding darkness, while I am racked with guilt and resentment and self-pity.

Now I understand why Neeve didn't let Hayden fix my legs. I have to develop the strength either to learn to walk or to learn to be contented without walking.

My battle is just as important as Neeve's with the darkness.

Going through this kind of process, helping each other cope with our various forms of baggage, will either blow us apart in a cataclysmic explosion or will draw us together in perfect harmony.

We are each other's destiny.

I kiss his palm again.

"Oh, Karissa," he begs, "don't. Not until you're sure."

"I am sure. I've been drawn to you from the first time you glanced in my direction. The pull has been continuous, relentless, and ruthless. For some reason, our lives are already intertwined. I can't imagine a future without you. I can't imagine loving anyone else." I spread out my hands in a plea for understanding. "I'm not saying it very well, but I know we belong together."

He surprises me by laughing. "It's not exactly the declaration of devotion I've always hoped for, but it's a beginning."

We hold hands and gaze at each other for a long moment. I've never been in love before, but I think this is real. The emotion permeates me, makes me feel complete.

"Tell me the rest about your uncle," I say. "What did he carve into your back?"

He starts to protest.

I hold my hand up in a *stop* gesture and don't let him finish. "My father says there's nothing that can't be spoken. He says words have no power that we don't give them. Whatever your uncle wrote, it has no meaning in either of our worlds because it's a lie."

"How do you know?" His voice is a rough, pleading whisper.

I realize there is a lot I don't understand about Neeve and his people, but there are some things I know I know.

"Because," I tell him with certainty, "you said it was a vulgarism, and there is nothing vulgar or coarse or crude about you."

Neeve looks at the tabletop, the floor, and then the ceiling. He swallows hard a couple of times. He gazes out the window at the far end of the room.

Finally he forces the words out. "It says *Prince Mud-Hugger, son of Justus IV."* He bites his lip and closes his eyes. "Mud-hugger is a vulgar term for one of us who has lost his wings."

I open my mouth to reaffirm my stance that it's a lie, but before I can comment, there is a soft tapping on the little window in the door.

The lady from the checkout desk sticks her head into the room. "I got you as much time as I could, honey," she says, "but this next group is quite insistent. I'm sorry."

I glance down at my watch. We've been here over three and a half hours.

"Oh, I didn't realize it was so late," I say. "It was kind of you to arrange for us to have the extra time." I really mean it. Considering how emotional our conversation has been, it would've been awful to be interrupted earlier. "We'll gather our things and be out in just a minute."

She closes the door.

"We can go over to Starbucks," I suggest.

"No." Neeve voice is soft, but it is also emphatic, leaving no room for discussion. "I can't talk about these things in public." He rubs his stomach. "Despite your mother's excellent breakfast, I'm starving. It must be about lunchtime. I'll have Brenlyn pick us up. We can grab some fast food and then go over to his workshop to talk."

"You don't want to open a doorway to Bigger Burgers?" I ask.

He looks down at me and rolls his eyes. "It requires stealth to use doorways during the daytime, especially in places where people congregate. I think your chair is a little too conspicuous."

He pulls out his cellphone.

As I retrieve my own, I say, "I'll call Mom and tell her we're going to be out a couple more hours."

Thirty minutes later, we're sitting in Brenlyn's shop at Neeve's worktable, ready to eat.

Getting fast food with Neeve is a unique experience.

I order a hamburger, French fries, and a Diet Coke. He gets a salad. The only thing that saves him as a dining companion is that he accompanies the salad with a super-sized chocolate marshmallow milkshake.

Brenlyn and Talitha stand in the hallway.

"We're going to catch a movie," Brenlyn says. "Lock up if you leave. Or if you want to hang out until we get back, I'll drive you both home."

"Thank you, Bren," Neeve says.

I take the wrapper off my hamburger, dump my fries on the paper, and then open a couple of packets of ketchup and squirt them into a puddle for dunking.

# Echoes: A Modern Fairytale

As soon as I hear the front door close, I say, "Tell me about the echoes."
Neeve gapes.

I smile innocently, like I didn't say anything at all significant. "You told your mother I hear the whispering of echoes. You told your father that you need me to listen to them for you. What are they?"

He looks at me with admiration.

"I really am impressed with your memory," he says. "You must be extremely bright to be able to remember so much of what you heard during such dire circumstances." I feel myself blushing. He takes a huge drink of milkshake before he begins talking again.

"All worlds with strong magic resonate. The vibrations can sometimes be felt or heard on other worlds by people who are particularly receptive. You're one of those people. It shows in the pictures you draw and the story you wrote. Your mother reacted so strongly to the piece I wrote for the violin that I believe she is one, too. Many of your culture's myths and legends are based on our history, written down by people who didn't understand what they were experiencing when they caught snatches of our echoes."

"What parts of our myths and legends?" I ask.

While he drinks his milkshake and thinks, I take a bite of my hamburger.

"Mermaids," he finally says. "You have legends about mermaids. My world actually has merfolk, but they don't have fish tails. They are people, not so different from everyone else, who can breathe in both the air and the water, and who for their own reasons have chosen to live under the sea."

"Hmm." I pick up a French fry and doodle in the ketchup. "Give me another example."

He must have been thinking while he talked, because he has this one ready.

"To you, Heracles (or Hercules, as he was known to the Romans) is a mythical demigod who had to accomplish twelve acts of penance for the death of his family. In my world he was a great warrior who performed a dozen miraculous feats during one of our ancient wars. The name Heracles is right, and the number of deeds is right. Even a few of the specific tasks are correct. The rest of your legend is pure fiction."

Neeve picks at his salad, finally spearing a cherry tomato and popping it into his mouth.

I finish my hamburger. The fries are cold and greasy, so I wad them up in the burger wrapper and stuff them into the paper bag they came in. After I wipe my mouth and fingers on my last napkin, I wheel over to a trashcan beside the backdoor and dump them.

"It doesn't sound like the echoes are very accurate," I say on my way back to the worktable. "Why do you need me to listen to them for you?"

Using the plastic fork, Neeve stirs the remainder of his salad around in the Styrofoam bowl. I guess he doesn't like what he sees. He gets up and

120

throws it away.

He hangs onto the milkshake.

"Have you ever painted ceramics?" he asks.

He wanders over to the bookcase where the miniatures are and picks up a white ceramic angel that's about eight inches tall.

"When Brenlyn made this one, I asked him if I could keep it. I think she looks like you."

"The hair is similar," I admit.

He hands the angel to me, so I study it for a few seconds.

She looks like every other ceramic angel I've ever seen except for two things: the length of her hair and the cut of her gown.

For some reason most angels are depicted with long curls that hang halfway to their waists, and they usually wear robes that drape in graceful folds down to their feet and have billowy sleeves.

My angel has short fluffy hair and is wearing a gown with elbow-length puffed sleeves, a high waist decorated with diamonds, and a flowing long train in back. Her wings are gorgeous. They arc up on the sides higher than her head and then taper down to points that touch the ground at her feet.

My only complaint is that like all angels her wings are covered with feathers. I've always thought that was absurd, unless there are secret Biblical writings somewhere that indicate that angels and birds are related.

I give the figurine back.

As offhandedly as possible, I ask, "Is this your way of telling me you've finished talking and you're not going to answer any more of my questions?"

"You just won't be distracted, will you?" he says, half serious and half teasing.

I shrug. "It's one of the disadvantages of having a psychologist for a father. Although I hate it when he does it to me, he's taught me how to spot a person's defense mechanisms. It would be better if you just told me you were all talked out for now."

Neeve reaches over and fingers back a wisp of my hair that's been dangling in front of my left eye. "I wonder if your father knows how influential he is in your life. You look like your mother, but you think like him."

I open my mouth to get him back on track, but he puts his finger against my lips to shush me.

"I'm not going back on my word. I'll answer your questions, but I need a break. It is difficult for me to talk about all of this. It's even uncomfortable when I discuss it with Brenlyn and Talitha, and they already know everything." He gives me that special, tender look, and I melt inside. "And I'm not even in love with either of them."

I don't know what to say. It's impossible not to respond physically and emotionally to such a statement. I have a strong urge to throw my arms around him, but I'm cautious enough to wonder if this isn't merely a better and more effective distraction.

"So, you want to paint ceramics for a while?" I ask.

"Would you mind?"

"Not if you teach me how—and if you promise we'll get back to the issues later."

"I promise," he says, raising his arm like he's reciting the Boy Scout Oath. I wonder where he learned that. He flips a hand at the ceramics. "Choose one you like."

The items on the left are dark gray and the ones on the right are white like the angel.

"What's the difference between these?" I ask.

He picks up one of the dark figures. "This is called greenware. It's what the pieces look like after they have come out of the molds. They have to be cleaned before they can go into the kiln." He shows me where the seams from the two halves of the cast are visible, plus little bumps and dimples that need to be smoothed away.

"After they've been fired, they're called bisque." He points to the white ones. "Now they're ready to be painted or glazed."

As I sort through the bisque, he glances around and then starts digging through some boxes on the shelves.

I decide the cottages, lighthouses, and other buildings (which are all enhanced with grass, flowers, trees, and small animals or birds) need too much detailed work for a beginner.

There are several kinds of creatures: foxes and bears, cats and dogs, horses, unicorns, and dragons. But they look kind of boring. I mean how many shades of brown can you paint on a single bear? And unicorns are always white, aren't they?

I look at the holiday pieces: Easter bunnies, ghosts and goblins, pilgrims hunting turkeys, and many different Santa Clauses.

Finally, in the back of the second-to-the-bottom shelf, I find a cute little sprite sitting on a toadstool. One leg is extended. The other is bent with the hands clasped around the knee. His hair is pulled back in a tail, and he has long arms and legs and a lovely face. He doesn't really look very much like Neeve, but by carefully selecting the colors I use, I think I can create the illusion of resemblance.

"May I do this one?" I ask.

Neeve glances up from the box he's rummaging in.

He quirks an eyebrow at me, as if he can read my plan on my face, but then he nods.

He shoves the boxes back into place.

"I get sloppy when I paint," Neeve says, "so I always cover the table with newspaper." He jams his fists onto his hips and glares at the room. "Bren usually has a stack or two stashed somewhere, but I can't find them."

I wheel over to a stool beside the big table where I dropped my backpack.

"I picked up the newspaper in the study room," I say. "It isn't stamped with the library's logo, so I know it's not a library copy. I was going to take it home and toss it into the recycle bin." I dig in my bag. When I find the paper, I roll it up, bend it in the middle, and toss it to Neeve.

He sticks up his hand and catches it.

By the time I've replaced my backpack, turned around, and wheeled back over to Neeve, he has covered about half of the table. Something must have caught his eye, though, because he is bent over, reading.

He has a real smirky look on his face.

I join him so I can see what he's found that's so interesting.

On the front page in the column on the left that's reserved for late breaking news is a story that reads:

## Football Players in Crash

Eight players from Millard Fillmore High School's championship football team were injured early this morning when the three cars they were traveling in collided near Aspen Hills Mall.

The drivers, Kenneth Nelson Jr., Michael Ray Olson, and Tolliver Jones, all 18, appeared to be intoxicated at the scene.

With them were Stanford Mills and Manuel Rodriguez, also 18, as well as three juvenile passengers.

All eight young men were taken to Mountain View Hospital for treatment.

Officer Denise Brewster said, "Considering the mangled condition of the cars, these boys are lucky to be alive."

I glance up from the article.

"You and Brenlyn did that?" I ask.

"Only partially," Neeve says with a little shrug. He hands the front page to me and then finishes spreading the rest of the newspaper across the tabletop.

"The boys chose to drink alcohol and to attack us. We merely set the stage in such a way that they would be held accountable for their drunkenness and be blamed for their own injuries."

# Chapter Nineteen

Neeve gets an empty jar from a shelf and fills it with water at the utility sink. After he sets it on the worktable, he picks up the coffee can of paintbrushes and trades it for a different can of brushes that was on a shelf with the ceramic molds.

When he makes the switch, I notice one can is labeled *oils* and the other is labeled *acrylics*.

He notices me noticing.

"The oil based enamel is for the lead soldiers," Neeve says, pointing at a rack that holds many little jars with screw-on lids. The jars are filled with vibrantly colored paints.

"The acrylics are water based, and we use them on the ceramics." A second rack holds plastic bottles with flip-top lids. The shades of color are softer, gentler, than the oils. "Each kind of paint requires its own brushes."

He gives me a round tray with six shallow depressions around the outer edge and one large well in the middle. "This is a watercolor palette. You can mix or dilute colors in it. The more water you add to the paint, the smoother it goes on, but the lighter the color gets."

He picks up a small bottle of paint and squeezes a pea-sized amount onto his palette. "This is a premixed flesh tone. You can make it paler by adding white, ruddier by adding red, tanner by adding brown, or sallower by adding yellow. It depends on what you want."

I watch him dip a rounded brush in the jar of water and then just barely touch the tip of the brush in the paint.

He strokes the brush a few times in the center well, I suppose to mix the paint and water, and then he applies the color to the angel's face. He repeats the process until he's painted the face, neck, arms, hands, and feet all in a delicate peachy-pink.

He puts a tiny dot of red in one of the cups and drips water onto it from a smaller brush. When the paint is very thin, he uses it to add a hint of blush to the cheeks and lips.

"Go ahead," he tells me.

"I'm afraid I'll make a mess and ruin it."

"Don't worry. If you make a mistake, we'll just wash it off. Or if the paint has dried, we can cover it with white. Then you can redo it. Everything is fixable."

I mimic his actions, and when I paint the face of my sprite, it doesn't look too bad. I do all the exposed skin. Then I choose a sandy shade of yellow and add some white plus a touch of pecan brown. I can hardly believe how close I've come to matching Neeve's wheat-colored hair.

The stresses of last night and today diminish.

I'm enjoying myself.

Naturally that's when Neeve decides to drop his next bombshell.

"One of the things our two cultures have in common," he says while he paints the angel's wings with half a dozen pastel colors that flow in and out of each other, "is the acknowledgement of an eternal soul. When my uncle mutilated me, he severed a part of my spirit, the part that is my strongest connection to the light. But he couldn't destroy it. No one can destroy our souls except ourselves. I need to find my missing part. If I do, and if I can re-absorb it, the darkness will no longer have power over me."

I finish painting the sprite's shirt a pale blue, and then I rinse the paint out of my brush and put it down.

I stare at Neeve.

He continues speaking: "I have to find that piece before the evil inside me gets so strong that my severed spirit can't recognize me anymore. If that happens, I'll be beyond redemption. That's why I need you to listen to the echoes. If you're in tune with me, you'll hear the whisper of my echo within your world. That echo will lead us to the rest of my soul."

I take the news calmly.

Everyone goes hunting for missing chunks of their souls. Simple as pie. Happens all the time!

"You know it's here?" I ask, stifling the mental sarcasm. "Are you sure it's not still in your world?"

"I'm sure. It wants to reunite with me as badly as I want it to. Undoubtedly it followed me, and it won't be far away. By that I mean it's not on the other side of the planet or on the moon. But I can't hear its echo and neither can Brenlyn or Talitha. We come from a world that creates powerful echoes, so we've become habituated to them. They are part of our ordinary background noise."

He puts down his brush and kneels beside the wheelchair so we can look into each other's eyes without me straining my neck.

"Will you help me?" he asks.

"This is the quest in your story, isn't it?"

"Yes," he answers.

"What's the price?" I ask. "You said there was a price to pay."

He drops his head and shivers. "I think what my uncle did to me was the price. Without that, my mother would never have opened the doorway to this world and I would never have found you." He glances at me again. "But I don't know if it was the full price. There might still be dangers and roadblocks ahead of us. I don't think we'll find the way easy."

I don't either.

Once upon a time, everything in my life was simple and straightforward, although I didn't recognize or appreciate it.

Since the accident, everything has been complicated and challenging.

Why should this be any different?

"All right," I say, daring to stroke his cheek with my fingertips.

He leans forward. I think he's finally going to kiss me on the mouth, but he doesn't. He very lightly presses his lips against my forehead.

Grrrrrr!

I might have to get strong enough to stand again, just so I can intercept his lips.

"We should go back to your house now," Neeve says. "It'll be snowing quite hard by the time Brenlyn gets here. If we leave now and hurry, we'll reach your place while the flakes are still big and fluffy, before they turn to ice and the wind makes everything cold and miserable."

"How do you know?" I ask.

"Just one of my talents," Neeve says lightheartedly. "I have a strong weather sense."

He puts the angel and sprite on the bottom shelf of the bookcase where there are a few other partially completed projects. He tosses the newspaper into a box and then pours the dirty water down the drain of the utility sink.

I'm reaching for my jacket, but Neeve steps right in front of me. Tipping his head to the side, he studies my chest. I've had lots of guys ogle my breasts before, but never this openly.

He frowns, which makes me a little angry. I have a nice body, not counting the legs that don't work.

I glance down to check myself out.

My t-shirt is puckered and wrinkled from when he was crying on me.

"I'd better take care of that," he says. "I don't know what your parents would say if you came home with your clothing disarrayed."

He snaps his fingers.

All of a sudden, not only does my shirt look freshly laundered, but it also looks as if it's been ironed.

Neeve still doesn't seem pleased. He stares at my chest again until I'm quite self-conscious.

"I really don't like that shade of green on you," he says. "It has too much yellow in it."

He snaps his fingers one more time and my shirt changes to a deep emerald green, which just happens to match the color of Neeve's eyes.

He's showing off for me, I realize. Now that I know about his world and magic and all that, he's taking advantage of the moment to let me see what he can do.

I'll admit I'm impressed.

"That's much better," he says, grinning.

I glare at him. "My parents are pretty broadminded, but I think they'll worry if I start coming home wearing something different from what I left in."

"You could tell them I gave it to you."

"That would be worse. We've known each other for just a few weeks, and we've only been on one date. That's too soon for a guy to start giving a girl gifts of clothing."

"All right," he says with a shrug, "You win." He snaps his fingers and my shirt goes back to yellowish green.

I am immediately suspicious.

"You gave up too easily," I insist. "What's the catch?"

He gets the blank expression that means I've used a term he doesn't know, so I say, "The catch: the loophole, the trick, the snare, the snag, the drawback."

He laughs at me. "Has anyone ever told you that you're really good with synonyms?"

"Yes," I say dryly, "all the time. Now, what's the catch?"

He gives me a martyred look and sighs.

I frown and sigh even louder.

He shakes his head. "You're the only one who can see the original color—but honestly the dark green is much more flattering."

"Change it back for real," I tell him. "Someday when all this mess is over, you can give me something that color and I'll wear it whenever you want."

"Really?"

"Yes."

"I'll hold you to that."

The twinkle in his eye makes me a little nervous.

When we're out on the sidewalk headed toward my house, I ask Neeve to tell me about magic.

"What do you want to know?"

"Well," I say, "how much magic do you have?"

"It's not a commodity that you can measure," he answers.

We come to a street corner, and I wait until the traffic has passed and we've crossed to the other side before I ask the next question. "I guess what I really want to know is what you can do. Also, can Brenlyn and Talitha do the same things—except for opening doors in space?"

127

The first fluffy snowflakes begin drifting down.

"Each of us has at least one area in which we can do what you call magic with a mere thought. Brenlyn understands and can manipulate anything with moveable parts, whether manual or mechanical. It's why his repair shop is so successful. He prefers to fix things by hand, because he thinks it's fun, but if he has a tough problem, he might do some magical tweaking.

"Talitha can accomplish anything having to do with flowers. She could grow you a black daisy or a sky blue rose or a pansy that smells like bubble gum. My talent is with fabrics, natural or synthetic, knit or woven or felted, cloth or fur or leather."

We pass a yard where half a dozen kids are trying to catch snowflakes on their tongues. I remember when Jeremy, Bennett, and I used to do that. In fact, it wasn't so long ago.

When we're past them, I ask Neeve, "What do you do with fabrics, besides turning my shirt different colors?"

"Whatever I want," he says. "My clothing never gets stained or dirty or torn or even wrinkled. It never wears out unless I get bored with it and let it go. My sisters were always begging me to change the color or style—and sometimes the size—of their gowns, especially when Father told them they couldn't have something new made. My foster mother says she doesn't need to look at the schedule to know when I've taken my turn doing the laundry. She can tell because everything comes out cleaner and brighter."

"You said you could do it with a thought," I say. "What was all that finger snapping for?"

"Showmanship," he answers smugly. "In addition to manipulating fabrics, I can do some minor spells, like enchanting the elevens in World History, but nothing spectacular. I haven't been trained as a sorcerer."

"What about the music? Do you do that magically?"

"I wish," Neeve says. "I have some natural ability, but most of it is the result of thousands of hours of hard work. My mother loves music, and she insisted that my siblings and I take lessons. I practiced every spare moment I had, partly because it made her happy," he blushes and looks sheepish, "and partly because it got me out of some of the more disagreeable chores around the palace."

The wind is starting to pick up, and Neeve pauses to zip his jacket. I pull up the hood to my parka.

After we're moving again, I say, "I thought princes spent half their time studying weapons and horsemanship and the other half learning courtly dances and how to flatter the ladies."

"Not my father's sons," Neeve tells me. "Our country does not lie peacefully among its neighbors. There is no way to predict how long the throne will stay in our family. My father insists that his sons and daughters know how to survive in exile if it should ever come to that. Why do you think

I know how to cook?"

Before I can think of a snappy response, he continues.

"I can also make a pair of shoes, plant, weed, and harvest a garden, make bricks and mortar, and use them to build a house. I know how to erect a barn from lumber I have hewn and planed myself. I can use a forge to make horseshoes, swords, knives, and armor.

"I know how to chip arrowheads and spearheads from obsidian, carve a bow out of yew, reverse twist my own hemp bowstrings, and make arrows from birch or ash and fletch them with feathers.

"I can shoe a horse, sew my own clothing, weave a basket, knit a sweater, kill, skin, and roast a wild boar, thrash and grind wheat, tan leather, and dig and reinforce a well, plus a dozen other things my father thinks are important.

"I'm sure you can see why I preferred to take music lessons. Also, the better I got, especially on the violin, the more protective my mother became of my hands. Practicing for long hours on stringed instruments might be hard on the fingertips, but it is preferable to mucking out the stables or repairing the stone walls that surround the palace or chopping down trees. All of which I've done many times."

We're just turning into the driveway when the wind swoops down out of the north and strafes us with little pellets of ice.

I'm shivering uncontrollably by the time we reach the house.

Neeve follows me through the door.

The kitchen is wonderfully warm, and it smells great.

Mom is taking a tray of cookies out of the oven.

"I was just going to call you," she tells me. "The Weather Service has issued a storm warning until 9:00 tomorrow morning. Neeve, I've talked with Janet. She and Brian are coming to dinner Thursday evening." It's just like my mom to be on a first name basis with Neeve's foster mother by the end of a telephone conversation. "She also asked if you could spend the rest of this afternoon here."

"Did she tell you why?" he asks.

"Apparently there has been some trouble among the boys."

Neeve pulls out his cellphone.

"She said she or Brian would call you this evening. Before she hung up, I could hear a ruckus in the background. I've got a feeling that she's quite busy right now."

Angry frustration flashes across Neeve's face, but it is fleeting, and I hope Mom doesn't notice.

He slips his phone back into his pocket.

He smiles at Mother. "Thank you for letting me stay."

"We're happy to have you," Mom says.

Then Neeve smiles at me, too. I think he's trying to reassure me that he's in control of himself. However, his next comment lets me know that he's thinking about something completely different.

"Karissa, now you can play the flute for me. Then we can decide what we're going to perform at the recital."

"You don't really expect me to accompany you, do you?" I ask plaintively.

"You said you'd try."

"The flute and violin are both downstairs," Mom says. "So are Jeremy and Bennett. Since everyone is at home today, all practicing has to be done in the basement. I don't think I could stand the commotion of different instruments playing different tunes on different floors, no matter how exquisite the music might be."

I glance up at Neeve.

There is only one way for me to get down to the basement.

I hope he remembers he offered.

"Let's go park your chair in your room," he says, "then I'll carry you."

When he picks me up, he whispers in my ear, "I think your mother likes me."

# Chapter Twenty

When we get to the bottom of the steps, I turn the doorknob and push.

It's like in the movie *The Wizard of Oz* when Dorothy steps out of the tornado-wrecked house, and the film goes from black-and-white Kansas to multi-colored Oz.

I thought Dad and the boys had enclosed one small portion of the basement to make a game room.

I was wrong.

The little room that they put the sheetrock around is the bathroom. The door is open and I can see a toilet and sink inside, but just a bare spot where the bathtub should go.

The rest of the basement is wide open.

There are some columns here and there, which I suppose couldn't be removed because they support the floors above. They're painted dark brown, like tree trunks.

The bottom three feet of the walls is painted tan. Then there is a six inch stripe of dark brown, one of burgundy, and one of yellow. The top part of the walls is pastel blue. The ceiling is made up of white acoustic tiles. The floor is covered with half a dozen carpet remnants in various shades of brown, sewn or glued together.

It's gorgeous.

Neeve turns in a circle with me still in his arms so I can get a good look. The floor space is divided into three sections, not counting the bathroom.

The focus of the largest area is an entertainment center that houses a television, DVD and CD players, and various electronic games. Bookshelves that are made of cinderblocks and planks hold DVDs, CDs, and video game paraphernalia.

Throw pillows are scattered on the floor.

A brown fake leather sofa and two matching chairs look like they came from a secondhand furniture store, but they're in good condition. They constitute the rear boundary of the entertainment section.

The next area must be the study or the library.

The boys have moved both their desks down here and then pushed them together so they face each other.

On one desk are the computer and printer they share.

Neatly arranged on the other desk are two stacks of paper, one ruled and one plain, a box of paperclips, a stapler, a roll of Scotch tape, some crayons, and a jar full of pencils and pens.

Another bookcase made of cinderblocks and planks leans against the wall behind the desks. On the top shelf are a dictionary, a thesaurus, and a five-part children's illustrated encyclopedia, which has a different volume for animals, people, plants, geography, and astronomy.

The rest of the shelves are filled with books the boys have received over the years as birthday and Christmas gifts, everything from Dr. Seuss to Sherlock Holmes, from biographies to Sudoku.

The final section is made up of a card table, four folding chairs, and another cinderblock bookcase, this one stacked with games and puzzles.

"Wow, guys," I say. "This is great. No wonder you like hanging out down here. How'd you do it?"

Neeve places me gently on the sofa and then settles beside me.

Jeremy plops down on a chair, and Bennett sits cross-legged on a big green pillow on the floor.

They start talking over the top of each other, each trying to detail all the steps they took to fix up the room.

They are really proud of how much of the work they did themselves. I don't blame them.

I'm proud of them too.

Mom's voice yells from the kitchen, "Why don't I hear any music down there? You only have five days to get ready."

My brothers and I sigh. Neeve looks amused.

While Jeremy and Bennett set up a couple of music stands, Neeve picks up my flute and hands it to me. I drop it on the couch as if it is a rattlesnake.

I assume my most wretched, pathetic, poor-pitiful-me expression and turn it full force on Neeve. "Really, I haven't touched it in three years. You don't need any accompaniment."

"You said you'd try," Neeve reminds me, not at all sympathetically.

"I brought down your old music books," Bennett says.

Neeve picks up one and flips pages. Apparently nothing in it appeals to him. He puts it down and picks up the next one. After thumbing halfway through the book, he presses it open and sets it on one of the stands, which he resituates so it's right in front of me.

"Can you play this?"

It's "Lullaby and Goodnight."

Although I sang it to him in the library while he cried, that was because it was the first song that popped into my head. Mom used to play the guitar and sing it to me when I was little and had trouble falling asleep. I have happy memories associated with the song, but I don't particularly want to make a fool of myself by trying to perform it on the flute.

"Can you play this?" he asks again.

"Maybe," I say, sounding a bit sulky even to me.

He picks up my flute and hands it to me again.

I glower at him.

He is unmoved.

With ill grace I take the flute from him.

I hold it up to my mouth and practice lifting and placing my fingers in the right spots. I glance up at Neeve, and he's got the violin under his chin and the bow ready. He nods at me.

Shaking my head ruefully, I try to remember how to hold my lips in order to produce a pure tone. One of the reasons I gave up the flute was the difficulty I had shaping my mouth correctly. It's harder than it looks. It's not like blowing into a kazoo or a recorder.

I sneak a quick glimpse at Neeve. He's waiting patiently.

I close my eyes and inhale.

I exhale.

Encouraging my unconscious mind to search for long ignored memories, I look at the music, blow softly, and let my fingers find the right notes.

The timing is awkward, and the pace is too slow, but I play the melody from beginning to end.

When I finish, Neeve says, "Again."

There are no congratulations, no praise for a job well done, no warm-fuzzies of any kind.

Just "Again."

As I go through it a second time, Neeve joins me on the violin. He improvises harmony in counterpoint, turning my infantile rendition into something charming.

"Again."

After the third time, Jeremy says, "That was really good."

"I knew you could do it," Neeve says. "All you need is a little practice to refresh your skills."

My heart is racing as if I just finished a two-hour concert in front of a full house at Carnegie Hall.

It's not just post-performance anxiety.

It's because I shouldn't have been able to play that well. I suspect Neeve did something to me or to the flute or to us both.

With my brothers present, I can't confront him.

I can't do anything except sit there and marvel at how good we sounded together.

133

# Echoes: A Modern Fairytale

Neeve turns to Jeremy, "What are you going to play?"

"I haven't decided yet—something Benny Goodman did in the big band era, 'Bugle Call Rag' or 'Swingtime in the Rockies' maybe."

"Why don't you play them for us?" Neeve suggests. "Perhaps we can help you choose."

Jeremy stands up and breezes through both pieces as if he had been born with a clarinet in his hands. He doesn't even use sheet music—and the idiot would rather play football! Go figure.

We applaud. He deserves it.

"Is there a reason you can't do both of those?" Neeve asks.

Blushing, Jeremy says, "I don't want to hog all the time."

"Neither one is overly long," Neeve continues. "I'll be playing one number with Karissa and one by myself. I don't see why you shouldn't do both pieces. You're very good. No wonder your mother doesn't want you to quit."

"Thank you," Jeremy says with just a little strain in his voice. Obviously Neeve's comment reminds Jeremy of the music vs. sports dispute. He avoids dealing with the subject by turning our attention onto Bennett.

"Have you decided on anything yet?" he asks.

Ben shrugs nervously. "I'd really like to do 'La Vie En Rose,' but Karissa would have to sing the words. It's not nearly as pretty without the lyrics."

"Don't be silly," I tell him. "It's beautiful as a trumpet solo."

I doubt my protest sounds very convincing.

I love this song, as did my junior high school band teacher, who introduced our class to it. I still go to YouTube and listen to Louis Armstrong's version at least a couple of times a month. I always sing along.

The first time Bennett came into my room while I was listening to Louis Armstrong, he was absolutely speechless.

We were still in Chicago then, and he hadn't been taking music lessons very long. It changed his whole attitude toward the trumpet. He began practicing in earnest because he wanted to reproduce Louis Armstrong's sound.

I searched all over the Internet until I found the sheet music for "La Vie En Rose" arranged as a trumpet solo, even though it still included the words.

I gave it to Bennett on his next birthday.

When I glance up, I find all the guys staring at me expectantly.

Singing doesn't frighten me the way that playing the flute does. I only wish I could sing "La Vie En Rose" in French like Edith Piaf (which is another great performance on YouTube).

"I'll do it," I tell Bennett, "as long as you agree to play something else too."

"Like what?" he asks. "My repertoire isn't very big, not like Jeremy's."

I don't even have to think. "You could play 'March of the Wooden

134

Soldiers' from *Babes in Toyland*. You know that one."

His eyes light up. Doing "March of the Wooden Soldiers" for an audience would give him an excuse to play as loud as he wants without Mom telling him to quiet down.

"We'll each perform twice," Jeremy says, "even Karissa since she'll be playing the flute with Neeve and singing for Bennett. That's only six numbers. At an average of four minutes per piece, that's less than half an hour. That's not too long."

"Oh, oh, oh," Bennett says, waving his arms in the air, "I just had an idea. Why don't we wrap up the program by playing 'Row, Row, Row Your Boat' or 'Three Blind Mice' as a round? All four of us. Or if you don't want to do it on the flute, Karissa, you could sing it. It would probably end up being funny, and it's always good to end on a laugh."

"I like it," Jeremy says.

"Me too," Neeve and I say at the same time.

"Ben," Neeve says, "I'd like to hear you play 'La Vie En Rose.' If you would."

"I don't have it memorized." He looks at me. "Do you know all the words?"

"I know them, but sometimes I get the order wrong," I admit.

"We can share the sheet music for now."

While he gets his trumpet, I take 'Lullaby and Goodnight' off the stand. Neeve slides over on the couch and pulls me into the middle so there's enough room for Bennett to sit on my other side.

Like Louis Armstrong, Bennett plays the song all the way through and then does a short introduction.

I begin to sing:

> "Hold me close and hold me fast,
> The magic spell you cast
> It is La Vie En Rose . . . "

One of the hardest things to do on the trumpet is to play softly. I have a nice voice but it's not particularly strong, so Bennett pretty much drowns me out. He stops in the middle of the second verse.

"This isn't going to work," he says, frowning.

"I don't need to sing," I tell him.

"But—"

"Ben, may I play it with you?" Neeve asks. "When we get to the vocals, I can play the accompaniment for Karissa, and you can pick it up again when she's finished."

"Super," Bennett says with a big grin. "That ought to sound good." I think he's suffering from a severe case of hero worship.

## Echoes: A Modern Fairytale

After Bennett has gone through the first verse solo, Neeve comes in on the violin. He enriches the melody with subtleties. Bennett doesn't have a lot of practice playing duets, so the sound of the violin distracts him for a few seconds. But he keeps going, fading out right before the vocals.

I sing to Neeve's violin.

My voice has never sounded better.

Bennett rejoins Neeve after I complete the last verse. Then Neeve fades out and lets Ben play the final high notes alone.

It doesn't go as well as Jeremy's numbers, or even as smooth as me on flute and Neeve on violin. But if we get it right—between the crystal clear tones of Ben's trumpet and the flourishes added by Neeve's violin—it's going to be a showstopper.

In fact, when I glance up and see the expression on Jeremy's face, I realize he is feeling a little—well, jealous isn't the right word; disappointed is more accurate, I think—anyway, he looks sad about being left out.

"Let's do it again," I suggest, thinking that maybe I can come up with a way to include Jeremy.

I don't need to.

After the second time through, Bennett says, "It still needs something." He runs his finger along the page, indicating the flourish that comes after the vocals. "I think it needs a clarinet to come in right here to make the finish stronger. What do you think?" he asks Jeremy.

"Sure." Jeremy beams as if he's been given his Christmas gifts early. He stands behind the couch and leans forward, so he can look at the music over my shoulder.

It was generous of Bennett to include Jeremy, but the fact is that the addition of the clarinet gives the ending new depth.

"You know," Neeve says, "this is really lovely. I think maybe we should begin the program with 'Row, Row, Row Your Boat' and end with this."

"It would be a powerful finale," I say.

We're going through it for the fourth time—and it is sounding better and better—when there is a loud, banging clatter against the basement windows.

"The storm is getting worse," Neeve says.

While Jeremy and Bennett rush over to the window, Neeve picks me up and carries me so I can see too.

The wind is blowing the snow horizontally and picking up bits of rubbish with it.

It is pure white outside.

"Kids," Mom calls down the stairs. "You need to come up now."

Neeve carries me, of course.

When we get upstairs, the television is on in the living room.

"Storm Warning" is flashing across the top of the screen in big red letters.

A meteorologist points at a map of the state to show where two storms are converging. Then he begins quoting projected snow depths for the weekend. It looks like we're going to get hit hard.

After the meteorologist finishes, someone else comes on camera and starts talking about emergency measures. He tells everyone to stay indoors and off the roads. He warns about carbon monoxide and the need for ventilation if using gas or log fireplaces for heat.

He reminds middle-aged men, when they go outside to shovel driveways and sidewalks tomorrow, to rest often because of the risk of heart attacks.

He reminds mothers to be cautious about letting children play in the snow after the storm passes. He cites statistics about children who have suffocated because the tunnels they were digging in snowdrifts collapsed and about other children who have been hit by cars or snow-removal equipment while sledding.

This guy is just a ray of sunshine.

Dad is talking softly to someone on the telephone. I recognize his reassurance-voice.

Neeve has a faraway look on his face, and I get the feeling that his hearing is good enough to pick up on Dad's conversation. He doesn't look at all surprised when Dad hands him the phone.

Neeve doesn't say much. Mostly he listens and mumbles "I understand" and "okay" a lot. His face is completely blank when he hangs up.

Dad takes over.

"We need to prepare for the storm. Neeve is going to be staying with us. His foster parents are involved in a difficult situation right now. They wouldn't be in any position to come get him even if the roads were passable, which they're not.

"Jeremy and Bennett, I want you to get the sleeping bags and extra bedding together. You can stack everything in the corner at the top of the stairs until we know if we're going to need it. Then gather all of the flashlights and check the batteries."

The boys gallop up the stairs to the second floor.

"Kari, you and your mother need to get busy with dinner. And, Sharon," he says to Mom, "you might want to consider what you can cook ahead for tomorrow in case the power goes out tonight. I'm going to bring in extra wood for the fireplace."

"I'll help you," Neeve says.

Dad starts to reply, probably to suggest that Neeve help the boys instead.

Neeve is quicker. "An uninvited guest has obligations to his host. Bringing firewood in from outdoors will be cold, heavy work. Together we'll finish twice as fast."

"All right," Dad says.

While Neeve gets his coat from the rack in the kitchen, Dad rummages around in the hall closet.

He comes in with his arms full.

Mom has begun handing me stuff from the refrigerator.

I hear Neeve's voice, "What are these for?"

Dad sits down at the kitchen table, kicks off his slippers, and puts on heavy leather boots.

"You can lose one-third of your body heat through the top of your head," Dad says. "You need to wear a hat. The galoshes are for your feet. I hope they'll fit. You can't go out in this weather in those shoes. Your toes will get frostbite."

"Yes sir," Neeve says. He sits down and pulls on the galoshes. I'll bet his talent with fabrics works on rubber too. The galoshes fit over his shoes just fine.

# Chapter Twenty-one

By the time dinner is ready to go on the table, we have a Dutch oven full of potatoes cooking on the stove. A dozen hardboiled eggs have been rinsed in cold water and are cooling on a wire rack on the counter. A casserole of homemade baked beans is in the oven next to the roaster, which has two whole chickens in it. Turkey vegetable soup is simmering in the crockpot, set at its highest temperature. A macaroni and tuna salad is chilling in the refrigerator.

The poor microwave has been worked to capacity thawing out meat from the freezer.

We have just finished eating our meal of halibut in cheese sauce over brown rice when the lights flicker out for the first time.

"Jeremy," Mom says, "go fill the sink with hot water and dishwashing liquid. We'll need to do the dishes by hand."

There's a box of fat candles on the bar between the kitchen and dining room. Mom lights two and hands one to Jeremy.

"But Mom," Jeremy says.

Mom cuts him off.

"I won't have dirty dishes sitting in the dishwasher or on the counters for heaven-only-knows how long. We could be without power for days. That would cause enough mess. I don't want to start out with one."

"I'll wash," Neeve offers. He picks up a candle and lights it from the one Mom is holding.

"I'll dry," I volunteer.

"I'll put away," says Ben, taking another candle with him as we file into the kitchen.

"I guess," Jeremy says as we pass him, "that means I'll clear."

I don't look back as I wheel behind Neeve, but I would guess my parents are left with their mouths hanging open. I don't know if the guys feel the same way that I do, but it seems like an adventure to me to do dishes by hand in the candlelight.

139

Neeve starts whistling 'La Vie En Rose,' and Bennett and Jeremy join in. Neither one whistles as well as Neeve does. Big surprise!

I sing along with them, humming whenever I'm not sure of the words.

We can still hear the howling of the wind and the pinging of icy snow crystals hitting the windows.

Dishes are washed, dried, and put away in about twenty minutes.

The lights come back on shortly after that.

Mom and I check on the food we left cooking.

The potatoes are done, so I dump them into a colander to drain and cool. The baked beans are ready to come out of the oven. The chickens and the soup both have at least another hour before they'll be finished.

Mom sets the timer.

No one wants to go to bed.

"Why don't we play spoons?" I suggest. This has been my favorite card game since I was tiny.

"Spoons?" Neeve asks. He's leaning on the bar, lining up candles in two parallel rows.

I explain the rules. "You put a spoon in the middle of the table for everyone who is playing except for one. The dealer deals four cards to each player, including himself. The goal is to be the first person to get four of a kind.

"The dealer sets the remainder of the deck face down on the table and goes through the cards one at a time. If he doesn't want a card, he passes it face down to his left. If he comes to a card that he does want, he passes one from his hand.

"Then the next person has to decide whether or not to keep the card or pass it. You can't ever hold more than five cards: the four in your hand and the one that you're deciding about. However, you can have less.

"The first person to get four of a kind takes a spoon. After that, anyone can grab one. If you don't get a spoon, you get a letter on the score sheet. Usually we choose a word to spell like 'stupid' or 'skunk' or—"

"Or not," Jeremy says. "When Bennett was little, Dad always made us spell 'horse' because Ben cried if he ended up the skunk, but he didn't mind being a horse."

"So?" Bennett says good-naturedly, "I was a sensitive kid."

"Each time you don't get a spoon, you get another letter," I continue. "The game ends when someone spells out the whole word."

"What you want to do," Jeremy says, "is keep the cards moving as fast as possible so people get confused about what they're keeping and what they're passing."

"While trying not to get confused yourself," says Bennett.

"Once you set a card down to pass it," I add for clarification, "you can't pick it up again. So if you accidently give away a card you wanted to keep, you're out of luck. If you drop one or knock one onto the floor, you call *freeze*. Everyone has to stop what they're doing until you pick it up and say *unfreeze*."

"This ought to be fun," Neeve says.

He starts to sit down next to me.

I tell him, "Because the table is a rectangle, we always make the two people with the longest arms sit at the ends. I think that's got to be you and Dad."

"Why?"

"If someone with short arms is at the end, he has to stand up to grab a spoon. Your arms will reach the middle of the table without having to jump for it."

"Sounds fair."

I roll over to the china closet. Whereas most people probably keep their good silverware in the top drawer, our family uses it for a dozen decks of cards, the canasta tray, the cribbage board, the backgammon set, and a box of double-twelve dominos.

I choose a deck of cards, pull out the jokers, shuffle, and then spread the cards in an arc on the tabletop.

"Whoever draws the highest card deals first," I say.

"Are aces high or low?" Neeve asks.

"High," I tell him.

We all take a card.

Dad gets the king of spades. He scoops up the cards and begins shuffling. I'm on his left and Jeremy is on his right. Bennett is next to me. Mom is next to Jeremy. Neeve is across the table from Dad.

After Dad deals, I look at my cards. What a mess, not even a pair!

The members of my family always seem to prefer collecting face cards, so I generally go for low numbers. It's no fun holding onto something, like two jacks, when you know someone on the other side of the table is probably saving them too.

Dad starts passing cards to me. One of them gives me a pair of threes. I slide the rest of my cards over to Bennett. Now all I have to do is watch the spoons and wait for threes.

Different people use different strategies.

Jeremy always goes for two pairs first. He waits until he gets the third card to make three of a kind, before he dumps a pair.

There is no conversation as people look at cards and pass them on.

The threes I need show up almost together.

I keep passing cards while I unobtrusively sneak a spoon.

Dad's hand shoots out a second later as he grabs one.

There are only two spoons left.

Mom, Jeremy, and Bennett scramble for them.

I glance at Neeve, and he is already holding a spoon. I have no idea how he got I it. I didn't see him move.

The boys knock a spoon to the side. Mom snatches it.

Jeremy and Bennett scuffle for the last one.

Jeremy wins.

We decided to spell skunk.

Mom is always scorekeeper.

Ben gets an *S*.

I deal the next hand.

Some people think the dealer has an advantage since he gets to see the cards first. I always feel at a disadvantage because I have to divide my attention into thirds: peeling off the top card of the deck in front of me, watching for what I want to collect, and keeping an eye on the spoons.

I'm lucky it's Bennett who gets the next four of a kind. There is nothing subtle about the way he reacts. He's so excited he knocks spoons all over the table while he's trying to grab the first one.

After that, it's a free-for-all. I manage to steal the last spoon from Mom before she gets a firm grasp on it, which is allowable.

We're all laughing.

We get through three more hands before the timer goes off in the kitchen.

While Jeremy deals, Mom rushes to take the chickens out of the oven and to unplug the crockpot. She barely sits down again when the lights go out.

We play by candlelight until the electricity comes on again.

"I think we all ought to go to bed," Dad says, "while we have lights to get ready by. We can finish the game tomorrow if anyone is still interested."

Jeremy is the only person without at least one letter, so he is declared the winner. Bennett and I are tied for last, each of us having *S-K-U*.

I'm tired. It's been a busy day.

But instead of heading for my room, I follow Mom into the kitchen to help her get everything put away and cleaned up.

Dad and the boys come too.

Jeremy fills the sink with soapy water again. He starts washing the pans the potatoes and the eggs were cooked in. Neeve dries, and Ben puts away.

After I dump the potatoes into a big plastic container and snap on the lid, I hand Jeremy the colander. Dad puts the hard-boiled eggs in a bowl, passes me the cooling rack, and I give it to Jeremy.

While Mom rearranges things in the refrigerator, I wrap the chickens in foil and dig out the lid that goes on the casserole the baked beans are in. I hand them to Mom, and through her clever manipulation, everything fits inside the fridge including the crockpot.

"Neeve," Mom says, "you can sleep upstairs in Karissa's old room. My brother left a set of sweats here when he visited us before Christmas. They ought to fit you close enough. He's not quite as tall as you, but nearly." She doesn't give Neeve a chance to respond. "Kids, all of you need to sleep in warm clothing. The way the wind is howling, we probably won't make it through the night without the power going off again."

"If any of you wake up and the house is cold," Dad says, "come get me. We can gather around the fireplace." He looks at me with concern. "I hate leaving you down here alone, Kari."

"I could carry her upstairs," Neeve suggests. "The sofa looks comfortable. I could spend the night down here."

"No," I say. "I want to sleep in my own bed. If the power goes off and the house gets cold, I don't imagine I'll be down here by myself very long."

"I can bring you one of my walkie-talkies," Bennett says. "I'll sleep with the other one on my pillow. If you need anything, you can call me."

"For that matter," I say, "I can call any of you on my cellphone." I turn my chair and head for my bedroom. "I'll be all right. Good night, everyone."

It usually takes me about half an hour to go through my bedtime rituals. Tonight, knowing everyone is getting ready for bed at the same time, I just wash my face and brush my teeth. I'm already wearing sweatpants. All I have to do is pull on a sweatshirt.

Since the lights are still on, I decide to read about Lark and Jaydon for a few minutes. I want to add more illustrations, but I'm not sure where they would fit best.

I flip to the page where the corner is turned down. That's where I left off last time. Queen Alexis had just told Lark that her husband and two eldest sons were missing and had asked her to help Jaydon find them.

The lights go out.

I sigh and set the papers back on my desk.

I wheel over to the window, open the blinds, then park the wheelchair so I can pull myself into bed.

I watch the storm.

Knowing Neeve is upstairs, almost directly above me, makes me feel strangely excited.

*Good night, Neeve,* I think.

*Good night, Karissa,* I hear inside my head.

My breath catches in my throat.

*You didn't tell me that you could talk to me as well as listen,* I say in my mind.

*Sorry,* Neeve answers, *it didn't occur to me that you wouldn't realize that it went both ways.* His mental voice sounds nervous, unsure. *You spoke to me first. I wasn't eavesdropping.*

*Rrrrrright,* I say, drawing out the word skeptically. *You just had the radio on, waiting to see if I'd start to broadcast.*

*Precisely. I was thrilled to hear you tell me good night.* He pauses a second then goes on hesitantly. *I can tune out the radio if you want me to.*

143

I consider for a moment. *No. It's actually kind of comforting to know you can hear me.* I look out the window. The top of the pine tree in the front yard is bent over so far I'm afraid it will snap off. *The storm is a little scary.*

*May I come down?*

*You think my parents aren't upstairs, straining their ears, listening for stealthy footsteps?*

*I won't use the stairs.*

*Oh. All right then, just for a minute.*

He appears in my room as if he has stepped from behind a curtain. There is no slit in reality, no tear, no seam. No wonder his dad said he did a sloppy job before.

He is wearing Uncle Leon's burgundy sweat suit. He has obviously made some adjustments in length and width because it looks good on him. Usually sweats aren't that flattering.

He sits down in my wheelchair, which is right beside the bed.

"The storm is going to be a bad one," he whispers. "If you want, I can stay with you. Your chair is comfortable enough to sleep in."

"I don't think so," I say, grinning, keeping my voice low. "I'm sure my parents will check on us off and on all night."

"Uh oh," Neeve says. "Your mother." He gives my palm a strawberry flavored kiss before sliding out of view.

There is a knock on my door.

"Come in," I call.

"I wasn't sure if the boys left you a flashlight," Mom says. She sets one on the bedside table. She gives me a quick hug before she leaves.

Neeve's voice comes into my mind. *If you need me, just call. I'll leave the radio channel open.*

# Chapter Twenty-two

When I wake up Sunday morning, the house smells like we're camping out. Dad arranged kindling and logs in the fireplace last night so all he'd need to do if the power went out was strike a match.

I'm warm under my pile of blankets, but when I push them back, I can tell the furnace isn't working.

Still, it's not too cold.

Before the accident, I slept with my windows cracked open a couple of inches all winter. Back then, I could jump out of bed and slam them shut on my way to the bathroom.

I wonder how many years it will take for me to stop labeling occurrences *before* or *after* the accident.

I pull myself into my chair and roll over to the window.

Snow is still falling, but the terrible wind has stopped. Broken branches poke up through snowdrifts that look as if they're five and six and seven feet deep. It is impossible to tell where the driveway is, or the road.

After my usual morning routine—minus the shower since the house is all electric and there won't be any hot water—I take a few extra minutes to perk up my hair and put on a little makeup.

Usually I wouldn't bother with cosmetics this early on a Sunday morning, but Neeve is somewhere in the house.

When I wheel into the living room, I find Dad and the guys sitting on the hardwood floor clustered around the rectangular area of ceramic tile in front of the fireplace. My brothers and Neeve are wrapped up in sleeping bags, and Dad is wearing his bright orange-and-black-checkered hunting jacket (something he enjoys even though he's never been hunting in his life). They act like they're in the wilderness, roughing it.

Dad must have been up for quite a while because the fire has burned down to a comfortable level. An old coffee pot is dangling from what looks like a metal coat hanger hooked to the handle of the flue.

Jeremy and Bennett have the big cutting board balanced between them on

145

their knees. Ben is chopping onions. Jeremy is slicing cooked potatoes.

Dad has a roll of aluminum foil. He rips off a square, sprays it with cooking oil, grabs a handful of potatoes and some diced onions, centers them on the foil, folds the edges together, and works the bundle into the embers under the fire. Then he does another packet.

Neeve has the small cutting board and is dicing celery, green onions, and red peppers. A carton of eighteen eggs is beside him, as is a cereal bowl half full of grated cheese.

The camp stove, which uses small canisters of propane, is on the tile in front of him, and there is a skillet waiting on the floor beside it.

This is what Mom calls a testosterone moment: the men taking charge and providing survival necessities for their womenfolk.

She is nowhere in sight.

Not wanting to intrude on the male-bonding process, I head for the kitchen. On the way, I think *Good morning, Neeve.*

He looks up and smiles at me. *Good morning, Karissa.*

Mom is in the kitchen.

She is in the early stages of making potato salad. I offer to shell the hardboiled eggs for her.

Breakfast isn't too bad, even though my packet of potatoes and onions is scorched on one side. The scrambled eggs that Neeve cooked are perfect. While we eat, a pot of water heats on the camp stove.

Although we use paper plates, flatware and pans still need to be cleaned. Mom uses the hot water to fill the sink. She washes. I dry.

Dad and the boys put on their coats and boots so they can begin the long process of digging us out.

"I was a fool not to buy a snow blower in the fall," Dad grumbles as he follows my brothers outside.

"I don't think it would've done much good this morning," Neeve says as he's closing the door. "There's too much rubbish mixed in with the snow. The debris probably would've clogged up the blades and ruined the machine."

As soon as everything in the kitchen is cleaned up, I go into the living room and park by the picture window to watch the guys.

Jeremy and Bennett are at work on the driveway.

Dad and Neeve are gathering broken branches and pinecones, which they toss into a pile over by the fence.

At least it's chilly enough that the snow is powdery. Moving heavy, wet snow is backbreaking work.

I wish I could be out there with them, just to feel the bite of cold on my face and to breathe in the fresh air.

After a few minutes, Neeve disappears.

When I spot him again, he has an old coal shovel and a broom. He attacks the snow on the front porch. After he gets it down to a manageable level, he sweeps the rest of it away.

Then he knocks on the door.

When I answer, he says, "I thought you might like to come out for a while."

I grin at him, do a 180 with my chair, and go get my coat.

By the time we come in, Mom has heated water in a pot by the fire. It looks as if she's decided to conserve propane in case the blackout lasts a couple of days.

While Dad and the boys change into dry clothes, she makes hot chocolate to warm us up. We have cold chicken, baked beans, and potato salad for lunch.

Still no electricity.

The sun comes out from behind the clouds for a while, and the light reflecting off the snow fills the house with brightness.

Neeve, Jeremy, Bennett, and I play Scrabble.

Jeremy wins, but not because he has the biggest or best vocabulary. He just consistently draws the letters worth the most points. It doesn't matter how smart you are if you only have one-pointers to work with.

Neeve and I are at the dining room table working on our history report when we hear the snowplow scraping our street.

Thirty minutes later Neeve's foster father shows up.

Neeve stands when Mom and Dad usher Detective Taylor into the dining room.

"Hi, Dad," Neeve says, smiling. "Karissa, this is my foster father, Brian Taylor. Dad, this is Karissa."

Detective Taylor is a little older than my father, about the same height, but heavier. He has the beginnings of a potbelly. What little hair he has left is dark brown with a few streaks of gray.

He offers me his hand. "How are you doing, Karissa?"

"Very well, thank you. I'm pleased to meet you." I try to keep my face relaxed and pleasant, but—

a) Mr. Taylor is a policeman and I have guilty knowledge about Kenneth Nelson's so-called accident Friday night, and

b) I'm shocked to hear Neeve call his foster father *Dad*, since I have seen Neeve's real father, and he is alive and well and majestically intimidating.

"Is it time for us to go?" Neeve asks.

Detective Taylor pulls out a chair and sits down at the dining room table with us. "Not quite. I need to talk with Karissa and her parents for a moment."

Mom and Dad, looking confused, sit down at the table too.

"What's going on?" Dad asks.

"Friday night," Mr. Taylor says, "some local boys were in a three car accident. Karissa's name came up during the investigation."

My heart stops.

"Kari," Dad says, "do you know what this is about?"

I shake my head. I don't trust my voice.

Dad looks at Detective Taylor. "Did someone accuse Karissa of being involved in some way?"

"No, it's nothing like that."

Neeve's foster father turns his eyes on me, and I'm scared.

I don't know why I should be.

If the truth came out about Friday night, I would be cast in the role of victim not villain.

But the truth can't come out.

Our world is not ready to learn about people like Neeve and Brenlyn and Talitha—or about their world, where people have wings and magic is real.

If the government found out about them, they'd be locked up in a laboratory somewhere. What Neeve's uncle did to him would be nothing compared to what the scientists would do.

Maybe Neeve could open a doorway and get them all out safely—if he wasn't strapped to a gurney and kept unconscious or something—but I wouldn't want to count on it.

I try to look curious without looking terrified.

Detective Taylor continues. "What I'm going to tell you hasn't been made public." He interrupts himself. "I don't want to frighten you, Karissa."

My mouth goes dry. I swallow hard before I say anything. "Why should I be frightened?"

"After the boys were taken to the hospital," the detective continues, "when the cars were being pulled apart so they could be towed away, one of the officers at the scene found a gun among the debris scattered in the street."

*Neeve,* I cry out in my mind.

*Take it easy,* Neeve tells me. *When the police asked the guys about the accident and the gun, a couple of them admitted that Kenneth Nelson had threatened to kill you because of Josie Peters.*

*But I saw you crush the gun.*

*I had Brenlyn fix it. I was afraid if Kenneth Nelson missed it, he might remember what happened. Hayden didn't erase memories. He just superimposed new ones over the old. The right kind of stimulus could cause the true memories to surface.*

"A gun?" my mother repeats.

"What does that have to do with Karissa?" asks Dad.

"All of the boys involved in the accident were interviewed, at least all of them who were in any condition to talk. The gun belongs to the father of one of the boys, and that boy apparently has a grudge against Karissa."

"How can anyone have a grudge against Karissa?" Mom asks. "She didn't have time to make friends, let alone enemies, before the car accident."

"It was because of the accident," Mr. Taylor says. "The girl who died, it's her boyfriend, Kenneth Nelson, who has made threatening comments about Karissa."

"Should we worry?" Dad asks. "Do you think she's in danger?"

"Well, I'll tell you," Mr. Taylor answers, "I'd be a lot less worried if there weren't a gun involved and if the accident had been somewhere else."

"Where was the accident?" Dad asks.

"Only a block away from where Neeve works part-time." Detective Taylor looks at his foster son. "After the movie Friday night, did you go over to Brenlyn's shop?"

"Yes," Neeve answers.

"I wanted to see the miniatures," I interject. After all, I was the one who suggested it. "Brenlyn said it was on the way home."

"Did either of you notice Kenneth Nelson or any of his friends? Could they have been following you?"

Neeve and I look at each other, surprised. We hadn't stopped to wonder how the football players had known where we were. Too much happened that night.

"I didn't see them in the restaurant or at the movies," Neeve says.

"A couple of cars pulled out of Mama Mia's right behind us," I say. "At least one of them followed us all the way to the mall, but when we turned into the parking lot, it went on by."

"Why didn't you tell me?" Neeve asks sharply.

I see a look flash between my parents. The tone in Neeve's voice is possessive, too possessive for after one date. I suppose Mom and Dad are wondering how far along my relationship with Neeve has progressed.

I try to minimize the situation by appearing annoyed when I answer. "They passed on by, Neeve. It was probably just a coincidence. I shouldn't have mentioned it."

I don't know if Neeve taps into my mind or the minds of my folks, but he backpedals and does some damage control.

"I didn't mean that to come out the way it sounded," he says apologetically. "I'm just frightened. The newspaper said they were all drunk. If they had a gun, and if they followed us—"

My parents seem reassured by Neeve's contrite response—at least reassured about the status of our relationship—but it's clear that they're still worried about everything else.

"What happens now?" Dad asks Mr. Taylor.

"I'm not sure," he answers. "The first officers on the scene were a couple of women who are both fairly new to the area. They've cited all three drivers for driving under the influence.

"It's caused an uproar at the station. I hate to admit it, but if one of the good-old-boy football fans had been there first, I doubt the drivers would have been written up. With a DUI on Kenneth Nelson's record, the college football recruiters might drop him. If it weren't for the gun, I think the official stance would be to sweep it under the rug."

"Regardless of the threats?" Dad asks.

"As far as we know, it's all talk, no action."

An inarticulate sound, maybe a groan, pops out of my mouth before I can stop it. Kenneth Nelson shot me. He wanted to kill me. He would have succeeded if Neeve hadn't taken me to wherever his home is.

The police are like Principal Haskell. They don't want Kenneth Nelson to take responsibility. Not even for drunk driving!

"Kari?" Dad asks.

"This is just one more reason Kenneth Nelson will have for hating me."

"What is?"

"Getting a DUI and not being able to play college football. He blames me for Josie Peters' death, even though I didn't ask her for a ride and I wasn't driving either car. If he was out looking for me Friday night, and the end result is that he doesn't get a football scholarship, he's going to blame me. He's going to want me dead even more than he did before."

"Oh, Karissa, honey," Mom says.

"That would be pretty convoluted thinking," Dad, the ever-lasting logical psychologist, states. "He can't blame you because he was out drinking and driving."

"We don't know if he actually intended to harm you," Detective Taylor says. "This is all supposition."

"Right," I say. "Excuse me for a moment." I head for the den.

When I return, I have the shoebox with me. I dump the letters on the dining room table.

*Good thinking,* Neeve says. *Now is the perfect time to let your parents know what's been going on.*

All of the adults reach for an envelope.

The sun is setting, and the room is getting dark.

Detective Taylor pulls a small flashlight from his pocket and flicks it on for better illumination.

Dad gets one from the kitchen while Mom lights half a dozen candles and sets them in a grouping in the middle of the table.

After Dad reads several letters, he looks at me with hurt in his eyes. "Why didn't you show us these before?"

"There wasn't anything you could do," I say. "There still isn't."

"We could have gone to the police."

"Then what?" I get tears in my eyes. "Didn't you hear what Detective Taylor said? The police don't even want to hold Kenneth Nelson accountable for drunk driving. Do you think they're going to care about a few pieces of paper?"

All the stress of the past few months hits me, and I start to cry.

Between sobs I tell them about everything: the hostile looks I get from the jocks at lunchtime, Kenneth Nelson and his friend bullying me in the hall and the principal ignoring it, and Kenneth Nelson and his football player friends threatening to drop me into the lake, or maybe something even worse.

Dad gets a box of tissues and hands it to me.

I wipe my eyes and blow my nose.

"Kenneth Nelson told one of the guys to go get his car. He came back driving a faded red Mustang," I say sniffling. "I don't know what would've happened if Neeve hadn't shown up and scared them off."

Mom scoots her chair over by mine so she can put her arms around me. She doesn't tell me not to worry, or that I misunderstood the situation, or that everything will be all right. She simply hugs me and pats my back and strokes my hair.

I just love her sometimes.

Detective Taylor is still reading. He doesn't say anything.

"Well," Dad says, "regardless of what the police do or don't do, there are steps we can take. We'll start by getting a restraining order against Kenneth Nelson and his whole crowd. I'll meet with the principal and let him read a copy of the order and maybe a handful of these threats. I'll tell him that we expect his complete support at school. Then I'll call Uncle Frank and see if we can do anything in the courts."

Dad's eldest brother, Frank, used to be a lawyer in Denver. Now he's a State Superior Court judge.

"Kenneth Nelson is legally an adult," Dad continues. "Maybe we can charge him with harassment or stalking. I don't know. Maybe we can sue him for being a bully. We will certainly sue the school district if we don't get one hundred percent cooperation from the principal."

He doesn't sound like a psychologist. He sounds like a dad. Sometimes I just love him too.

"I don't think we should handle these letters anymore," Dad says. He begins sweeping them into a pile. "We need a couple of plastic bags. Frank might want them."

Detective Taylor says, "You should let me take them."

"I don't think so," Dad tells him, "not unless you know how they can be used to bring charges against Kenneth Nelson and his friends."

Mr. Taylor slowly shakes his head. "We can't prove who's responsible for these. They're all unsigned. But we might need them in case—" He stops himself before he says anything insensitive like *in case he kills Karissa in the future*. He stammers a bit before he adds "—in case something happens later."

"They're of no use to you," Dad says, "and they might be to us. I'll make copies for you before I send them to my brother. If the originals are ever needed, they'll be available."

"I'll get the bags," I tell Dad.

"Good. Bring a pair of those disposable gloves too. We've probably messed up any physical evidence, but we might as well be as cautious as possible from now on."

I take a candle from the table.

Neeve follows me through the kitchen and into the pantry. Storage bags from snack-sized to gallons are in a metal rack that's attached to the back of the door. It also holds trash bags, plastic wrap, and aluminum foil. The disposable latex gloves are on a shelf with the cleaning supplies.

As soon as we're inside the little room, Neeve closes the door and crouches down in front of me so we're pretty much eye to eye.

"I'll have to leave in a few minutes," he says, "but I want you to know that being here, having spent this much time with you, has meant a great deal to me. If I could, I'd conjure up a storm every weekend so we could get stranded somewhere together." He takes my hands and turns them over so he can give each of my palms a strawberry flavored kiss.

When he lets go, he stands up with his hands behind his back. Clearly he doesn't want me to reciprocate by kissing his palms.

Maybe he still doesn't believe that I know how I feel about him. Maybe that's why he won't kiss me on the lips.

When we return to the dining room, Dad and Detective Taylor are having a heated discussion about what to do with the letters.

Dad pulls on the gloves I hand him and begins stuffing the letters into bags.

Detective Taylor watches with his lips fixed in a tight line.

There is a lot of tension in the room.

Neeve goes and gets his coat.

"Thank you for your hospitality," he says to my mother. He kisses her hand just as he did the first time he came to dinner. "I realize the circumstances weren't ideal for having a guest. You have been gracious and kind."

He shakes hands with my father. "Thank you for welcoming me into your home. I've had a pleasant time, sharing your table and being with your family."

He goes into the living room where Jeremy and Bennett are playing Jenga on the coffee table. The only light comes from the fireplace and two candles that are on an end table beside the couch. I'm sure the dim lighting adds to the excitement of trying to remove the little logs without knocking over the entire stack.

For some reason the atmosphere in the dining room changes as Neeve makes his farewells. Maybe it's because he looks so serious and sounds so formal—he has been trained to behave like a prince after all. But even if you don't know that, you can't help but like someone who tries so hard to be polite.

My parents and Detective Taylor are wearing similar expressions. I've seen that look before. It means something like: *Kids can be so surprising. Sometimes they're worth all the trouble.*

The power comes back on, which helps brighten the mood too. (No pun intended.)

The adults smile at each other.

They aren't going to fight anymore.

Detective Taylor stands.

Mom and Dad accompany him to the door.

"Is it safe for Karissa to go to school tomorrow?" Dad asks.

"I'm sure it is," Neeve's foster father answers. "I doubt if any of the boys will be back to school before next week. They were all banged up pretty bad. Kenneth Nelson will probably be out even longer. He had the most serious injuries."

Dad opens the front door. Mr. Taylor steps through.

"Don't forget that you and Janet are coming over for dinner on Thursday," Mom says. "Neeve, too, of course."

"We're looking forward to it."

"I'll see you in the morning, Karissa," Neeve says to me. He follows his foster father out of the house.

After Dad closes the door, he turns and frowns at me. "We need to discuss those letters," he says.

"I know," I say, "but they'll still be here in the morning, and I'm so tired."

"All right," Dad says, "but don't think you're off the hook. I've got some serious questions for you."

# Chapter Twenty-three

Despite what I told my dad, I'm too restless to sleep.

So much has happened in just a few days that I'm in overload.

I try to watch a little television, now that we have power again, and then I try to lose myself in one of my favorite fantasy novels. Unlike some people, I love rereading books I've enjoyed before.

Not tonight.

If I can't focus enough to watch television or to read a book, the next option is art.

I try to draw a fairy castle sitting inside a daylily with pollen-heavy anthers dangling in the air like multiple oval-shaped moons.

I can see the picture clearly in my mind.

I can't make my pencil go where I want.

Finally, I pick up my story.

What was going on last night when the power went off? Ah, yes, Lark had just told the queen she would help Jaydon look for his missing father and brothers.

A few minutes later, there's a knock on my door. When I call come in, my Dad does and perches on the side of my bed. I maneuver the wheelchair around so I face him.

"Can't sleep?" he asks me.

I shake my head.

"Me either." He doesn't say anything else for a few seconds. Then he asks, "When did you get those letters?"

For a moment I wish I had turned off the light and gotten into bed even if I couldn't sleep. But this conversation wouldn't get any easier by putting it off. Might as well get it over.

"They started coming as soon as I was moved from the ICU."

"I don't understand why you didn't show them to your mother and me," he says. "Even if there was nothing we could've done to stop them, we could have tried."

Connie A. Walker

I shake my head. "You had enough going on with your new jobs, the house, unpacking, getting the boys to and from school, and still managing to spend time with me whenever you could get to Denver."

"You must have been frightened, Kari. We could have at least taken steps to help you feel a little bit more secure."

I wheel closer to him so I can take his hand.

"I know you and Mom would have done everything you could think of, Dad, but you'd have figured out soon enough that none of it made any difference. All you could've done was worry about me, and I was already doing that all by myself." I smile a little. "I intended to show you the letters eventually, after I knew if there was really anything to worry about."

"And tonight?" Dad asks. "What made you go get the letters tonight?"

I crinkle my brow as I choose my words. I don't exactly lie, but I can't tell him the whole truth. Is a half-truth a lie?

"It occurred to me that those guys might have been planning to hurt Neeve to get at me. Then they might have come after you or Mom or the boys. Suddenly I was more afraid for the rest of you than I was for myself. I couldn't carry that much responsibility alone."

"I'm glad it's out in the open now," Dad says. "Until this is resolved, all of us need to take precautions. I'll talk to Jeremy and Bennett in the morning. In the future, Kari, if you have a problem, try to trust your mother and me. If we can't help you come up with a solution, we can at least provide you with moral support."

I feel as if a heavy weight has been lifted from my shoulders.

"I will, Dad."

He kisses my forehead.

I hug him and tell him goodnight.

Monday morning when I get to school, Neeve is waiting for me.

The roads have been scraped and salted, and snow is piled everywhere. Some of the least used sidewalks around the school are still impassable, but the parking lot has been cleared and a wide pathway has been opened between it and the main doors.

The sky is bright blue, and the sun has turned the snow into sparkly fields of diamonds.

The air is delicious and bitingly cold. One big advantage we have over Chicago is that the wind has stopped.

As soon as Neeve and I enter the school building, we hear Kenneth Nelson's name whispered again and again.

It is mostly preceded by "Did you hear about—?"

Occasionally it is followed by "Serves him right," accompanied by a few snickers.

Maybe he isn't as popular as I've always assumed. But it figures. If he

155

and his buddies are comfortable bullying a cripple in a wheelchair, they're probably comfortable harassing other kids too.

None of the comments I hear make any reference to Neeve or me, so I guess whatever suspicions Detective Taylor might have about why the guys were in that neighborhood have remained private.

"Do you have to join your friends for lunch today?" Neeve asks me.

"Not really," I answer. "Why?"

He bends over so he can speak quietly. "We need to work on the quest."

I guide the wheelchair over to the side of the hall and stop next to a big display case full of football trophies.

Neeve crouches down beside me so he can keep his voice low.

"Friday night, during the fight with the football players, the darkness almost overpowered me. Spending the weekend with your family, surrounded by love and peacefulness, helped me get back into balance.

"Now that I've returned to the Taylors' house, I can feel my control slipping again. The anger and restlessness of my foster brothers is like a contagion. In addition, my foster dad is hounding me with questions about you, about Kenneth Nelson, and about Friday night. If the pressure continues, I might go berserk. Time is running out for me. I can feel it."

"What a mess," I say.

"Another thing," Neeve says, "I'm puzzled by the attack Friday. When Kenneth Nelson and his friends were bullying you on Tuesday, they took off like a bunch of scared toddlers as soon as I joined you. So why did they start a fight when we had two extra people with us? If they were after you, why not wait until they caught you by yourself again? If they wanted to beat me up for interfering, why not wait until they could get me alone?"

"They had been drinking and doing drugs," I tell him.

"I don't know much about alcohol and drugs in your world," he says softly. "Is it possible to be drunk or drugged enough to cause irrational thinking and yet be sober enough to drive cars and follow us through all that traffic by the mall? They had the baseball bats with them. They were looking for a fight, but—?" He pauses and shrugs.

"I don't know much about alcohol and drugs myself," I answer. "I do know that different people react to them in different ways."

"It just seems strange to me. I wonder—"

First bell rings. I almost jump out of my skin.

Neeve gets to his feet. "I'll meet you outside of your Calculus class. We can talk some more at lunch."

When I roll into homeroom, Mr. Ullom isn't there yet.

Juanita is.

I tell her I won't be joining the group in the cafeteria.

"Neeve and I have to figure out what we're going to do about our research paper," I explain. "Seems like every time we try to get together to work on it something interferes."

"Is he your boyfriend?" Juanita asks, sounding almost embarrassed to voice the question, but obviously curious.

I laugh nervously and shake my head. "Friday was our first date."

"Still," she raises her eyebrows skeptically, "he meets you out front every morning and then walks you to homeroom. Also he takes you home after school. That's got to mean something."

I'm trying to figure out how to answer her when a scuffle breaks out on the other side of the room.

Two guys, one a dark-haired baboon and the other a redheaded scarecrow, shove each other back and forth.

From the mutterings I hear, they're arguing about whether or not Kenneth Nelson and his buddies could possibly have been drunk enough to have a three-car pileup in a residential area.

"They couldn't have been going very fast on those roads," the baboon says. "How did they bump into each other hard enough to cause that much damage?"

"I've got it!" the scarecrow says sarcastically. "The guys were beamed up by aliens. But the aliens didn't want the cars, so they dropped them in a heap. Then the aliens decided they didn't want the football players either. The guys were injured when the aliens tried to beam them back into the wrecked cars. Or was it a Sasquatch who smashed the cars together?"

The baboon punches the scarecrow, knocking him into the wall. The scarecrow responds by kicking the baboon a couple of times in the shins.

Luckily Mr. Ullom enters the room and separates the boys, preventing bloodshed. He sends them both off to the principal's office.

It's a long morning.

I get through it somehow.

I can't concentrate on things as mundane as the underlying meaning of D. H. Lawrence's story "The Rocking Horse Winner." And Calculus seems totally irrelevant to the rest of my life.

All I can do is worry about how Neeve and I will find the missing part of his soul during a 45-minute lunch break. The very thought of trying makes my stomach hurt. Also I didn't bring a sack lunch from home, which means we'll have to use part of the time getting me something to eat so I can take my medication.

The first thing Neeve says to me when I come out of Calculus is, "I checked with Brenlyn. He and Talitha are out on a service call. He said we could go over to his place and raid his refrigerator."

"Okay," I say, "but we only have forty-five minutes. We'll have to move fast."

Neeve winks at me while he pantomimes ripping a hole in space.

I smile and nod.

Next to the auditorium is a little alcove that leads backstage.

That's where Neeve and I go.

He draws a line in the air with his finger, takes hold of one edge of nothingness and lifts it as if it were a curtain, and motions me forward.

When Talitha carried me through the magical doorway to Neeve's home world, I wasn't in any condition to notice how it felt. This time I'm wide-awake and alert.

As I wheel through the opening, I feel like I'm on a rollercoaster just as it plunges down the first drop. I'm rushing through space so fast that my stomach detaches from my body and gets left behind.

Then I'm in Brenlyn's kitchen.

I'm still catching my breath when Neeve steps into the room. He lets the flap of nothingness fall back into place. The seam seals itself.

Immediately Neeve starts pulling things out of the refrigerator: sliced turkey, lettuce, tomatoes, cucumbers, mayonnaise, and grapes. He gets a loaf of bread from a cupboard and is making a sandwich before I can even offer to help.

"There is milk, cranberry juice, and bottled water in the refrigerator," he says to me. "I prefer juice."

I roll over to the fridge and take out the juice and a bottle of water. I set them on the little drop-leaf table.

A moment later, Neeve hands me a plate with a thick sandwich on it.

I lift the top piece of bread. Besides the turkey, lettuce, and tomato, which I expected, I discover that Neeve has included cucumber slices and grape halves.

I take a bite. The different flavors combine pleasantly together. I'm chewing my third bite when I notice that all Neeve has on his plate is a slice of turkey, half a tomato, and four grapes.

He pours himself a tall glassful of cranberry juice before he picks up a grape and pops it into his mouth.

Doesn't he ever really eat?

I don't ask out loud.

"What I need you to do," Neeve tells me while I devour my sandwich, "is learn to sense me. When you can tune into my aura, you'll be able to feel me plus a faint echo. That whisper of echo will be the other part of my soul."

"Uh huh," I say. "How do I do that?"

"Finish eating and I'll teach you."

I've barely swallowed the last bite when Neeve takes the plates, rinses them off, and puts them in the narrowest dishwasher I've ever seen.

He arranges us so that we are sitting almost knee to knee. He has me hold out my hands, palms up.

"Close your eyes," he tells me.

He places his hands on top of mine and applies a little pressure.

158

"Can you feel my hands?"

"Uh huh," I murmur.

"Hold your hands steady and keep your eyes closed. Focus on the point of contact between us."

In minuscule increments I feel the pressure of his hands on mine decrease. "Can you still feel me?" he asks every few seconds.

I mumble affirmatives.

Then his touch is gone.

"Can feel me now?"

"No."

"Try," he says. "Picture the space between us as merely an extension of my body."

By the time we go back to school, I'm thankful that the lunch period is only forty-five minutes long.

Holy crud.

Learning to sense Neeve is like trying to learn how to smell with your fingertips, or hear through your toes, or see with your hair. It sounds crazy, but it has to be possible. After all, I taste his strawberry kisses in the palms of my hands.


Tuesday at noon we try it again.

It goes better.

Wednesday is better still.

Something in my brain clicks into place.

I sense Neeve even when our hands are several inches apart. That may not sound like much, but to me it's amazing. Not only can I still feel him, but I can also recognize the position his hands are in, whether the palms are up or if they're down or if he is holding them sideways so the thumbs are on top.

Being aware of Neeve without using my five senses is sort of like the feeling you get when you suddenly realize you're not alone in a room or when you sense someone is watching you.

I don't understand how it works, and it's not easy to do on command.

But now I have a glimmer of hope.

# Chapter Twenty-four

Usually, I have physical therapy at least three a week, and always on Thursdays and Saturdays, but today my team is involved in some kind of workshop or conference. If I had wanted a session, they said they could arrange for a qualified private therapist to work with me.

(Ha. Ha. Those silly PTs, what will they think of next?)

Even without physical therapy, I don't get to spend a stress-free evening.

Tonight Neeve and his foster parents are coming to dinner.

Mom bought me a really pretty blue dress to wear. It has short sleeves, a rounded neckline, and a flared skirt long enough to cover my legs but short enough that the hem won't drag and get caught under the wheels of my chair.

At first I didn't want to wear it.

Not because it isn't pretty and not because I don't like dresses, but because I can't put it on by myself.

After I pull it over my head and get my arms through the sleeves, then what? I can't stand up, pull the skirt down, zip up the back, and arrange the skirt so it'll hang gracefully over my legs while I sit.

I hate being a burden to my family.

When I'm all ready except for the dress, Mom comes in to help me. She doesn't seem to mind.

"Slide forward in your chair," she tells me. She lifts my feet, flips the footrests out of the way, and arranges my feet flat on the floor. "Now hold up your arms," she tells me.

When I do, she drops the dress over my head. I slide my arms into the sleeves.

She gets the shoulder seams and the waist in place, and then she bends forward and glides her arms under my armpits.

"Put your arms around my neck and hold on," she tells me.

Slowly she stands up, taking me with her. While I'm hugging her, she zips up the back of the dress. She takes a step backward so the skirt can fall into place, then she takes a step forward so she can ease me back into my chair.

Connie A. Walker

She flips the footrests down and sets my feet on them. I feel a brief stab up the back of my calves. It passes before I panic. I'm never quite sure if the pain is real or just a memory.

Mom stands back and gazes at me.

"You look lovely, Karissa," she says. Her eyes fill with tears, but before they can drip down her face, she turns and sniffs a couple of times. "I'd better go check on the rotisserie chickens," she says.

"Thanks, Mom," I call after her.

I wheel into the bathroom so I can see myself in the full-length mirror.

I do look nice.

The color of the dress brings out the blue in my eyes.

I touch up my makeup, fiddle with my hair for a few minutes, dab a little perfume behind my ears and on my wrists, and return to my bedroom.

I wheel over to the bookcase where I keep my jewelry box.

For my birthday, when I turned sixteen years old, which was shortly before we moved here, my parents gave me a delicate teardrop shaped pendant outlined with sixteen diamond chips and with a single pearl centered at the bottom. It's set in platinum and has a sterling silver chain.

There are two matching earrings with smaller pearls and three diamond chips each.

It's the only real jewelry I own.

I didn't have a chance to wear it before the accident, and I haven't had a reason to wear it since.

Until tonight.

The doorbell rings while I'm putting on the final earring.

When I roll into the living room, the first thing I see is Neeve. He is wearing dark slacks, his beige sports coat, and an emerald green turtleneck that matches the color of his eyes. Once again his hair hangs loose and fans out over his shoulders.

He takes my breath away.

Before I can say anything he sends his thoughts to me.

*You are beautiful,* he says.

*You look quite wonderful yourself,* I think back.

He smiles his special smile at me and then turns to the side. He makes a motion with his hand to draw my attention to a woman standing beside my father and Detective Taylor.

"Karissa," Neeve says, "this is my foster mother, Janet Taylor. Mom, this is Karissa."

Although Mrs. Taylor is probably in her mid-thirties or early forties, like my parents, she lacks the perky, bouncy, youthful aura that my mom has. Instead she projects a mature, comfortable, motherliness that practically shouts of kindness, loyalty, and protectiveness.

She's only a few inches shorter than Dad and probably outweighs him by twenty pounds.

Nevertheless, it looks good on her, making her appear shapely, healthy, and athletic rather than chubby or overweight. Her long brunette hair is held back with barrettes just above her ears. She is wearing a glittery soft brown sweater set, a just-below-the-knees dark brown wool skirt, and low-heeled pumps—simple, sensible, and yet stylish.

I remember feeling sorry for Neeve after I heard Heather and her friends talking about his being in foster care. I remember thinking a person couldn't get much love and support from someone who was paid to take care of him.

All I have to do is see the affectionate way Mrs. Taylor looks at Neeve and the friendly way she smiles at me to know I was wrong. This woman doesn't take foster kids into her home for the money. She likes teenagers and wants to see us succeed and find happiness. It shows on her face.

I like her.

I wheel forward, and she takes a few steps to meet me halfway. She offers me her hand.

"I'm so pleased to meet you, Karissa," she says.

"Thank you," I answer. "I'm glad to meet you too."

Mom comes in and tells us that dinner is ready.

The meal progresses predictably.

The food is delicious, and everyone says so.

Mom might not like to cook, but she's good at it.

While my younger brothers eat as if they've been starved for weeks, Neeve and I pick at our food—him, just because that's the way he eats, and me, because I have to sing later.

I never eat much before I sing, and I choose my foods carefully. It's hard to control the diaphragm with a full stomach, and some foods cause throat mucus or dry mouth.

I'll be nervous enough just performing for Neeve's foster parents without making myself physically uncomfortable too.

The adults engage in most of the table talk, asking and answering questions about their careers and interests, getting acquainted. I'm fine with that. I think the other kids are too.

Neeve sits across the table from me, and as I look at him I am flooded with feelings: respect, desire, hope, admiration, and love—true love, forever love, all-my-heart love.

As often as I've dreamed about falling in love, I never guessed it would feel like this, like the sum of all my positive feelings combined together and wrapped around one person. I know I am going to spend my lifetime loving Neeve. If an afterlife actually exists, I'll continue loving him after I die, now and for always. That knowledge makes me feel terribly vulnerable and completely secure at the same time.

For one brief moment I am so keenly aware of Neeve's presence that I can't tell where I end and he begins. I feel as if we are two halves of one whole.

Then I notice something else: a spiral galaxy of tiny sparks dancing between Neeve and me. This swirling brilliance intensifies and magnifies the sense of oneness I feel with him. It floods me with ecstasy—not the kind that results from overworked hormones but rather the kind that comes from contact with the divine.

In a flash of insight I know what the sparks are.

I guess my facial expression changes.

*What?* Neeve asks me mentally.

I'm about ready to burst into tears from pure happiness. *The echo of your soul just brushed against me. It's floating between us. Can't you see it?*

*No.* Neeve is holding his glass of water, and his hand begins to tremble so badly that he has to set it down.

We both glance around the table. Apparently, no one else sees the twirling sparkles either. Maybe that portion of Neeve's soul can show itself to me because of how strong my feelings for him are and because those feelings are pure and innocent and uncontaminated.

*You wouldn't tease me about something this important, would you, Karissa?*

*Never,* I assure him. I'm too thrilled with the sensations I'm experiencing to be offended by his question. *If we practice tomorrow at lunchtime, maybe I can call it to me again.*

He doesn't respond for a moment. When he thinks *Thank you* at me, it sounds just like *I love you.*

I am so nearly overwhelmed that I don't dare look at anyone. I stare at my plate and stir mixed vegetables and brown rice together into a nice swirly pattern like the spiral galaxy of Neeve's soul.

Are all souls as glorious, as awe-inspiring, and as heavenly as Neeve's is? If just a tiny segment of his spirit is so magnificent, what must the total be like?

I try to calm my heart before I burble over with joy and make a complete fool of myself in front of Neeve, his foster parents, my mother and father, and my brothers.

"Karissa," my mother's voice slices through my distracting emotions. She waits a moment before she repeats my name.

I try to compose myself.

Finally I'm able to look up at her.

"It's your turn to clear the table. Do you want to do it now or after the entertainment?"

"After," I manage to say. I'm too keyed up to do something as routine as clearing the table. I hope I can convey some of what I'm feeling in the music. Something this powerful needs to be shared.

I put the wheelchair into reverse. Everyone else pushes back his or her chair.

While Mom and Dad usher the Taylors into the living room, Jeremy and Bennett set up three folding chairs facing the couch, plus one music stand.

The music stand is for me.

The guys are all so good on their instruments that memorizing their pieces was no big achievement for them, but five days weren't enough time for me to relearn how to play the flute and also learn the song Neeve and I are going to play together.

All the musical instruments are in my bedroom. Neeve and I go to get them. I am wheeling over to my desk when I hear the door close softly behind me.

I stop and turn.

Neeve kneels in front of my chair.

"Thank you for being everything I knew you would be when I first saw your face." He takes my hands and kisses my palms. He smiles his special smile at me, and then he stands. "Let's go make some music."

# Chapter Twenty-five

The second time Neeve, my brothers, and I practiced together, we decided to have Jeremy act as the master of ceremonies.

He's the most extroverted of us and is always comfortable in the spotlight.

The guys also decided unanimously that since I must remain seated, whether I'm performing or not, that they would too, except that Jeremy would stand when introducing the numbers.

He stands.

"Thank you for coming to our little recital," he says. "We're going to warm up by doing a familiar round."

He sits and blows a *C* for me on the clarinet.

I start singing.

"Row, row, row your boat gently down the stream."

Neeve comes in on the violin.

"Merrily, merrily, merrily, merrily, life is but a dream."

Jeremy joins us on the clarinet.

I go through the first line again, and Bennett comes in on the trumpet.

After I sing the last line, I stop, and the three guys go on without me.

They drop off one by one until Bennett ends the song, sustaining the sound until his face is almost purple.

When he releases the note, he does an exaggerated "Whew!" and wipes his brow.

Everyone laughs like they're supposed to.

Jeremy stands.

"First on our program will be 'Lullaby and Goodnight' performed by Karissa on flute and Neeve on violin." (I asked if we could go first so I could get this ordeal over.)

"After that I will do 'Swingtime in the Rockies' on the clarinet, followed by Bennett doing 'March of the Wooden Soldiers' on trumpet." Jeremy sits down.

Neeve does a short introduction on the violin before I begin the melody.

# Echoes: A Modern Fairytale

My nervousness disappears as soon as I blow into the flute for the first note. I make no mistakes.

I'm relieved when we finish.

I smile as the parents applaud.

Jeremy does his number to more applause, and then Bennett does his.

When the clapping dies down, Jeremy stands up again.

"Tonight," he says, "we're privileged to hear Neeve's newest original composition: 'Auravale Homecoming.' When he finishes, I'll do 'Bugle Call Rag.' Our grand finale will be 'La Vie En Rose,' featuring Bennett on the trumpet and Karissa doing vocals."

As Jeremy sits back down, Neeve situates the violin under his chin.

He runs the bow over the strings and then pauses to tighten a peg before he begins.

Every time we practiced, Neeve played something different as his solo, saying he hadn't decided yet what to perform.

When he plays tonight, I realize he simply wanted to keep his piece a surprise—because it tells with music the story of the night I got shot.

It begins with a soft and gentle melody: our first date. There is a sense of newness, of discovery, of little surprises.

Then he plucks the strings and produces a BANG that sounds more like a gunshot than I would have guessed was possible on a violin.

The piece becomes frenetic.

Neeve portrays his fury at being attacked, his savagery as he fights back, his battle with the darkness in his soul when Brenlyn keeps him from killing Kenneth Nelson, his victory over his rage.

Returning to the original sweet melody, he transposes it into a minor key, giving it a worried, mournful sound as he fears for my life.

This is followed by the sharp dissonance of his ripping a hole in space, his frantic efforts to get me help, and his bittersweet feelings about going home. He poignantly expresses his yearning to feel his mother's touch and his mortification and contrition at seeing his father.

Briefly I wonder how Neeve could write such a magnificent piece of music without access to a violin, but then I remember he told me he was able to do a complete composition in his mind while his uncle tortured him—in fact it was during that awful experience that he wrote the piece he played on Mom's violin the first evening he was here.

Tonight's melody captures us and takes us on an emotional roller coaster ride. When the feelings become almost unbearable, Neeve returns to the gentle little tune he began with, but he enhances it until it becomes a proclamation of love and an entreaty that his devotion be reciprocated.

The final notes fade away.

Neeve drops his head and then puts the violin and the bow in his lap.

Suddenly I realize I have tears running down my face.

I glance up and see that Mom does too.

Dad, Mrs. Taylor, and Detective Taylor all seem a little misty around the eyes, but they don't let their feelings run away with them.

I swipe the moisture from my cheeks before I face Neeve.

The room is silent.

Jeremy and Bennett look stunned, as if they've been hit over the head with a couple of bricks.

Then with surprisingly mature composure, Jeremy stands up and says, "We're going to take a short break now. Feel free to get up and walk around. We'll continue in about ten minutes."

He puts his clarinet on his chair and goes into the dining room. I hear him beginning to clear the table.

Bennett jumps up and rushes off to help him.

I don't know what to say to Neeve, so I merely take his hand and give it a squeeze.

He turns to look at me.

"Did you like it?" he asks under his breath.

"Oh yes," I whisper back. "It was heartbreakingly beautiful."

By this time the parents have recovered from whatever they were experiencing.

Mrs. Taylor comes over and puts Jeremy's clarinet beside the trumpet on Bennett's chair so she can sit down next to Neeve.

"That was incredible," Mrs. Taylor says. "Why didn't you tell us you were a musician?"

Tapping the side of his head, Neeve answers, "Memory problems. I didn't remember until Jeremy brought up the subject of music that first evening I came here to dinner." He grins a little. "After that, well, I didn't want to ruin the surprise."

Mrs. Taylor laughs. "As far as surprises go, I've got to admit that was one of the best. Where did you get the violin?"

Of course that's Mom's cue.

She begins by telling Mrs. Taylor about hearing Neeve play and wanting to give him her violin.

"It's very generous of you," Mrs. Taylor says, "but not all of the boys in our care have good boundaries. I would hate for you to give Neeve the violin and have it end up destroyed."

"Surely there's a solution," Dad says. "It's a shame for someone as gifted as Neeve not to have access to an appropriate musical instrument."

Mom nods. "At first I wanted to give him the violin simply because he plays it so well, much better than I did even when I was at my best. But after hearing a sample of his compositional skills, good heavens, the boy belongs at Julliard. In lieu of that, he at least needs a violin of his own so he can develop and explore his talents."

167

# Echoes: A Modern Fairytale

Mrs. Taylor returns to the couch and puts her hand on her husband's shoulder. "What do you think, Brian?"

Soon all four adults are trying to figure out how to allow Neeve to accept the violin without putting the instrument at risk.

"Let's go help Jeremy and Bennett," I suggest softly to Neeve.

He puts the violin in its case before he gets up.

In the kitchen we discover that the boys have not only cleared the table but have also filled the dishwasher.

"I've decided not to do 'Bugle Call Rag,'" Jeremy tells us. "It would be anticlimactic after Neeve's solo, but I still want to do 'La Vie En Rose.' We began the program together. I think we should end it together."

Bennett nods.

I smile.

"Let's do it," Neeve says.

We enter the living room in a line, Bennett first because his chair is at the far end. He picks up his trumpet and Jeremy's clarinet and stands in front of his seat. When Jeremy joins him, Bennett hands the clarinet to him. Next comes Neeve.

The guys all remain standing until I'm in place, then they sit down in unison.

The parents stop talking and watch us.

Without any introduction Bennett begins. He is just a kid but he plays the trumpet like a pro.

When Neeve takes over on the violin, I begin to sing.

I know there are other people in the room, but I sing only to Neeve. It is my reply to the question he asked at the end of his piece.

Jeremy and Bennett come in strong as they join Neeve for the build up to a powerful climax. At the height of the music Neeve and Jeremy stop playing and let Bennett do the last few measures alone. He finishes on one pure, clear high note.

There is no English equivalent for the French idiom "la vie en rose."

The literal translation is "life in pink." I've heard people say the closest we can come to it is "a happy life" or "a rosy life." Most Americans try to make it match one of our own idioms, "Looking at life through rose colored glasses."

But it's more than that.

I have a friend in Chicago whose family spent three years in France before she started high school. I asked her once what the expression meant. She said that when everything is exactly as it should be, joyous and fulfilled, that's "la vie en rose," that's life in pink.

I hope she's right, because that describes how I feel tonight.

The parents give us a standing ovation.

Jeremy and Bennett take the folding chairs and music stand back

168

downstairs while Neeve sits and talks with his foster parents. Dad and I help Mom get everything set up so dessert can be served.

By the time the Taylors and Neeve leave, they have come up with four possible scenarios that will allow Neeve to accept the violin safely. Mrs. Taylor will explore them, and then she and Detective Taylor will decide which is the most feasible.

# Chapter Twenty-six

With the recital out of the way, Neeve and I actually plan to work on our research paper Saturday morning. When he arrives at the house, he is bursting with excitement. "Where's your mother?" he asks.

"Kitchen," I say.

He heads that way, and I follow.

Mom is filling the dishwasher, but she pauses when she sees Neeve.

He goes to her and kisses her hand.

"Janet has arranged an audition for me with Mr. Chandler, the orchestra teacher, Monday morning before school. He said they were badly in need of someone for First Chair. Thank you so much."

As Mom offers her congratulations, I'm thinking that Neeve obviously knows very little about the rivalry and jockeying for position among musicians.

He's not going to be too popular in the orchestra's string section if he comes in as a brand-new violinist and automatically gets First Chair.

Although Mom is smiling, she has a slight crease between her eyebrows, and I suspect she's thinking the same thing. Like me, she chooses not to mention it. No need to rain on Neeve's parade. He'll learn soon enough.

He and I go to the library.

The same woman is at the checkout counter who was there before.

I ask if there are any free study rooms.

"We're booked really tight today," she tells me.

I guess I shouldn't expect special treatment again, but I do. I must look disappointed, because she comes from behind the counter and motions for us to follow her.

She talks in a whisper as we cross the lobby then go down an aisle between the stacks. "There's an empty room back here. It was used for storing damaged and donated books, but the basement has been remodeled, and all the extra books have been moved downstairs. Admin hasn't decided how to use the space yet. Right now, there's only a small table with a couple of chairs in it."

When she opens the door for us, I'm pleasantly surprised. The room is small, but it's in a corner and has windows on two walls, so it doesn't feel claustrophobic.

"It's perfect," I tell her. "Thank you so much."

After Neeve and I spend a couple of hours writing about the Brothers Grimm, we work on my sensing his aura and reaching out to his soul.

I thought it would be easier after the experience at dinner Thursday, but I guess the missing piece of his spirit doesn't hover around him all the time. Neeve is disappointed. I am too, but I put on an optimistic face for his benefit.


Monday morning the guys pick me up early so I can watch Neeve's audition. When Mom hands him the violin, she kisses him on the cheek for good luck. Neeve looks like he could float to school on a cloud.

I can't believe there's any darkness left inside of him.

I assume that Neeve will play for Mr. Chandler in one of the music rooms.

But no! When we get to school, Neeve is told that his audition will be held in the auditorium. Since it has stadium seating, I have to take the elevator down to the lower level and enter through a side door that opens onto the space between the stage and the first row of seats.

Neeve opts to accompany me.

Waiting for him, seated in the middle of the third row, is the complete musical faculty—Mr. Chandler, orchestra, Ms. Christopherson, band, Mrs. Gilles, choir—plus Mr. Haskell, principal, Mrs. Fulton, vice-principal, and Ms. Granger, school counselor.

I wonder if they're here hoping to see Neeve succeed or fail.

A few students are scattered around the auditorium too, mostly kids who come to school early because their parents drop them off on the way to work.

Students aren't allowed in the classrooms until after the first bell rings, but they have the option of waiting in the cafeteria or in here. The ones who choose the cafeteria are mostly the ones who want to meet with their friends and get rowdy. The ones who prefer the auditorium generally read, play games, or listen to music on a variety of electronic devices with their earbuds effectively shutting out the rest of the world.

There is a short staircase on each side of the proscenium.

Mr. Chandler waves Neeve onto the stage.

Looking calm and composed, Neeve climbs the stairs on the left and takes his place next to a music stand, which is the only object already on stage. He waits until the faculty stops whispering among themselves. Then he steps forward and says, "I'll be playing Caprice No. 24 in A Minor by Paganini."

I'm disappointed. I had hoped he would play something he had written himself, but after a few minutes, I understand his choice. He selected this solo because it demonstrates his mastery of the violin, and it shows that he has been classically trained.

I recognize the piece because David Garrett plays it in *The Devil's Violinist,* a movie about the life of Niccolò Paganini. Although the film is R rated, Mom and Dad let me watch it because of the music and the cultural value.

Briefly I wonder how Neeve came to know something written by an earthling composer, but it's just a fleeting curiosity. He told me part of his royal education had included Earth Studies.

His long fingers dance up and down the length of the violin's neck while he glides the bow across the strings. I am awed.

The faculty members all have that deer-in-the-headlights look: eyes wide, mouths slack, bodies frozen.

No matter what they expected, this isn't it.

When Neeve finishes, he holds his pose for a few seconds before he lowers the violin and the bow. He drops his head forward.

The room is silent.

Probably a full minute passes before Mr. Chandler clears his throat. "On the music stand you'll find the sheet music for Violin Concerto in E Major by Bach. I'd like you to play the first several measures. I'll tell you when to stop."

Neeve adjusts the height of the stand and then begins to play.

If this is a test of his sight-reading skills, he aces it.

He plays the piece by Bach with the same confidence and ease that he did the one by Paganini.

"That's fine," Mr. Chandler says. His voice sounds calm, but I can tell by his facial expression and his body language that if he had been a little girl he'd have been jumping up and down and squealing.

"How long have you taken lessons?" he asks.

Neeve's facial expression is neutral, and he shrugs. "I'm not sure," he says. "I only recently remembered that I could play at all. My impression, however, is that I started quite young. I seem to recall a very small violin."

Mr. Chandler stands up. "Welcome to orchestra. We meet during the last class of the day. Since you have that time as a study period, it won't interfere with your current schedule. I would like you to play the Paganini piece for the class this afternoon."

"As you wish," Neeve says. "Thank you." He dips his head again and leaves the stage. He and I exit the auditorium together.

"How did I do?" he asks as soon as the door closes behind us.

"You were terrific," I say. "You took my breath away." I nod toward the auditorium. "Theirs too, I'd say."

He smiles down at me.

"That was the goal."

As we wander through the halls, waiting for the first bell to ring, we notice that a few "car accident" football players have come back to school.

It's been over a week since that traumatic Friday night.

All of the returning footballers show signs of lingering (but not too serious) injuries: some bruises, a few bandages, a wrist brace, and a little limping.

One of the guys is wearing a whiplash collar, which surprises me because I never even knew he had a neck. Although I'm not a great football fan, and I was in the hospital or rehab center for most of the season, I think I remember someone pointing this guy out and saying he was the fullback. He's so big that his head just sort of flows into his shoulders, which makes the whiplash collar look a little extraneous.

All of the footballers appear surly and defensive.

Maybe they're embarrassed that the story in the newspaper exposed their drunkenness.

Or maybe they catch snatches of the whispers that follow them wherever they go, things like: "Serves them right," "It's about time they got caught," "We're lucky football season was over before they did something this stupid."

Conspicuous by his absence is Kenneth Nelson.

He is still in the hospital.

He broke his nose and his jaw, which everyone assumes happened when his face slammed into the steering wheel. He's going to need reconstructive surgery. He also has some internal injuries, as well as a broken arm and some cracked ribs.

Oddly enough, none of the airbags in the three automobiles deployed.

It's a mystery no one understands.

I hear Kenneth Nelson's parents are threatening to sue the manufacturer of the car Kenneth was driving.

One thing makes me uneasy.

As Neeve and I head for World History after lunch, we pass a couple of the football players, and they give us hostile looks.

"Is it possible that they remember some of what happened?" I ask Neeve. "Maybe the false memories that Hayden gave them aren't working."

"I don't know," Neeve says, sounding unconcerned. "Human bodies and human chemistry are very similar to ours, but they're not exactly the same. I suppose Hayden could have miscalculated the depth he needed to implant the memories, but with the alcohol, the marijuana, and the physical injuries, I suspect their memories are fairly scrambled anyway."

"Having them look at me like that scares me," I tell him.

"Don't worry about them," he says. "I doubt they'll be motivated to make much mischief now. They've been humbled."

I tilt my head and look up at him. "One problem with humans is that sometimes after we've been humbled we strike out to prove that we still have power."

"Nevertheless," Neeve says, "I doubt these guys will do anything violent without Kenneth Nelson to goad them along." He flashes an evil grin. "And I expect him to be down at least a couple more weeks, maybe a month."

# Chapter Twenty-seven

On the drive home after school, I ask Neeve about his first day in orchestra.

He pauses to think before he answers.

"At first I was uncomfortable. Mr. Chandler waited for me outside of the orchestra room, and we entered together when the second bell rang. Chairs and music stands were arranged in four rows, with no empty seats, and that seemed odd to me.

"Mr. Chandler introduced me as soon as the normal classroom chatter died down, and then he asked me to play the Paganini piece. I sensed a lot of antagonism coming at me because of First Chair.

"After I finished playing, one of the girls in the violin section stood up, and the whole section moved over one seat. The last person went and got a folding chair that was leaning up against the wall. Mr. Chandler motioned me over to the empty chair, and that was that. The mood in the room was still tense, but not as hostile. I don't understand."

He frowns as he looks over at me.

"What's the significance of First Chair? Do you know?"

"I'm afraid I do," I say. "First Chair in the violin section is reserved for the best violinist in the orchestra. He's also called the concertmaster. He makes sure instruments are tuned up before practices and performances, and all the other violinists match their bowing to his. After a concert he stands and shakes hands with the conductor. It's a position of high-status. Mr. Chandler will meet with you and tell you what your responsibilities are."

"The girl who got up and moved? She was the best until I arrived?"

"Uh huh," I mumble.

Neeve frowns. "I'm not going to be popular for displacing her, am I?"

"Maybe not," I tell him, "but she acknowledged your superiority when she moved down a seat." I pat his hand. "Don't worry. Even the kids who resent you will appreciate how much stronger a good First Chair violinist makes the whole orchestra sound, especially with the Spring Concert coming up."

"I hope you're right." Neeve lifts my hand and kisses my fingers. "It feels great to play again. I almost think I could conquer the darkness with the violin alone."

The next few weeks pass smoothly.

Neeve and I make really good progress on our Brothers Grimm report. Writing their lives' story like a fairytale and illustrating it like a children's book has made the usually boring research process a lot of fun.

During the lunch period, we alternate between working on the quest and eating lunch with Juanita, Maren, Deedra, and John. They all seem to like Neeve, and he seems to like them, too, which makes me feel good. I always resented my friends who dumped me as soon as they got a boyfriend.

When Valentine's Day comes around, instead of going to the Sweetheart Ball at school, Neeve and I double date with Brenlyn and Talitha again. We go to dinner at The Casablanca, the fanciest restaurant in town, and then to a live theatre production of the musical *Once Upon a Mattress* at the University. It's a lovely evening, and I think it is worthy of ending with a kiss on the lips.

Nope.

I go to bed less than happy.

If Neeve doesn't kiss me on Valentine's Day, maybe he never will.

As I drift off to sleep, it occurs to me that kissing on the mouth might be taboo in Neeve's world. If so, I can anticipate many frustrated years ahead of me.

Monday, I have an appointment with my physical therapy team to update my treatment plan. I don't know how to react.

I want to walk. I really do.

But I can't stand up without support.

It hurts to try, and I don't want to hurt anymore. Besides, it's scary and makes me feel vulnerable. As long as I'm in my chair, I feel safe.

They schedule an accelerated gait training session for tomorrow.

When Neeve and Brenlyn pick me up Tuesday morning, I tell them about the PT appointment I have after school today.

"I've got orchestra practice this afternoon," Neeve says.

Brenlyn glances over at me. "There's no reason I can't take you to your appointment," he offers. "If need be, I can pick you up and take you home afterward too."

That's the longest speech I've ever heard Brenlyn make.

"Thank you," I tell him. "Let me call my mother."

After I explain Brenlyn's offer, Mom is clearly relieved.

"Tell him I'd really appreciate it if he drove you over to the hospital, but

I should be finished with my last client by the time your session is over. I can pick you up at the PT unit."

It's all arranged by the time we pull up in front of the school.

Before Brenlyn and Neeve open the van's doors so they can get out and fetch my wheelchair, I clutch at their arms to stop them.

The day I've been dreading has arrived.

Kenneth Nelson gets out of the Suburban that's parked in front of us.

Gossip has been floating around the school, saying that his jaws have been wired shut so the reconstructed bones can heal. I can't tell if it's true from this distance. His left arm is in a cast and he moves awkwardly, but the injuries don't make him look any less intimidating.

Half a dozen of his football buddies climb out of the Suburban right behind him.

I hold onto Neeve and Brenlyn until after the footballers have gone into the school building. The two guys barely get my wheelchair out of the van before we hear the first bell.

I zip up the ramp at top speed, hoping to make it to class before the tardy bell rings. Neeve rushes ahead to hold the door open for me.

We almost run over Kenneth Nelson and his friends. They're in a little cluster right inside the door.

When Kenneth sees me, hatred burns in his eyes.

Neeve and I duck around him.

When I get to my desk in homeroom, just under the bell, I have a new and sudden epiphany.

I understand why the football players have been giving Neeve and me the evil eye, and why Kenneth Nelson glared at me so vilely this morning. Although Hayden implanted false memories of a car accident over the memories of the fight with Neeve, Brenlyn, and Talitha and of my being shot, that was all he did.

That night was so significant to me that it altered my perceptions of life, of reality, of science, of metaphysics, and of the paranormal.

I felt as if everything was different everywhere for everyone.

Actually the only changes were within me.

From the points of view of the football players, on that Friday night, they had been on their way to incapacitate Neeve so Kenneth Nelson could kill me. Then somehow their cars had crashed into each other, and they ended up in the hospital. In their minds they have an unfinished task ahead of them.

When the insight hits me, I begin to shake so hard that Mr. Ullom notices.

"Karissa, are you all right?" he asks.

I can't make my tongue work.

I shake my head.

"Juanita, will you take Karissa to the nurse's office?"

"Yes, Mr. Ullom, " she answers. She stuffs my English book into my backpack and then slips a strap over her shoulder so she can carry it for me. When we're out in the hall, she asks, "Do you want me to call your Mom for you? Or your Dad?"

"No," I tell her. "I'll be all right in a few minutes."

She doesn't look convinced.

"I didn't sleep well last night," I lie. "Maybe if I rest a little while, I'll be okay."

What I really want to do is talk with Neeve.

Juanita walks me to the nurse's office and then goes back to class.

"I just feel a little dizzy," I tell the nurse. "I didn't sleep well, and I had to rush out of the house without eating much. My morning medication always makes me sick if I skip breakfast."

She gives me a couple of packets of saltines.

When I've eaten the crackers, she lets me park my wheelchair in the examination room. She offers to help me onto the table and get me a pillow and a blanket, but I tell her I'm fine where I am.

She turns on a nightlight and turns off the overhead ones.

As soon as she closes the door behind her, I call out to Neeve.

*Are you all right?* his silent voice asks inside my head.

*I just realized why the football players keep staring at us. The last memories they have before the supposed three-car pileup is of them planning to get you out of the way so Kenneth Nelson could shoot me. They're probably trying to decide when to try again.*

Neeve doesn't say anything right away. Then his voice, soft and thoughtful, comes into my mind. *I think you're right, and with Kenneth Nelson back, I imagine it will be soon.*

*What are we going to do?*

*For starters we're going to be extra careful. I'll meet you after all of your classes. I don't want you going anywhere alone. You probably ought to tell your folks that Kenneth Nelson has returned to school. I'll tell Brian and Janet. Has your father met with the principal about the restraining orders yet?*

*Yes, he did it right away. Mr. Haskell wasn't thrilled, but he agreed to enforce the orders to the best of his ability during school hours.*

*At least that's something,* Neeve says. *Let me know when you're ready to leave the nurse's office. I'll meet you there.*

I'm frightened all day.

Going to physical therapy after school is actually a relief.

The therapists support my weight while my feet rest on the floor.

I have a therapist on each side of me, and they help me move so my body will remember how to walk. It feels odd.

I wait for the panic to wash over me as I remember the car accident.

It doesn't come.

Maybe I'm ready to let go of my fears and risk failure in hopes of success. Or maybe I'm just so afraid of being shot again that everything else pales next to it.

Before I leave, Abby Madison, the therapist I like best, tells me that I'm doing well.

"Lots of clients try slowing down at this point," she says, "but I'm not going to let you. So, no excuses for not showing up. I want you to walk out of here on your own two feet. Deal?"

"Deal," I say.

At the dinner table I repeat what she said.

"Does that mean you're going to walk again?" Jeremy asks.

"I hope so," I say. "I'm going to try."

"Can I have your wheelchair?" Bennett asks.

"What on earth would you do with a wheelchair?" Mom wants to know.

"I'd paint it red, put a Chicago Bears pennant on one side and a Denver Broncos pennant on the other, and zip around the neighborhood."

"A wheelchair isn't a toy, Bennett," Dad says.

"Besides," Jeremy inserts, "those two pennants would clash with a red wheelchair. Chicago Bears colors are navy blue and orange and Denver Broncos are royal blue and orange. Instead of those teams, you ought to go with the New York Giants and the Buffalo Bills. Both of them are red, white, and blue. Or if you'd just like to go with blue and white, you've got the Colts and—"

"That's enough, Jeremy," Dad says. "I repeat: a wheelchair is not a toy!"

"Besides," I tell Bennett, "even when I can take a few steps by myself, I'll want the chair for school. My legs aren't very strong, and I'll need time to build up stamina."

Bennett shrugs and returns to eating.

As soon as he's finished, Bennett gets up and takes his plate to the kitchen. It's his turn to clear the table, and he never bothers to make sure everyone else is done. A moment later, Jeremy gets up. It's his turn to fill the dishwasher.

As soon as both my brothers are busy, I tell my parents Kenneth Nelson is back at school.

Mom gives Dad an alarmed look.

"I'll call Mr. Haskell in the morning," Dad says, "and remind him about the restraining orders against Kenneth Nelson and his friends. I might also casually mention our intention to sue if all reasonable precautions aren't taken to keep Karissa safe."

# Chapter Twenty-eight

When Mom drives me to school in the morning, I try not to act like a complete coward. If I let my parents see how afraid I am, they might think I'm overreacting.

Or maybe not.

Detective Taylor told them about the gun.

But they don't know that Kenneth Nelson has shot and almost killed me once already.

Regrettably, I do know it, and I'm terrified.

Neeve escorts me everywhere all day.

Kenneth Nelson and his buddies avoid us like the plague.

When we pass each other in the halls, they don't even look in our direction. Maybe Principal Haskell has put the fear of God into them—or at least the fear of the legal system. But I'm still frightened that they'll ambush us somewhere, like they did before, and Neeve and I won't have Brenlyn and Talitha to help us this time.

My days fall into a routine.

Mom drives me to school.

Neeve walks me to my classes, even second period. While I check in at P.E., he waits and then walks me to the library even though it makes him late to his class. He doesn't get into trouble, so I assume he's doing something magical to prevent being noticed.

Brenlyn takes me home or to physical therapy every day regardless of Neeve's schedule.

On PT days, either Mom or Dad picks me up when my session is over.

The footballers continue to ignore us.

After two weeks of this, Neeve starts to relax. He thinks the guys have given up on their vendetta and we're safe.

"Now that the truth has come out about Kenneth Nelson's threats and bullying," Neeve tells me, "he's probably decided that the risk of getting caught and punished outweighs his desire for vengeance."

I don't believe it.

I'm hypervigilant at school, at home, at physical therapy—everywhere, all of the time.

I can't relax.

I have nightmares.

I jump (figuratively) at shadows.

Neeve's time after school is fully occupied with orchestra. The concert is scheduled for the last Saturday before spring break starts, and he's thrown himself into rehearsals and practicing. He takes his role as First Chair seriously and will not allow himself to make a single mistake. Also he has a solo he has to prepare for.

We get together for a few hours on Sundays so we can finish our World History project on the Brothers Grimm. Since the deadline is almost upon us, we don't have time to discuss other things.

I feel almost as lonely and afraid as I did the first day I came back to school.

"Can't you just touch Kenneth Nelson's mind and see what his intentions are?" I finally ask Neeve in a moment of desperation.

He doesn't answer right away. When he does, he looks embarrassed. "I tried," he says softly, "the first day he came back, and then again the next week, but his soul is as black as Uncle Maldon's. I don't dare try again."

"I'm sorry," I say. "I should've guessed."

He takes my hand and kisses my palm. It seems like a long time since he's done that.

"As soon as the concert is over," Neeve says, "we'll start on the quest again. If I regain the light, neither of us will have anything to fear from Kenneth Nelson or his friends ever again. Divine light can overcome even their darkness."

Days pass.

Talitha starts accompanying Brenlyn when he comes to pick me up in the afternoons. At first, I think she's uncomfortable because Brenlyn is spending so much time with another female. I realize I'm wrong when she begins talking to me about Neeve, about the missing part of his soul, and what will happen if they are not reunited.

"Immersing himself in the music has helped stabilize him for now," Talitha says, "but there will be great danger when this concert is over."

"Why?" I ask.

"Because there will be an emptiness where all the excitement and anticipation of the musical performance has been. Darkness will rush in to fill the void."

"But he'll still have the violin."

"True, but he won't have the same focus. Little problems will become big ones in his mind. He will slip into rages easier than before."

"What can I do to help?" I ask.

Talitha smiles her movie-star-smile at me.

"Perhaps on the afternoons when you don't have physical therapy, we could spend a little time driving around town to see if you can catch the echo of Neeve's soul. Because the music is making him particularly happy right now, it will strengthen the missing part."

Brenlyn interrupts. "It sounds strange to talk about a missing part. It is called the *enaid*. It means *that which will make him whole*. We search for Neeve's *enaid*."

"That does sound more positive, doesn't it?" Talitha says. Then she goes back to complete her thought. "Since the *enaid* will be particularly strong right now, and because Neeve won't be here to distract you, you might be more susceptible to the *enaid's* feel."

She reaches over and takes my hand.

"I wish you could have known him before the mutilation. He was like a beam of sunlight, bringing brightness and warmth to all those around him. Playing the violin is not his only talent. I doubt you've heard him sing or been exposed to his wonderful sense of humor. He is worth every effort we can make to save him."

By touching me, Talitha reinforces her words through her fingertips. In the same way that Neeve's kisses taste like strawberries in my palms, her touch on my hand tastes like lemon honey.

"I'll do everything I can," I say, "but if I find the missing piece—" I stop and correct myself. "If I find Neeve's *enaid*, how do I help them reconnect with each other?"

Talitha hesitates and Brenlyn answers. "When you find it, when it recognizes your bond with Neeve, it will show you the way."

"All right," I say. "When do we start?"

Brenlyn answers again. "As soon as you have made arrangements with your parents so they won't worry if you arrive home a little later than usual."

I call Mom and tell her that I'm going to run an errand with Brenlyn and Talitha and will be home before six o'clock.

No problem.

Neeve and I finish the story and the illustrations for our report. I scan the pictures and insert them into the text. I edit and polish "Lark and the Secret Doorway" and write a brief explanation about how the classic fairytales have influenced my writing. I proofread, make corrections, add the footnotes, put together the bibliography, and print out a copy.

I ask Neeve if he wants to go over the finished product.

"I don't have time right now," he says. "I won't have until after the concert. I promise I'll read it that weekend. The paper's not due until the next Wednesday. We'll have time to correct any mistakes I find." He squeezes

my hand. "I doubt I'll find any, though."
I hardly see Neeve anymore.
I miss him. I hadn't realized how central he's become to my life.
At least I have the time with Brenlyn and Talitha. It helps. Because they are from his world, being with them makes me feel closer to him.
Physical therapy helps to distract me too.
My legs are getting stronger, I can move them if the therapists help support my weight. Awkward baby steps are all I can manage, but six months ago I didn't believe I'd be able to do even that much.

The evening of the concert finally arrives.
My whole family attends.
We sit in the back row where there is room for my wheelchair. It gives us a great view of the stage. In my purse I have the opera glasses that I inherited when my Grandmother Baker died. I brought them so I can focus on Neeve.
I see Detective and Mrs. Taylor enter the auditorium with four teenage boys in tow.
A few minutes later, Brenlyn and Talitha come in and sit just across the aisle from us. I have the opportunity to introduce them to my parents and brothers.
The lights dim and the curtains open.
The orchestra is arranged on tiers in an arc that covers nearly the entire stage. An aisle down the middle divides it into two halves. Everyone is dressed in black. The guys wear black suits, white shirts, and black bow ties. The girls are in long black dresses. They all look so grown up, so professional.
When the music starts, I'm surprised.
I guess I expected an Easter-themed performance since Easter is only two Sundays away. Instead, Mr. Chandler exposes himself as a true romantic. The orchestra plays some of the most beautiful music ever written.
They start with The Blue Danube by Strauss and then follow it with Rhapsody on a Theme of Paganini Variation 18 by Rachmaninoff.
Next they perform Clair de Lune by Debussy. The girl on the piano is excellent.
Then, on the lighter side, they do a medley of show tunes by Rogers and Hammerstein, and then another medley taken from the music of Andrew Lloyd Webber.
During the applause that follows "All I Ask of You" from *Phantom of the Opera,* I see Neeve get up and leave the stage.
Anxiety floods me.
Has something gone wrong?
Is he sick?
I try to calm myself down

## Echoes: A Modern Fairytale

Maybe he broke a string.

I saw a video on YouTube where David Garrett broke a string during a concert in New York City. At the time, he had been playing a piece called "Asturias," which is a whole lot faster, a whole lot more energetic, than anything written by Andrew Lloyd Webber. Breaking a string in a piece like that makes more sense than breaking one during a love song.

I glance over at Brenlyn and Talitha. They don't seem worried.

I try to spot the Taylors. I can't see them.

Where is Neeve?

My heart starts pounding erratically.

Why hasn't he come back?

The stage lights dim.

A spotlight flickers on.

Neeve, with his hair fanning over his shoulders, gradually comes into view as he ascends a set of stairs from behind the orchestra. When he reaches the top, he begins playing Paganini's Caprice 24. He continues playing as he walks down the aisle between the two sections, slowly moving toward the front of the stage.

The scene resembles the one David Garrett does in *The Devil's Violinist*, except in the movie Garrett (as Paganini) enters the concert hall from the back and walks through the middle of the audience before he climbs the stairs to the proscenium and joins the orchestra.

(One other difference: Neeve's pale wheat-colored hair is perfectly straight and smooth, and in the movie David Garrett's dark brown hair is wavy and artistically mussed.)

The orchestra provides a soft accompaniment, which enhances Neeve's performance without distracting from it.

The sullen, angry, anguished boy from my World History class is gone, replaced by this magnificent, poised, radiant young man.

Neeve said once that he might conquer the darkness inside him with just the violin. Looking at him tonight, I think maybe he's succeeded.

Surely Brenlyn and Talitha's fears are unfounded.

After doing Caprice 24, Neeve returns to his place as First Chair.

The orchestra performs a few more pieces, but I only half hear them.

In my mind's eye, I am still seeing Neeve in the spotlight—his face the countenance of an angel, and his hair a golden halo—as he immerses himself in the genius of Paganini and projects his delight to the audience.

The notes still echo in my mind.

Then the concert is over.

The curtains close to thunderous applause.

They open again.

Neeve stands and shakes hands with Mr. Chandler. The members of the orchestra applaud their conductor, and he nods his head and applauds them.

184

People continue clapping.

I expect the curtains to close again, but they don't.

A girl from the audience takes Mr. Chandler a bouquet of flowers, and without warning there is a stampede of people going up the stairs on both sides of the stage. Never having been to a concert at this school before, I don't know if this is normal or not.

People cluster around Mr. Chandler.

Other groups interact with various musicians.

Admirers, young and old, surround Neeve.

Kids who never paid any attention to him before suddenly speak to him.

I watch a little jealously. Because of my wheelchair, the stairs, and the crowds, I can't get to him to add my congratulations. I'm afraid he'll stay on the stage accepting kudos forever.

I ought to know him better by now.

Neeve steadily works his way through the people and comes straight to me. He is beaming with joy.

"How'd I do?" he asks me.

"Superb!" I tell him. I feel both humble and proud that after all of the attention he's gotten from others that it's my opinion that matters.

Then my family, Brenlyn and Talitha, and the Taylors demand his attention so they can add their praise to all the rest.

Neeve and I spend most of Sunday together at my house. He reviews our paper on the Brothers Grimm and finds two typos. I correct them and reprint those pages. We watch a DVD with Jeremy and Bennett, and Neeve accepts an invitation to join us for an impromptu turkey-hot-dog wiener roast in the backyard.

Spring has come to the Rockies, and although it's still a bit chilly when the wind blows, Dad can hardly wait to pull the propane fueled barbeque grill out of the garage.

While he digs it out from under half a dozen empty boxes, Jeremy and Bennett uncover the patio furniture and wipe it down. I volunteer to put together a relish tray, and Neeve talks Mom into taking him to the grocery store so he can get the ingredients for his favorite fruit salad. They pick up graham crackers, marshmallows, and chocolate bars too.

We have a great time.

Neeve says he's never eaten a Hershey's S'mores before, and the highlight of the evening is watching his face as he takes his first bite. He closes his eyes and looks as if he's been transported to heaven. He eats four of them.

The bleak letdown that Brenlyn and Talitha feared doesn't happen.

The school week after the concert is a short one because of spring break. Mom says they used to call it Easter break, but non-Christians complained, so it was renamed.

On Wednesday, the last day of classes for a week and a half, Neeve and I turn in our research report.

Unlike most of the other students, who have their papers either stapled together or in folders, Neeve and I put ours in a one-inch, three-ring binder. The pages are in plastic paper protectors (odd and even numbered pages are back-to-back) so it can be read like in a book. We named our report "A Grimm Tale of Two Brothers."

At the end of last period Neeve meets me.

We're almost to the front office when he stops abruptly.

"I forgot there's no school tomorrow," he says. "I left the violin in my locker in the orchestra room. I'd like you to take it home with you so I can come over during the break and practice—if that's all right with you."

"Sure," I say.

"Stay here where the staff in the office can keep an eye on you while I run and grab the violin. I won't be more than a minute."

In a blink he's gone.

I wheel a little closer to the office and wait.

Five minutes pass.

Ten minutes pass.

Where is he?

I try to be patient. Maybe he bumped into Mr. Chandler and got talking.

Fifteen minutes pass.

The halls are empty.

Could he have forgotten me and gone outside to wait for Brenlyn?

Twenty minutes.

No. He wouldn't do that.

I edge closer to the front doors.

Thirty minutes.

I see Brenlyn's van. Talitha has the window down and is shading her eyes with her hand, looking at the school. For the first time since I met her, she is frowning.

I push open the door and wheel outside.

Talitha sees me.

She and Brenlyn jump out of the van.

"Where's Neeve?" Brenlyn demands as he rushes toward me.

"I don't know," I say. Tears form in my eyes. "He forgot his violin and went to the orchestra room to get it. He hasn't come back."

"Show me," Brenlyn says.

I lead the way.

Brenlyn walks on my right side and Talitha on my left. I don't know if I should feel like a criminal or a VIP under guard.

When we get to the orchestra room, I'm afraid to pull the double doors open.

Brenlyn steps forward and does it.

Through the opening I can see that the room is a mess. Chairs and music stands are strewn all over. In the middle of the chaos is a pile of rubbish and splatters of red.

Moving closer, I see that the trash is the remains of my mother's violin and case, splintered and smashed.

The red is blood.

# Chapter Twenty-nine

I can't stop crying.

I cry while Talitha pulls a chair over next to me and holds onto my hand, patting it occasionally.

I cry while Brenlyn calls Mrs. Taylor on his cellphone and asks if she's heard from Neeve. I cry while he describes the scene in the orchestra room.

"She's going to call Detective Taylor," Brenlyn says after he disconnects. "She said I should tell the principal that Neeve is missing and that the police are on their way." He looks at Talitha. "Will you be all right? Do you want to—?"

"We'll stay here," she says. "We'll be fine."

"I'll hurry."

Brenlyn props the doors opened with a chair on each side, maybe so he can hear us if we scream, and then dashes down the hall.

"Can you sense Neeve?" Talitha asks me. "You've practiced listening for his echo. Can you feel him?"

I shake my head.

The tears flow harder, and I cover my face with my hands.

Talitha grabs me by the shoulders.

"Stop that," she says. "I know you're worried and you're frightened, but the crying isn't helpful. Soon this room will be crowded with people, and it'll be hard for you to concentrate. Calm yourself. Reach out to Neeve. The blood on the floor is his. I can sense that much. I need you to tell me if he's still alive."

I feel as if she's thrown a bucket of cold water over me.

Does she think Neeve is dead?

As soon as I saw the overturned chairs, I knew Kenneth Nelson and his gang had jumped Neeve and he'd fought back. I was afraid he was hurt somewhere, and I didn't know how to find him.

Never once did it occur to me that they might have killed him.

I wipe the tears away with the sleeve of my sweater. I dig through my purse until I find a packet of tissues so I can blow my nose. I sniff and gulp a couple of times.

I stop crying.

"That's better," Talitha says. "Close your eyes and concentrate on the feel of Neeve's mind. I know you and he have talked to each other silently. Reach out to him."

I close my eyes. *Neeve, can you hear me?*

Silence.

I try to shout mentally. *Neeve! Can you hear me?* I pause.

I shout again. *Neeve, damn it! Answer me!*

A weak whisper sounds in my head. *Karissa?*

*Yes. Where are you?*

*I don't . . . I don't . . .*

His mental voice fades, but I still sense his personality or his life force or his—his something.

"He's alive," I tell Talitha. "He responded when I called to him, but then he stopped. I think he passed out. He didn't die."

She slips her arm around my shoulders and gives me a squeeze. "Thank you."

"Can't you touch his mind?" I ask her. "He told me that your people don't really need oral speech, that you use it as a courtesy so you don't violate each other's privacy."

"Not all of our people can speak mentally," Talitha says. "Luckily, I am one and so is Brenlyn, but it is not always a safe way to communicate. Right now, the violence will have stimulated the darkness inside Neeve, and if I open myself to him, he could grab onto my mind like a drowning man will clutch at anything. The evil could overwhelm me. It could possess me.

"You're in no danger," Talitha continues, "because of how he feels about you. Love comes from divine light. Darkness has to grow very strong before it can overcome love. However, if we don't find him in time, the darkness will devour everything positive that's inside him, including his love for you."

We are interrupted when Brenlyn returns.

Principal Haskell and Mr. Chandler are right behind him.

A few minutes later, Detective Taylor arrives. He has a woman with him. He introduces her as Officer Brewster. Two other uniformed officers follow them in, but no one bothers to tell us their names.

Detective Taylor asks me to describe everything that happened at school today. Then he wants to know if I've seen anyone hanging around here or at home or at the library, someone who didn't seem to belong or who kept popping up in odd places.

"Like who?" I ask.

"Like anyone suspicious," Detective Taylor says. "It might have been an electrician or a delivery man or even a jogger who looked out of place.

Whoever took Neeve knew he was here."

"It wasn't a stranger," I tell him. "It was Kenneth Nelson and his friends. They were all in school today. I imagine since Neeve's performance at the concert they realize he has orchestra last period."

Detective Taylor looks at me like I'm naive. "I think it's more likely that the Satanists who tortured Neeve last fall have found him again."

"You're wrong," I insist. "I'll bet if you check, you'll find out that no one knows where Kenneth Nelson and his gang are right now."

Although Detective Taylor clearly has his own hypothesis, he tells someone to track down Kenneth Nelson and his friends.

There are two positive aspects of Detective Taylor's erroneous theory about the Satanists: (1) he is sure they will kill Neeve this time and (2) he is determined not to let that happen.

I sit in my wheelchair and watch Officer Brewster paw through the sheet music in Neeve's locker, which is still open. The orchestra lockers are about half the size of the ones that line the hallways, more like lockers you'd find at a private gym or at a public swimming pool.

Officer Brewster asks Mr. Chandler something, and I hear him tell her that not all orchestra members have individual lockers because there aren't enough to go around. Some students have to share. Neeve has a private locker because he keeps—or kept—his violin in it overnight.

Time blurs.

I go numb.

I don't know who calls my parents.

Suddenly Dad shows up and takes me home.

Thursday is the first day of spring break.

I sit in my room and search for Neeve with my mind.

I get quick flashes of information, but no words. He is in a building that is open to the elements but does not let in much light. He smells trees and water and small animals.

His arms are bound behind his back, but he is upright, tied to something that supports most of his weight.

He is thirsty and hungry.

Occasionally, just when I think I'm about to make verbal contact with Neeve, he experiences a sudden burst of pain, and his consciousness flees from me. Whenever that happens, I start crying again.

Kenneth Nelson is hurting him, and Neeve doesn't want me to know how much. I recognize Kenneth Nelson as the perpetrator. I can feel his presence and the evil that emanates from him. I sense a couple of his buddies too.

Neeve told me that Kenneth's soul is as black as the soul of his Uncle Maldon. I understand now. The blackness of their souls is not like the darkness that is growing inside Neeve. I've seen Neeve's rage and I've seen

190

his despair, and they are clean, honest feelings that result from his circumstances.

Maldon and Kenneth Nelson have muddy, vile, nasty souls because they take delight in the physical pain and the emotional turmoil of other people. Also, they don't get their enjoyment from passively watching misfortunes (like I'd enjoy seeing Kenneth Nelson hit by a train). They go out of their way to make bad things happen.

I've never hated before, not really, even though I've said that I did.

But I hate Kenneth Nelson with every fiber of my being.

For the first time in my life I understand the impulse to murder.

In the afternoon, I don't want to go to physical therapy, but Dad makes me. While the PTs take me through my exercises and then get me on my feet, I daydream about all the things I would do to Kenneth Nelson if I could walk.

Friday morning, I touch Neeve's mind.

He tries to say something to me, but he can't seem to organize his thoughts.

Instead I get a strawberry flavored kiss in my palm.

Then there is a sudden burst of pain, quickly followed by fury.

Neeve withdraws.

As hard as I try for the rest of the day, I don't get any response from him. He's still alive, but he is moving farther and farther away from me.

I start crying and can't stop.

I'm still crying when my parents come home from work.

Mom comes into my room, kneels down by my wheelchair, and gathers me in her arms. I lean against her and sob.

A little while later, Dad comes in with a bowl of chicken noodle soup and some crackers on a tray.

I can't eat.

Somehow I make it through another night.

Saturday I have physical therapy at nine o'clock in the morning. The session will be a long one because they are taking me to the pool.

After enduring the indignity of having a physical therapist, a female at least, help me put on a swimming suit, I finally get to slide into the water.

It is warm, and the buoyancy feels great.

Even though they won't let me just take off and swim laps, they help me stand and then walk me around a bit. They let me float and then walk me around some more. Before they take me out, they let me swim for a while. It feels so good to move under my own power.

It's over too soon.

Then I have to go through more indignity while the therapist helps me get the wet swimming suit off.

Before the accident, no one had seen me completely naked since I was old enough to take baths without my mother in the room to make sure I didn't drown. Since the accident, there have been doctors, nurses, interns, physical therapists—I don't know who else. I just have to turn off my brain and not think about it.

One nicety is that there is a heat lamp in the changing room, so I don't get chilled between the time I start peeling off my bathing suit and the time I am dry and dressed again.

On the way home I realize I'm hungry for the first time since Neeve was taken. Swimming has always had that effect on me.

After lunch, I'm ready to isolate in my bedroom to see if I can make contact with Neeve.

The doorbell rings. I turn around so I can answer it.

Standing on the doorstep is Talitha.

"Brenlyn and I are going for a drive. I thought you might enjoy getting out of the house for a while. Would you like to come with us?"

I hear the breath of a whisper in my mind. It's Talitha. *Please say yes.*

By this time, both of my parents have appeared.

"Talitha and Brenlyn have invited me to go for a drive," I tell them. "I think it might be good for me to get out of my room for a few hours. Do you mind?"

"I think it's a good idea," Mom says.

"Take your cellphone," Dad instructs, "so we can call you if we need to reach you for some reason."

"I will, Dad." I glance at Talitha. "Just let me grab my purse."

"How is she doing?" I hear Talitha ask.

"She cries a lot," Mom answers. "I don't suppose you've heard anything from the police or the Taylors?"

"No," Talitha says, "but we're very fond of Neeve, and we're praying for his safe return."

I don't hear the rest of the conversation because I decide I'd better take a moment to use the bathroom. Since I don't know what Talitha and Brenlyn have planned, I don't know what kind of facilities will be available later.

I wash my hands, grab my purse, and wheel back out to the hall.

Talitha is gone.

"I told her you'd go out the side door because of the ramp," Dad says. "She's waiting in the van."

"Thanks, Dad. I'll be back in a few hours."

When I get to the van, I expect to sit in the back seat like I usually do when Talitha is with Brenlyn while he drives me somewhere. But Talitha gets out and has me slide into the front. She helps Brenlyn put my wheelchair in the back, and then she climbs in next to me so I'm sandwiched between her and her husband.

As Brenlyn backs out of the driveway, I ask, "What is it you want me to do?"

Talitha takes hold of my hand. "We want you to try to sense Neeve's *enaid* again. Just as his happiness strengthened it, his misery will weaken it. If you concentrate on Neeve, if you focus on all the things you love about him, you might draw his *enaid* to you. Neeve has been wherever he is for three days. Right now there is probably more of Neeve's essence in you than there is left in him."

Moisture threatens to well up in my eyes as I think of Neeve suffering for three days, but I push the tears away. As Talitha pointed out before, crying isn't helpful.

"While Brenlyn drives," Talitha continues, "I'll try to link my mind with yours if you'll let me. With you focusing on the goodness you've seen in Neeve recently and me focusing on what he was like before the mutilation, hopefully we'll become a beacon for his *enaid* and attract it to you."

"All right," I say.

I don't know what to expect when she links our minds. Surprisingly it's like I can taste the same lemon honey flavor that I get when she holds my hand, except I taste it inside my skull just behind my eyes.

If I think too much about tasting through my skin or within my head, I fear my brain might explode. I simply have to accept the fact that sensory input from Neeve and his people is unusual by human standards.

"I thought I'd just crisscross through town," Brenlyn says. "Does that sound all right to you?"

"It sounds fine." I don't have any better ideas.

"Think about Neeve," Talitha tells me.

I do. I think about the first time he smiled at me. I think about his playing every musical instrument in our house the first time he came to dinner. I think about his cooking. I think about the fun we had writing and illustrating "A Grimm Tale of Two Brothers." I think about his playing Paganini's Caprice 24 at his audition and again at the concert.

I think about his golden wheat-colored hair fanning out over his shoulders and how much I want to run my fingers through it to see if it is as silky as it looks. I think about his emerald green eyes and how easily I drown in their depths. I think about his strawberry kisses in the palms of my hands. I think about how loving and gentle he is, and how protective of me.

In these moments of recollection I feel as close to Neeve as I did at the dinner table when his *enaid* touched me and then appeared between us. I remember its beauty, and I yearn for its return.

All of a sudden I know where it is.

"Brenlyn," I say softly, "head toward the Taylors' house. We need to go to the park that's in their neighborhood."

He takes the next right turn.

# Chapter Thirty

When we get to the park, we find families picnicking, children running and playing, teenagers tossing a Frisbee. They're taking advantage of the beautiful spring weather.

"It's here somewhere," I say. "It's attracted to the happiness, the playfulness, and the laughter."

Brenlyn and Talitha get my chair from the back of the van.

I can't help being amused every time I watch them do it.

I know that either one of them could pick it up alone—maybe with one hand tied behind his or her back. The night I got shot, Talitha picked up the chair with me still in and carried me into Neeve's world.

I wonder how hard it is for them to pretend to be human.

Once I'm in my chair, I start rolling through the park, trying to keep my happy memories of Neeve in my mind while I reach out to his *enaid*.

It brushes against me.

I feel it before I see it.

Then there it is, right in front of me, sparkling like a spiral galaxy.

It is still beautiful, but it's not quite as radiant as it was before.

It starts to move away.

*Stay with me,* I think as hard as I can. *I love Neeve, and that means I love you too. You're part of him.*

It's afraid.

It knows something is wrong.

*Neeve is lost right now, but we'll find him. When we do, I'll reunite you. But you have to stay with me. Neeve and I have been searching for you. Neeve wants you back as much as you want him. I'm the link that can bring you together.*

It is listening to me, but it is still afraid.

It wants to believe.

It wants to belong.

All of a sudden I realize I'm dealing with a child's fear.

The part of Neeve that allows him to experience divine light is the innocence of childhood—it is the part of him that recognizes the joys, the wonders, the miracles, and the marvels of life.

I stretch out my arms.

*Don't be afraid,* I tell it. *I'll keep you safe until you and Neeve are united. Come with me. Let me protect you.*

It rushes at me in the same way that a lost child might run to a sympathetic stranger who offers help.

When it hits me, I am surrounded by Neeve, a sweet, gentle, joyous, loving boy full of music and art, dancing and flying.

I wrap my arms around myself as if I could hug Neeve's *enaid* closer.

Talitha whispers to Brenlyn so softly that I almost don't hear her musical voice.

"She has it," she says.

# Chapter Thirty-one

I wake up Easter morning feeling as if I could soar without wings.

Neeve's *enaid* stayed with me all night long. I was afraid that it would drift away while I slept.

I don't know if it understands what I think, but maybe it understands what I feel. It doesn't communicate with me using words, only images and emotions.

For some reason I feel confident that, together, Neeve's *enaid* and I can find and save him, body and soul. I focus on that thought as I pull myself out of bed and into my wheelchair.

Even though my family isn't very religious and our church attendance is spotty at best, we usually make an appearance on Mother's Day, Easter, and Christmas.

Today I want to go.

I want to pray for Neeve.

Even though I know I can pray at home, or anywhere else actually, I've always thought prayers probably reached heaven easier if they were launched from a place of worship.

Mom makes us a nice late breakfast, and then we all put on our best clothes so we can go to afternoon services.

My brothers wear their seldom-used suits, and I wear the pretty blue dress Mom bought for me when the Taylors came to dinner. Since my parents usually wear suits to work, in order to make their wardrobes seem more spring-like, Dad wears a pastel striped tie with his gray suit and Mom chooses a pink silk blouse to wear with her beige suit, which has a skirt instead of trousers.

My favorite part of all church services is the music. I suppose most people feel that way, even when the minister gives a superlative sermon. Today's sermon is only so-so, but the choir is excellent and the congregation gets to sing three songs too.

While people are filing out of the chapel and my parents are talking with

196

the minister, I whisper to Jeremy. "I need to use the restroom. Tell Mom and Dad that I'll meet you guys in the foyer."

After I come out of the ladies room, I hear a voice in my ear. "Don't make a sound if you ever want to see your boyfriend again."

I slowly turn my head, and there bent over beside my chair is Godzilla, Kenneth Nelson's huge friend.

"There's a side door on your left," Godzilla says. "We're going out that way—no muss, no fuss—or lover boy won't make it through the day."

I know if I go with him I'll die, but I try to be brave. If I can save Neeve in the process, it'll be worth it, especially if I can reunite him with his *enaid* first.

At least that's the way I feel right now.

I don't know how I'll feel while I'm actually dying. However, I've nearly died twice already in less than a year. Maybe it'll be easier this time since I've had so much practice.

We go out the side door of the church.

The faded red Mustang is waiting for us with two guys in the front seat and one in the back. I had assumed the Mustang was destroyed in the three-car pileup, but I suppose it was left behind that night because it is so recognizable. I certainly would have paid more attention to what was happening on that life-changing Friday if I had spotted the Mustang following us.

Godzilla pulls me out of my wheelchair and throws me into the backseat of the car, wedging me between himself and Kenneth Nelson. They leave my wheelchair there in the church parking lot.

What Godzilla doesn't notice is that when he grabs me I manage to slobber on the sleeve of his shirt. When I slam into Kenneth Nelson, air whooshes out of my lungs and I spray him with spit also.

As I push myself away from Kenneth, I plant my palms flat on the vinyl seat, making sure each fingertip makes contact. I'm trying to leave as much evidence as possible on my kidnappers and in the car. Hopefully it will help the police figure out what happened to me and what probably happened to Neeve too.

Detective Taylor might have thought Satanists grabbed Neeve on Wednesday, but I don't think he'll believe they had a reason to grab me four days later. As soon as my parents find my wheelchair, they'll be on the phone with him. I'm certain they'll convince him to start his investigation by locating Kenneth Nelson and his bullyboy friends.

I mentioned the Mustang to Mr. Taylor right before I showed him the shoebox full of nasty notes I received in the hospital. If he puts two and two together and accurately gets four, I want him to know I was here.

None of the guys in the car say anything.

Fine.

# Echoes: A Modern Fairytale

I don't have anything to say to them either. My mind is racing a hundred miles a minute—that's a stupid expression, I realize. There's no way to measure how fast I'm thinking, but I'm going as fast as I can.

Suddenly, it occurs to me that maybe I can reach Talitha. I close my eyes and shout as loud as I can mentally.

*Talitha! The guys who took Neeve have me. They grabbed me from the church on Maple Drive. We're headed out of town going east on Highway 50. We're in a faded red Mustang. There are four guys in the car with me. The driver's name is Tolliver Jones. I think it's his car. Kenneth Nelson is here too. I don't know the names of the other two guys.*

The car hits a bump, and I throw myself forward so my face hits the back of the driver's seat. It hurts, but it's more evidence. As I try to regain my balance, I leave fingerprints on the backs of both bucket seats.

I call with my mind, again, and tell the Talitha the same information. I don't know if she can hear me. I listen for her mental voice, but between the racket that the Mustang's engine is making and the thumping of my heart, if she answers, I don't hear her.

The Mustang turns onto an overgrown gravel road.

The car shivers and shakes as it bumps over deep ruts.

"Almost there." Kenneth Nelson says his first words to me. His jaws are wired shut, so he sort of slurs, but I understand him well enough.

*Talitha, we've made a right-hand turn off the highway onto a narrow gravel road that's almost completely overgrown with weeds. I think it used to be a driveway. You can see the tire ruts if you're looking for them. At the turn off, at the beginning of the road, is a crumbling, square, brick pillar about three feet high. It might have been a mailbox stand at one time.*

The trees are thick enough to block the sunlight, and I shiver as we drive through them into twilight.

Godzilla puts his arm around me and pulls me against him. He leans over and licks my ear.

I want to vomit.

Kenneth Nelson slugs him. "Leave her alone."

"Come on. Let's have a little fun with her before we toss her to the maniac."

"Don't you watch any police shows on television?" Kenneth Nelson snarls. "You don't want to leave your DNA on her, do you? No matter what happens next, there will be an investigation. Do you want it to lead the police straight to you?"

"We'll tell them we were somewhere else," Godzilla says. "There'll be four of us telling the same story. They'll have to believe us."

"Not if they find your slobber all over her."

With a sulky pout, Godzilla takes a quick swipe at my ear with the sleeve of his shirt. He is none too gentle, and certainly not at all thorough.

198

"Maybe they don't need to find her," Tolliver Jones says, turning to look into the backseat over his shoulder. "I think we ought to come back tomorrow, pour gasoline all over the place, and set it on fire. It ought to burn great with all that old wood scattered around. Then all the evidence will fry—including the bodies. What do you think?"

"It's worth considering," Kenneth Nelson says.

The car pulls to a stop in front of an abandoned church.

*Talitha,* I call, *the road leads to a dilapidated old church. I'm sure the police will know about it. It looks like the kind of place where college kids would come to party and try to scare each other. Find a way to tell Detective Taylor: Highway 50 going east, crumbling brick pillar marks the turn onto an overgrown gravel driveway. It leads to a deserted church.*

I keep describing what I see in hopes that, if the police don't immediately recognize which church we're in, someone will be able to figure it out if they have enough information. Or maybe I want to focus on communicating with Talitha in order to keep from thinking about what's going on in the here and now.

*The steeple looks as if it has been struck by lightening. Most of the roof is gone, and there are big holes in the walls. Bits of broken glass look like jagged teeth in the window frames. The front door is off its hinges.*

The guys get out of the car.

After Godzilla climbs out, he grabs me and tosses me over his shoulder like a sack of potatoes. I slobber down the back of his shirt. I pray the CSI television shows are based on reality and the police will collect and test the clothing of the suspects.

Kenneth Nelson leads the way.

Godzilla and the two guys from the front seat fall in behind.

I can barely sense Neeve within the church. There is so little light left inside of him. I try not to envision what they've been doing to him since Wednesday afternoon.

Spring break was supposed to be a fun time for us, a week and a half of freedom from school. Instead of sleeping late and then hanging out at my house, Neeve has spent the past four days in agony, and his anger has almost driven him insane.

His *enaid* is afraid. I feel it fleeing from me.

*No,* I cry. *Stay with me. He needs you now more than ever. I'll find a way to reunite you. When you're with Neeve again, you'll both be whole. You'll both be safe.*

It hesitates.

*Trust me,* I plead. *I'll find a way to make it right. I promise.*

It doesn't return to me, but it doesn't flee either. I have just the tiniest tingle of hope.

We enter the church.

199

Debris litters the floor, and a few rickety pews still stand.

There isn't much light.

One of Kenneth Nelson's buddies flips on a flashlight.

He shines it into the deep shadows at the front of the chapel.

I see Neeve.

He looks as if he's suspended in the air.

In actuality, he is tied to a pulpit that's on a dais five steps high. He is facing the door. There are ropes wrapped around his body. They disappear into the shadows behind him.

He is covered with blood.

His clothing is in tatters.

His eyes are wild.

He howls and struggles against his bonds.

Darkness surrounds him like a shroud.

"Oh, Neeve," I whisper as I fight back the tears.

"Put her on the front bench," Kenneth Nelson says.

Like a good little robot, Godzilla does as he's told.

Kenneth Nelson sits down beside me. The rickety pew creaks.

"This is the situation, wheelchair girl," he says. "No one is going to make you pay for killing Josie unless I do it."

He has trouble enunciating his words with his jaws wired shut, but I'm listening hard to make sure I don't miss anything.

"I figure for things to be fair, you need to watch your boyfriend die just like I had to watch Josie die. He's stronger than she was, though, and it's taken us a while to soften him up."

He takes a gun from his pocket and turns it around in his hands.

"At first I was going to leave the gun with you. It's got one bullet in it. I figured you could take pity on your lover and put him out of his misery, or you could kill yourself out of guilt. But I decided that would be too easy.

"He can't last much longer. After he dies, you get to sit here and watch the flies and the crows and the other carrion feeders feast on him while you wait for thirst and exposure to take care of you."

He looks at me with loathing. "It's not enough to make up for Josie's death, but it'll have to do. I'm through with you now." He stands up and tells his buddies, "Give her the flashlight. He probably won't make it through another night, and we don't want her to miss the show, do we? In fact, give her two flashlights in case she needs one for backup."

A flashlight is shoved into my hand. The other drops onto my lap.

By the beam of a third one, Kenneth Nelson motions to his gang, and they file out.

# Chapter Thirty-two

I shine the light in Neeve's direction, but not into his eyes like Kenneth Nelson's buddy did.

He is slumped forward.

His chin rests on his chest.

His eyes are closed.

"Neeve," I call to him. He doesn't reply. "Neeve, can you hear me? Are you conscious?"

He growls, not a human growl, not even an animal growl.

It's more of a demonic growl.

He opens his eyes. The green is gone. His irises are completely black. Where the whites of the eyes should be, it's all red.

"Neeve," I say, "fight the darkness. Don't let it win. Think about playing the violin. Remember how happy it made you. Think of your mother. She loves you so much. Please, Neeve, don't die in the dark. So many people love you. I love you."

He struggles against the ropes that hold him. I don't need telepathic skills to feel the anger, the hatred, the darkness, and the pain.

I don't know what to do.

I don't know how to reach him.

I don't even know if I should try.

If he pushes back the darkness, won't the horror of his situation be worse? If he doesn't have the darkness to sustain him, won't he feel helpless, hopeless, and weak?

All I can think of is to offer what comfort I can.

I start to sing "La Vie En Rose."

With all the longing in my soul, I try to convey my feelings for him, to thank him for bringing magic into my life, to thank him for making the past months as close to heaven on earth as possible, to thank him for filling my heart with this new and wonderful love.

*Karissa.* I barely hear the whisper of his voice in my mind.

"Neeve."

*Don't mourn me,* he says. *Death will be a release. I want it to come. I can't fight the darkness anymore. It's won.*

"No, it hasn't," I insist, barely holding back the tears. "You're still fighting the battle. Despite everything Kenneth Nelson and his gang have done to you, I can still feel your goodness."

*I wish you were right, but the only thing that's kept me from ripping Kenneth Nelson into small pieces is the rope that binds me. If I were free, I don't even know if I could stop myself from hurting you. I feel a great need to lash out, to destroy, to kill. Brenlyn's father should have executed me as soon as he found me. Then at least I would have gone straight to the light.*

I start to cry.

I don't know if I'll ever stop.

*Sing to me again, Karissa. Maybe you'll kindle a tiny spark of light inside me. I don't want to spend eternity in the darkness.*

I howl at him. "You don't get to make me love you and then leave me behind. We'll both die tonight. We'll either go into the light together or we'll go into the dark together."

*No, Karissa. You have to—*

Suddenly I'm angry. How dare he just give up!

Dad says that emotions like anger, sadness, and fear are misunderstood and often condemned, but they aren't necessarily bad. They can be self-protective and motivating. He says the problem comes when people don't know how to use the feelings constructively.

Kenneth Nelson's hatred of me comes from his sorrow over Josie Peters' death and his anger at her for leaving him. If he had better coping skills, or if he'd had someone like my dad to help him deal with his painful sentiments, he wouldn't have to take them out on Neeve and me. (I'll admit knowing this doesn't make me feel any better about our current situation.)

I remind myself of these facts at this time because I am so irritated with Neeve. I'll admit I'm mad because I'm scared, but that's all right. I have a father who's a shrink. I know I can use the anger to make me strong.

I pull myself to the end of the pew where there is an armrest.

Since the physical therapists have accelerated my gait training, my legs have gotten stronger. I can stand briefly without assistance. I can hold onto the parallel bars and take several baby steps. I've even taken a few steps with just one PT holding my hand for balance.

I don't know how much I can do alone.

But I've never been more motivated to find out.

I flip on the second flashlight and put them both on the pew aimed in Neeve's direction.

Twisting at the waist, I grab the back of the bench with my right hand while I hold onto the armrest with my left. I pull with my right arm while I push with the left.

My body lifts from the pew.

I swing my right leg around the end of the pew and get my foot planted. I carefully shift my center of gravity so my foot is supporting part of my weight. I move my left hand to the back of the bench. Now, I can hold on with two hands, and my arms can bear most of the load while I get my lower body aligned. I lift my left leg and bring in around so it is beside the right. I shift my weight so my left leg is helping support me. I am now standing sort of hunched over facing the end of the bench.

I twist again and aim my feet in the correct direction.

I am still holding onto the back of the pew with both hands.

I'm scared.

My legs atrophied while they were in casts, while I was bedridden, and while I was wheelchair bound.

I haven't had time to rebuild much muscle.

My legs tremble.

*Karissa!* Neeve's voice comes into my mind. *The floor is covered with trash. If you fall, you'll hurt yourself—maybe seriously. I'm proud of you. I always knew you'd walk again. But now isn't the time. Sit back down.*

There is nothing like having someone think he can boss me around to make me really, really angry—which makes me less scared.

I let go of the pew with my left hand and pull myself erect.

I let go with my right hand.

I am balanced on my feet.

Baby steps. I remind myself to take baby steps.

I attempt to lift my right foot. I begin to lose my balance and I grab onto the back of the pew.

*Karissa, don't!*

I get my weight centered over my feet again.

I take one shuffling step forward then another. Then two more.

Breathing heavily, I pause. I'm too far forward to grab the pew again.

I shuffle another two steps.

When I move my right foot forward again, I come up against something solid. I don't dare dip my head to see what it is, or I'll lose my balance. I slide my foot to the side. I hit something else solid.

I slide my left foot in the other direction. The path seems clear that way. I sidestep until I'm past the obstacle.

I shuffle forward. I'm halfway to the pulpit.

My knees quiver.

I stop and breathe.

My legs buckle.

I land hard on my stomach.

It takes me a couple of seconds to catch my breath. I hear Neeve struggling against the ropes that bind him.

*Karissa!* His mental tone is full of anguish. *How badly are you hurt?*

"I'm all right," I say. I don't know how true my answer is. I have a burning sensation in a couple of places on each of my legs. I might have landed on some glass.

Carefully I brush at the debris on the floor, sweeping it away from my sides and from in front of me. I pull myself forward using my forearms.

I get more burning sensations in my legs.

I can't quit.

I feel the damage I'm doing to my arms.

I don't care.

I have to get to Neeve.

I inch forward.

I'm getting closer.

When I reach the bottom of the dais, I pull myself onto the first step. I slump to the side and rest.

*You silly, brave, remarkable girl,* Neeve says. *How I love you!*

*I love you too,* I think back at him.

Even though my strength is failing, I pull myself up the rest of the stairs. Anger isn't the only motivating emotion—love works just fine too.

Leaning my back against the bottom of the pulpit, I wrap my hand around Neeve's ankle. I feel him trembling.

I close my eyes. Now that I'm here, what am I supposed to do?

Twinkling lights flicker against my eyelids. I force my eyes to open. Dancing only inches away from my face is Neeve's *enaid.*

In my effort to reach Neeve, I had forgotten about it.

Luckily it hadn't forgotten about me—about us.

I think it is drawn to the love Neeve and I feel for each other.

*Now what?* I think at the *enaid.*

It seems to respond with an answer and a question.

It shows me the only shape that it knows how to take besides Neeve's wings, and it can't shape his wings without being reconnected.

It asks me if I know what to do with the object.

At first I'm not sure, but then the only possible answer comes to me.

*Yes,* I tell the *enaid. Form that shape and leave it on top of the pulpit.*

Using all my upper body strength, I haul myself up the side of the podium. Luckily it is one of the old, ornate lecterns that's bolted to the floor and has scrollwork I can use for handholds.

I pull myself up until my face is even with Neeve's.

*I want to hold you in my arms,* I tell him, *but my legs can't support my weight anymore. There's no strength left in them.*

*Put your arms around my neck,* Neeve says. *The ropes can support us both for the little time I have remaining. I want to feel you next to me when I die.*

I put my left arm around his neck while I reach for the top of the pulpit with my right. I pick up the *enaid* in the only shape it knows how to take besides Neeve's wings—the shape of the last thing that ever touched it.

A knife.

With one swift movement, before Neeve can sense what I'm about to do and before I can change my mind, I plunge it into his heart.

I don't know if it will kill him or heal him. If it kills him, I pray he will at least go to the light because his soul is whole again.

His muscles tense for one brief moment.

Then he goes limp.

I can't hold onto his sagging body.

I collapse, sobbing, in a heap at his feet.

My hand falls onto something cold—a long, skinny fragment of glass.

There is one last thing I can do for Neeve.

Clenching the glass between my teeth, I lug myself up the side of the pulpit again.

When I reach the top, I hook the edge of the lectern with my left elbow and forearm, letting them support my weight. Then using the glass, I saw away at the rope.

When the cord parts, Neeve's body drops and rolls down the five steps to the floor. I toss the glass away and lower myself until I'm sitting on the stairs. I squirm around so I'm on the bottom step with Neeve's head resting in my lap. I stroke his hair away from his face.

I feel his neck for a pulse.

I can't find one, but I don't know if that's because there isn't one or if I just don't know where the artery is.

I put my hand on his chest.

There is a tiny movement as he takes a breath.

His eyes open.

He moves my hand from his chest to his face so he can kiss my palm.

"Are you going to be all right now?" I ask.

*I hope so. My enaid could still reject me if the darkness is too strong, but with you here, I think the darkness is fading.*

His eyes close, but I can still feel him breathing.

I lift his hand and kiss his palm.

A slight smile curls his lips.

He dozes.

Time passes as I watch him sleep, and I marvel at how sweet and angelic he looks. I don't know if it is the magic of slumber or if it is the reunion of the parts of his soul that makes him appear so young and so vulnerable.

I shiver.

The night is getting cold.

We might not make it until morning. Death from exposure is still a threat. I am very tired.

My head droops forward.

The sound of tires on gravel wakes me.

Through the missing church doors, I can see lights flickering between the trees.

My heart skips a beat.

Has Tolliver Jones convinced Kenneth Nelson to come back and set fire to the church?

To burn it down with us in it?

I stare into the night.

A vehicle stops right in front of the doorway.

It flashes red and blue.

# Chapter Thirty-three

I wake in Mountain View Hospital.

My mom and dad and two brothers are there.

"Neeve?" I ask.

His wellbeing is the first thing on my mind.

"Just across the hall," Dad says. "He's been through a lot, but it looks like he's going to be all right."

My family crowds around my bed.

"Kenneth Nelson?"

He's the second thing on my mind, but only because I don't want him to have another chance to hurt Neeve or me.

"He and three of his friends have been arrested," Dad answers.

"How'd the police find us?"

"An anonymous tip, according to Detective Taylor," Mom tells me.

"Someone called 911," Dad adds, "and told the operator to let Detective Taylor know that you and Neeve were being held in an old church off of Highway 50 and that you both needed medical help right away."

*Talitha*, I think. *It had to be her. I doubt that any of Kenneth Nelson's buddies would have betrayed him—not now, not after supporting him all year.*

"Do they know who called?" I ask.

"If they did, it wouldn't be anonymous," Mom says.

She starts to pat my hand, but she stops herself. I look down and see that both of my hands are bandaged. So are my arms.

"How are you feeling?" Dad asks.

I smile wryly. "Maybe you ought to tell me. How banged up am I?"

Mom frowns at me. "You did yourself some damage when you fell onto the floor."

"And you compounded it when you dragged yourself through the rubble," Dad says. "In addition to the damage you did to your arms, you slashed up your legs pretty bad. The doctors had to dig out the glass."

"However," Mom adds, letting go of the frown and giving me a little smile, "they stitched you back together, and you'll be able to go to school when spring break is over."

Bennett edges in front of Dad. "Neeve said you can walk. Is he right? Can you walk now?"

"You've talked to Neeve?" I ask. "You actually talked to him?"

"Sure," Bennett says. "He woke up lots earlier than you did."

Jeremy pushes past the parents until he's standing beside Bennett. "Can you really walk?"

"I actually only managed a few steps," I say, "but now that I know I can do it, I'll work harder in the future." I look over at Mom and Dad. "May I go see Neeve?"

Dad lifts me out of the bed and sets me in a regular hospital wheelchair. I look down at the wheels and then at my bandaged hands.

"I'll push you," Jeremy offers.

"I'll go with you," Bennett says.

When we get to Neeve's room, I'm horrified.

I couldn't see in the dark how badly they'd hurt him.

His face is puffy and bruised, and he has a five-inch long bandage on the left side of his jaw. His arms are covered with cigarette burns and small cuts. The wounds have obviously been treated, but they've been left uncovered. I can see bruises around his neck where someone choked him.

His wrists are bandaged. I can only imagine what they must look like after being bound behind his back for four days.

An IV needle pokes out of his right arm.

He has obviously been bathed and his hair has been washed. Despite everything he's suffered, despite the bruises, the cuts, and the burns, he looks wonderful to me.

He opens his eyes.

They are emerald green again.

"Karissa," he whispers my name.

"He can't talk very loud," Jeremy tells me quietly. "I heard the doctor say his throat is raw from screaming."

I reach up and pat Jeremy's hand to let him know I appreciate him telling me. I can't take my eyes from Neeve's face.

When Jeremy has pushed the wheelchair next to the bed, I say, "Thank you. Would you give me a few minutes with Neeve alone?"

"Sure." He and Bennett leave, pulling the door closed behind them.

"Did it work?" I ask Neeve. "Is your soul reunited now?"

"Yes," he whispers hoarsely. "I've been home once already. An orderly helped me into the bathroom, and I opened a doorway from there. I had to take the IV stand through the veil with me."

"Why didn't Hayden heal your injuries? Surely he could do it."

"Not if I want to stay in your world," Neeve says.

He takes my hand, and despite the bandages, lifts it to his lips.

I taste his strawberry kiss in my palm as if the gauze and tape weren't there.

"I don't mind letting my body go through the natural healing process," he says, "if it means I can continue to live here, close to you."

I want him to remain with me, but I remember the longing on his mother's face. Is it fair for me to cling to him when I know there are people in his world who love him as much as I do?

"Do you really want to stay, Neeve? You can finally go home and be with your family and friends."

He grins at me.

"I still have to graduate from high school." He holds my hand next to his heart. "You and I can go visit my family whenever you want, after all they're only a step away, but I'm never leaving this world again without you."

I'm in the hospital over night, but the doctors keep Neeve for a week. He is discharged in time to go back to school. What a rotten way to spend spring break.

The school year continues.

Neeve takes me to Auravale so I can meet his parents, his twenty-two siblings, his fifteen brothers/sisters-in-law, and his thirty-seven nieces and nephews.

They accept me with open arms, wheelchair and all.

They consider me a heroine for everything I went through to reunite Neeve with his *enaid.* No one says it outright, but I get the feeling that not many people who have gone through what Neeve did are able to regain the light.

Summer is almost here.

The school magazine comes out the last week of classes.

"A Grimm Tale of Two Brothers" is the main feature.

# Epilogue

Three years later, Neeve and I get married in two worlds.

He insists that we marry in Auravale first, and I find out why he would not kiss me on the lips before the wedding.

When we share our first kiss, we are enveloped in a light so bright that everything around us disappears for a moment while our souls unite and become one. This a confirmation of our love, and it reinforces our marriage vows to the point that they can never be broken.

I am able to walk down the aisle in the great hall of King Justus IV's palace in Auravale, and I am able to walk down the aisle in the little church on Maple Drive in Shawon, Colorado.

Neeve's wings take over two years to grow back.

They are gold and green, like his hair and eyes, and they are strong enough for him to carry me in his arms and fly us to the lovely island cottage where we spend our first wedding night.

After our Colorado ceremony, we go to Disneyland for a week, a gift from my parents, the Taylors, and Brenlyn and Talitha.

Like the ending of all good fairytales, we live happily ever after.

Connie A. Walker was born in Blackfoot, Idaho, attended elementary school in Kansas City, Kansas, and graduated high school in Fairbanks, Alaska. She has been an insatiable reader and a compulsive writer since childhood.

She is the author of the prize-winning plays *The Light Still Burns* and *Nearly a Woman*, as well as the prize-winning children's book *Timmy and the K'nick K'nocker Ring.*

Ms. Walker has a B.A. in theatre/playwriting from Brigham Young University, plus a B.S. in psychology and an MSW from the University of Utah. She has worked as a graphic artist, a technical writer, a foster care worker, a clinical social worker, and a mental health program manager. Regardless of what she has done as her day job, there has never been a time when she stopped writing.